MW01047226

Second Chances

By

Nika Dixon

Dedication

For Greg and John, my heart and soul. Love, laughter and music, always and forever.
For Lisa, my BFF and co-conspirator.
And for my dad, who I still miss terribly.

This is a work of fiction. Names, characters, places, and incidents are products of the author's imagination or are used fictitiously and are not to be construed as real. Any resemblance to actual events, locales, organizations, or persons, living or dead, is entirely coincidental.

Second Chances by Nika Dixon

Red Rose™ Publishing
Publishing with a touch of Class! ™
The symbol of the Red Rose and Red Rose is a trademark of Red Rose™ Publishing

Red Rose™ Publishing
Copyright© 2009 Nika Dixon
ISBN: 978-1-60435-888-9
Cover Artist: Nika Dixon
Editor: Michelle Ellis
Line Editor: Mike Kay

All rights reserved. No part of this book may be used or reproduced electronically or in print without written permission, except in the case of brief quotations embodied in reviews. Due to copyright laws you cannot trade, sell or give any ebooks away.
This is a work of fiction. All references to real places, people, or events are coincidental, and if not coincidental, are used fictitiously. All trademarks, service marks, registered trademarks, and registered service marks are the property of their respective owners and are used herein for identification purposes only.

Red Rose™ Publishing
www.redrosepublishing.com
Forestport, NY 13338

Thank you for purchasing a book from Red Rose™Publishing where publishing comes with a touch of Class!

Prologue

The rain saved her life.

Cold drops fell on her upturned face, bringing her back to consciousness. Willing her eyes to open, Casey Marshall stared into blackness.

What an odd dream.

She moved her head and regretted the motion. Pain screamed and pounded with excruciating fury against the inside of her skull. Squeezing her eyes shut, she inhaled sharply and rode out the throbbing.

She was cold.

Wet.

It was raining?

Why was she in the rain?

Taking a deep breath, she re-opened her eyes, squinting as water bounced off her cheeks, scattering against her eyelashes. She tilted her head to the side, but all she could distinguish through the darkness and the rain was the vague outline of brick walls. She turned her head to look the other direction and squinted down a lopsided tunnel to where a half working streetlight struggled to cut through the gloom.

She rolled onto her side. Bile burned against the back of her throat, bitter and acidic, but she swallowed it down, fighting to ignore the howling demon in her skull.

A familiar shape loomed out of the darkness behind her head. A knapsack. *Her* knapsack. As she moved towards it, her left hand landed with a splash in a cold puddle. With trembling arms she pushed herself up onto her hands and knees, peering through the wet bangs that fell down across her face.

She was at the end of an alley, at least a half a block from the street and the solitary light hovering in the opening. Bags and boxes of garbage were scattered against the walls, and a long, toothless fire escape staggered up and disappeared several floors above. To her right, a recessed doorway loomed, half blocked behind a very full and overflowing dumpster. Even beneath the cleansing wash of the rain, the smell of stagnant, rotting food was overpowering. Casey sucked in a breath through her mouth and swallowed hard.

No car noises. No voices. No city sounds. Just a sharp ticking of rain off plastic.

Clambering to her feet, legs splayed and trembling, she lost her balance and automatically reached for something, anything, to keep herself upright. Her right hand found the side of the dumpster, slapping against it with a loud metallic clang that startled her.

She shook her head in confusion.

There was something in her hand?

She lifted her arm and stared down in shock at the dark object gripped between her trembling fingers.

A gun.

Shock tore through her, and she watched in horror as it clattered to the wet pavement.

What am I doing with a gun? She didn't own one and had no idea how to even *use* one.

Casey crushed the heel of her hand to her forehead, pushing back against the crescendo playing behind her skull while she stared wide-eyed at the object at her feet.

The gun lay with its handle half submerged in a small puddle, the barrel pointing at her in accusation. She snaked her foot forward and poked it with her toe. The barrel spun to the side. She squeezed her eyes shut, willing it to disappear, but it was still there when she opened them.

Casey looked around, desperate to find an answer. A violent shudder shook her bones, rattling her teeth. She pressed her fingertips to her temple, begging the pain to let her be long enough to think.

Nothing made sense.

Nothing past what she could remember last.

And what she couldn't remember after.

Her heartbeat kicked up, and the pain in her head marched along.

Help. She needed help.

Her eyes returned to the dark barrel.

And she needed the gun.

Sucking as much air as she could hold into her lungs, she bent and pinched the barrel between her thumb and index finger. The cold metal burned, and she flung it into the open pocket of her canvas knapsack.

Lifting the bag, she clutched it against her chest and straightened, feeling the encroaching crush of shadows and silence.

She had to get out of there.

Chapter One

Huddled in the doorway of a boarded up laundromat, Casey struggled to piece together the events that had brought her here.

She couldn't remember hurting her head.

She couldn't remember going into an alley.

She couldn't remember getting a gun.

In fact, she couldn't remember *anything* past her dinner with Carson Hale. The dinner where he'd asked her, *begged* her, to hand deliver a letter to his cousin as soon as possible.

At least he'd had the grace to apologize, knowing full well the level of dislike she afforded his relative. Then he'd kissed her cheek, shoved a small package across the table, and rushed through the double doors onto the street.

The image of Carson, his beige overcoat flipping behind him, was the last flash of her memory before the part where she'd looked up into the rain. She couldn't find the missing pieces. The pieces that put her in the alley with a gun.

Her limbs trembled with a sporadic rhythm beneath her wet clothing. Clutching her knapsack to her chest she tucked her knees closer and glanced down the row of brownstones to number 2427. It was Sunday morning, and he still wasn't home. Where the hell was he?

It had taken every ounce of willpower she had to make it this far without breaking down, but she was losing coherence.

The huge scrape on her scalp behind her ear was raw and tender. Casey could feel it with her fingertips, but couldn't see what was wrong. Not that it mattered. She had nothing to clean or cover it with anyway, and no painkillers. If she could keep her neck and head still, the area clotted and the bleeding stopped. But if she turned her head too quickly the wound cracked open, trickling blood down her neck and into the collar of her windbreaker, so she tried very hard not to move.

At least the pain helped to keep her awake.

Shifting the knapsack to the ground beside her, Casey threaded her arms around her torso and tucked her numb fingers under her armpits.

This was the last place she should be, but the only place she could be.

The one man she never wanted to see again was the one man she knew would help her without question.

"Damn it, Jackson." She shivered, staring past the driving rain at the brownstone down the street. "Where the hell are you?"

Jackson Hale cursed at the non-stop spring rain and slow-moving traffic. He never could understand how people forgot even the simple rules of the road the minute the pavement turned damp. There was a right to caution in this kind of wet weather, but no need to be idiotic.

He pulled his hand across the stubble on his jaw and made the final turn onto his street.

It had been a hell of a morning.

He'd received a frantic call shortly after three in the morning from his uncle. His cousin, Carson, had been in a car accident, and it was bad. The doctor wasn't sure he was going to make it.

For hours Jackson had paced a furrow in the hospital hallway, waiting. But since they were limited to one visitor in the ICU at a time, Uncle Wayne had finally ordered him home with the promise to call as soon as there was any change. He'd only agreed to go because Carson's parents and his sister, Meghan, were still there, standing watch over Carson's mummified body.

Jackson felt guilty for leaving, but he had never been one to sit around a hospital. The Marines trained him to stay awake for days in the field, but put him anywhere near medical buildings and he could fall asleep on his feet. They vampired his energy. He didn't understand it, couldn't control it, so he opted to avoid it.

Somehow he knew Carson would understand.

With a heavy sigh, Jackson navigated his large SUV into an empty spot just down from his brownstone. The clock on his dash read almost noon, but his body reacted as though it was after midnight. With a quick jog through the rain, he took the steps to his front door two at a time and let himself in.

Familiar silence settled around him, and he sighed. Removing his wet jacket and boots, he walked down the long hallway to the kitchen in the back.

"Carson, what the hell were you thinking?" He shook his head in disbelief.

Carson was a good driver. He knew better than to be caught without a seatbelt. So what the hell was he doing driving up on the twisted roads of the ridgeline over the city without his belt on? In the pouring rain?

Flipping on the pre-stocked coffee maker, Jackson leaned back against the counter and crossed his arms. His guilty mind slipped him images of Carson's bruised and battered body snaked with tubes.

It had been a good six months since they'd last talked, their conversation ending in a heated argument. Jackson had been unwilling to break the ice with an apology first, so they hadn't talked at all.

And now his angry words could very well be the final thing he had ever said to Carson.

Jackson rubbed his fingers over the knotted tension in his chest. They may have been only cousins in relation, but growing up they were as close as two brothers.

When Jackson was seventeen, they'd made a silly pact stating they would never let a woman come between them.

The rule stood unbroken for years.

Unbroken.

Until six months ago.

Six months of silence. Six months of denial. Six months of stubborn pride. Jackson refused to be the first one to call, even though he realized he'd acted like an ass.

Carson always said Jackson was too stubborn for his own good.

Tipping his head back, he stared up at his ceiling and pledged that when Carson woke up, the first words out of his mouth would be that apology.

The doorbell chimed, breaking through his thoughts. He sighed and ignored it, in no mood to deal with salesmen. After a few moments it rang again. And then again.

"Oh come on...!" With a frustrated curse, he shoved himself off the counter and strode down the hallway, fully intending to break the finger that was stuck on the doorbell button.

It rang again, and he cursed, loud enough to be heard outside. A flash of satisfaction pumped through his veins to see the figure on the other side of his door jerk and jump away from the doorbell, silencing the repeated ringing.

With another curse, Jackson ripped his front door open and froze.

Standing on his porch, soaked to the skin, was the last woman in the world he ever expected to see again.

Casey Marshall.

And she looked like hell.

"Jackson?" She exhaled with a startled squeak.

He blinked.

She stared up at him, her eyes wide. She opened her mouth to speak, but nothing came out. Then her eyes rolled back, and she toppled forward into his arms.

Chapter Two

Jackson's arms shot out to catch Casey as she collapsed. Gathering her up against his chest, he kicked the door closed and carried her to the couch.

She was deathly pale and soaked through to the skin. Her blonde hair was a wet, tangled mess plastered against her head, and dirt streaked her clothes.

Setting her onto the sofa, he reached down and placed his fingers against the side of her neck. Her skin was ice cold, but her heartbeat felt strong and steady.

He snapped into recovery mode, pushing all questions aside. She needed to get dry and warm, fast.

He threaded her arms out from under the straps of her knapsack and tossed the bag onto the floor. Pulling down the zipper of her windbreaker, he peeled it back to reveal a soaked through t-shirt and a very lacy bra pressing through the wet material.

He tore his gaze away from the slow rise and fall of her chest and cursed his own mental weakness. He never could think around this damn woman.

With her arms free of the clinging jacket, he scooped his right hand behind her neck, leaning her forward so he could slip the wet material out from behind her back. His fingers tangled in a matted tuft of hair along the side of her neck. Tilting her head, he slowly worked them loose and looked closer.

A long clump of mud glued the hair behind her right ear to her scalp.

No. That wasn't right.

It wasn't mud, it was *blood*.

Air expelled out of his lungs. He'd seen enough wounds to recognize the trough-like mark left by a grazing bullet.

A fraction of an inch to the left and she would have been dead.

Jackson released her head and straightened, his eyes locked on the blood-crusted wound. Anger ripped through him, concern and worry nipping at its heels.

"Damn it, Casey!" he whispered. "What the hell have you done now?"

Rubbing his fingers across the back of his neck, he pulled at the tension that knotted across his shoulders. He should take her to the hospital. Dump her off in the emergency room. Let the ER staff and the

12

police deal with whatever trouble she found herself in this time.

He should.

But he couldn't.

Because whatever it was, it wasn't good. Especially if she had come to *him* looking for help.

Casey Marshall hated his guts.

So if she was on *his* doorstep it had to be bad. Getting shot at kind of bad.

It would be a coward's move to leave her with the police. Not to mention the act would also ensure his backside ended up flat on a slab at the local morgue.

The man may be retired, but his former commanding officer and current boss, Colonel Thomas Marshall, would kick his ass to hell and back if Jackson didn't do everything in his power to help his only niece if she were in trouble.

The niece that was, at this exact moment, unconscious on his couch, with a bullet wound in the side of her head.

Jackson shoved his emotions back down into the dark pit they'd escaped from and concentrated on the task at hand. The wound needed to be cleaned, and he still had to get her out of the wet clothes.

Scooping her up into his arms he started for the master bedroom on the second floor. Once she was on the bed, he moved to separate her from the rest of her wet clothes. The shoes and socks came off easily, but he struggled to part her from her jeans. The infernal things were too tight to begin with and being wet only made them harder to peel. After folding them down over her hips, he wiggled them off her legs and tossed them into the growing pile.

Last to go was the t-shirt.

Jackson almost groaned. The see-through material of the white lacy bra was bad enough, but the tiny Hello Kitty tattoo peeking up above the edge of her bikini-underwear definitely taunted him.

He pulled her up the bed and drew the covers up to her chin. *Out of sight out of mind* was never meant to refer to Casey Marshall.

With a clearing shake to his head, he gathered up her wet things, walked into the bathroom, and unceremoniously deposited the sopping pile of clothes into the bottom of the tub. He dug under the sink for the first aid kit, then dampened a washcloth, grabbed a clean towel, and headed back to his room.

As he crossed to the bed, concern surged forward, washing his anger away. She looked so pale and fragile. A broken china doll someone had thrown out into the rain.

Too quiet. Too still.

Nothing like the little blonde hellcat he knew she was.

Crazy Casey.

Memories of bouncing blonde pigtails shuffled forward into his mind. From as far back as he could remember it had always been Casey in trouble. Casey stuck. Casey needing help. Casey needing rescue. And where Casey led, Carson's sister Meghan followed. The two of them had been inseparable since childhood. Best friends then, co-conspirators now. She had been trouble enough as a child, but when she hit puberty, it was no longer a state of being. Instead, trouble evolved into a collection of beings. Human beings. The male kind.

It didn't help that both women could make heads turn. Alone they were dangerous enough. Together they simply doubled the bet—a sexy blonde and a leggy redhead.

If there was any kind of order, rule or law, they'd break it. And it drove him, a man who functioned on discipline and decorum, completely insane.

It seemed to Jackson that he and Carson were forever bailing Casey and Meghan out.

Forever...until that fated night six months ago.

With a sigh, Jackson lowered himself to the side of the bed, guilt weighing heavily on his shoulders. He had always been there for both her and Meghan before. Always. Then one heated argument with Carson, and he ignored his own blood. Ignored the years. Ignored the history.

They were his only family. And he'd tossed them away like an obstinate child. All because of his stupid macho pride. Now Carson was in the ICU, and someone had hurt Casey.

Shot her.

A flash of white-hot anger radiated through his body.

The events could be unconnected....

No.

Coincidence will get you killed.

Two people he cared about in two days?

This was *not* acceptable.

Casey struggled out of a strange dream. Pictures of rain and bricks. Darkness and flashing lights. She grasped for the pieces, but they slipped away and disappeared.

She rolled over, pulling the warm blankets around her shoulders, drifting in the strange state of half-awake. Rain ticked in with an offbeat rhythm on the window, distracting her from the task of returning to sleep. She opened her eyes, the fuzzy edges falling away as she stared at the dark green comforter.

Her bedding was blue.

She blinked, confused.

That wasn't her nightstand. And why was it on the wrong side of the bed? And didn't her clock have red digits, not neon green ones?

The realization this *wasn't* her house, her room, her bed, shocked her body upright. With a gasp she launched herself into a seated position, confusion and panic of where she was slamming her heart into high gear. Sharp pain split her forehead. Everything tilted with carnival speed, and she pitched forward, desperate to get off the ride. Her body tangled in the bedding, trapping her limbs. She would have dropped face first onto the floor if her forward motion wasn't halted by a pair of very solid hands.

"Easy," a male voice growled.

Recognition shot down Casey's spine with a shiver, and she squeezed her eyes shut. Only one man had the power to break her body into goose bumps with something as simple as the sound of his voice.

She raised her head and looked up into the hazel eyes of the last person she'd ever expected to see again.

Jackson Hale.

Her arms fought free of the encumbering blanket as she struggled to put space between them, but his fingers continued to burn the flesh of her upper arms. He eased her back down onto the pillows and lowered himself onto the edge of the bed.

She knew she stared, but she couldn't stop. If Jackson was here...then the here was Jackson's.

"Painkillers," he supplied, releasing her arms to hand her a couple of small white pills followed by a glass of water.

She threw her concentration at getting the tablets onto her dry tongue, but had to use both hands to steady the glass while she gulped the water. After wiping her mouth with the back of her hand, she held out the empty glass.

He took it from her shaking fingers and set it on the nightstand without taking his gaze off her.

Trapped like the proverbial deer, Casey couldn't look away. Six months of faked ignorance and pretend normalcy fell away in a glance, leaving her feeling just as alone and lost as she was that night all those months ago.

His entire body was tense, a coiled spring ready to snap if the pressure wasn't soon released.

She wished he would talk, yell, shout. Anything but the silent stare he gave her right now. Casey read his face, the anger, the unasked questions reflected deep in his eyes. He may be able to still his mind and body, but those stormy hazel eyes betrayed everything.

He was still angry.

And he still blamed her.

She'd made a mistake in coming.

He wouldn't help.

Desperation welled up into her throat, and she dropped her gaze.

And realized she wasn't wearing her clothes.

With a shriek, she yanked the covers up to her chin. "Where are my clothes?" Her cheeks heated under his unconcerned expression.

"Laundry."

"Did you...?" She paused. "Did you take them off?" She was mortified to think he'd undressed her while she was unconscious. The burn spread to her ears.

"You weren't exactly in any condition to do it yourself," he pointed out. "What with you passing out and all."

Casey tried to portray casual, as though waking up in a strange bed, wearing nothing but her underwear, was a common occurrence. But the feeling of embarrassed fire across her cheeks and neck was not helping.

Jackson stood and crossed to the tall oak dresser standing against the far wall. Casey breathed a sigh of relief at the added space and squeezed her eyes shut, wishing she was still asleep. At the sound of a dresser drawer opening, she snapped her eyes open just in time to catch the wadded up t-shirt he flung at her.

She clutched the material over her breasts, her knuckles bunched around the cotton so tightly they turned white.

He crooked an eyebrow.

"Turn around?" she squeaked.

With an exasperated sigh, he turned his back.

Casey tugged the shirt down over her head and pulled the bottom hem over her thighs. Then she tugged the blankets back up to her chin.

"Okay," she muttered.

He faced her again but remained in the middle of the room, his arms crossed over his chest, watching with intensity.

Casey took a deep breath and held it.

Jackson Hale was one tall, dark, and sexy man.

Especially when he looked ready to strangle someone.

In this case—her.

His stance was wide, his legs braced. The well-worn jeans hugged his muscular thighs, and the light gray t-shirt stretched across his upper arms, accenting the raw strength and muscle of his torso. For years he'd kept his hair cropped short, military style, but now it was thick and wavy, the length almost touching his collar. His features were dangerous, rugged, and he needed a shave.

An avenging angel.

Just not hers.

Not anymore.

Dropping her gaze to the bedding, she ran a shaky hand through her tangled hair. Her fingers brushed against a piece of gauze taped behind her ear, and she winced. She picked at it, frowning.

"Don't pick at it," he snapped.

Her eyes jumped to his, her mouth open in reply, but her mind couldn't complete the order to speak, so she let it close.

Her stomach jumped at the silence and gave a long, slow burble.

Jackson's eyes narrowed.

Casey watched as his shoulders lowered and his arms dropped loosely along his sides. "I'll make you something to eat. Shower's through there. Towels are on the back of the door. Come downstairs when you're done," he ordered, then turned and walked towards the hallway. "And then I expect the details. *All* of them."

He left without looking back.

Just like he had half a year ago.

Covering her eyes with her hand, she flopped back down onto the pillows, unable to come up with a coherent answer to the question *now what*?

Her stomach growled again, and she sighed, arguing the pros and cons of leaving now versus later. He didn't want her here any more than she wanted to be here. But she couldn't go without her clothes, and what harm could a shower cause? Clean up first, and then she would collect her things and leave with at least part of her dignity intact.

So what if she drained his water tank first?

Sure it was petty.

But somehow the thought of leaving him with an icy cold shower gave her the drive to push off the covers and head to the bathroom.

Downstairs, Jackson listened to the water rushing through the pipes in the wall. He tried not to picture Casey, or the Hello Kitty tattoo, upstairs, in his shower, naked.

He occupied his mind with preparing some food. She'd slept for a good six hours, and he'd spent most of the time mentally frozen in the chair watching her. Now it was almost seven o'clock.

By the time the water shut off he'd inhaled an omelet of his own and finished cooking a second one for her.

When she entered the kitchen, he glanced up and almost dropped the knife he was using to butter her toast.

She stood in the doorway wearing his t-shirt and a pair of string-tied gym shorts she must have found in his dresser. The shirt was several sizes too big for her, and the bottom dropped as far as the hem of the shorts. The neckline had slid off one side, revealing a bare shoulder that showed him she was definitely not wearing a bra underneath. Her towel-dried hair hung halfway down her back, twisted upon itself forming a loose braid. A blonde tendril refused to be tied back and fell down the side of her face, coming to rest across her naked shoulder.

He thought back to the tattoo and swallowed.

Without makeup, she looked so young standing there. Innocent.

Lost.

Her blue eyes watched him, emotion swirling through their depths. Wariness. Confusion. Fear.

He wanted to reach out and wrap his arms around her.

Whisper words of comfort in her ear.

Hold her and protect her.

Then his gaze caught the now wet gauze along the side of her head, and he shut the emotions down.

This was Casey.

And she was in trouble.

Again.

Casey knew the instant he'd closed himself off. For a brief second she'd caught a glimpse of the old Jackson. The boy she used to know. The man she always thought she loved. His face softened, and his hazel eyes swirled with the tiniest hint of gold. Eyes that seemed to look right through her, deep into her soul, and straight to that lonely little girl she'd boxed away years ago.

Then he tuned her out and shut it all down.

She shook her head. It had been stupid to come here. To him. She didn't know what she had been thinking. No. Check that. She did know. She hadn't been thinking, she'd been reacting. And now reality was knocking her on the forehead. She was warm and rested, and no longer running on adrenaline and panic.

Yet she was here, and he was going to demand answers. Answers she couldn't give to questions she'd asked herself.

This was not going to be easy.

"First things first," he said, his voice curt. "We need to change that wet dressing." He picked up a small package of gauze and a roll of medical tape from off the counter and motioned for her to sit.

Casey perched on the edge of a kitchen chair, fingers gripping the sides of the polished oak seat. Jackson moved around behind her and eased the wet bandage away from her skin.

She wasn't noticing the heat radiating off his body, warming her skin like the summer sun. She wasn't noticing how gently his fingers changed the bandage behind her ear. She wasn't noticing the way her heart acted just a tiny bit sporadic.

Nope.

She wasn't noticing at all.

Instead, she distracted herself with the various objects around the kitchen. The two-seat café table she sat beside. An expensive, programmable coffee maker on the counter. An oversized stainless steel microwave that matched the other appliances. Hardwood floors and oak cabinets. Dark blue walls. Sheer curtains draping the window over the sink and covering the glass in the back door. When the pieces pulled together it was a comfortable space. Nothing unnecessary.

It suited him.

He moved away, taking his aura of warmth and leaving her feeling lost and alone. He opened the microwave, extracted a plate, and placed it in front of her next to a lone fork. Casey devoured the food, her gaze never leaving the plate.

As soon as she set the fork onto the empty dish, he removed it and dropped it into the sink.

Her eyes remained locked on the knitted blue placemat. She knew he watched her, leaning back against the counter, willing her to turn her head.

"Let's hear it," he finally broke the silence, his voice sharp and low. "Start from the beginning. Including who shot you."

"What?" Casey blinked up at him.

"You heard me."

"What are you talking about?"

A chair leg scraped. He sat across from her, close enough now that when he leaned forward, they were almost nose to nose. "What did you do to make someone take a shot at you?" he growled.

"Don't be ridiculous." Her voice worked, but somehow the tone wasn't as sure sounding as it should have been. "I...hit my head on something."

Jackson rested his weight on the table, his face so close she could feel him speaking. "I think I know a gunshot wound when I see one."

Casey stared at him, her fingers gripping the edges of her seat. Nervous laughter bubbled up into the back of her throat and caught on her tongue. He was wrong. He didn't mean it. He was just saying that to scare her.

Okay, fine.

It was working.

"What the hell happened?"

"I...don't remember."

"Try again." He scowled in disbelief,

"I'm serious!" she exclaimed. "I really don't remember. I just...woke up...in the rain...like this." She pointed to the gauze behind her ear.

His elbows hit the table. "Can the crap, Casey. I'm in no mood for your games."

"This isn't a game!" She shoved her chair back and turned away.

"Damn right it's not." Jackson stood, his fingers clamping down on her wrist, pulling her around to face him.

"Forget it," Casey hissed, wriggling her arm in a useless attempt to break free of his locked grasp. "You don't care so why should I bother—"

"You came to me."

"Yeah well obviously that was a mistake."

"*Obviously*." He glared.

She tried to peel his fingers off, but he wasn't letting go.

"You're not going anywhere until you tell me what's going on."

"Go to hell." She stepped back and extended her arm between them, twisting her wrist in an attempt to break his hold.

"Been there, bought the t-shirt," he countered, forcing her backwards towards her chair. "Now, you're going to sit down and tell me what's going on, or I'm taking you to the police."

Jackson knew he'd pushed the right button. The color fell from her face, and fear replaced the anger in her eyes. Guilt almost overrode the need for answers, but he pushed it away. Someone shot her, and he needed to know who and why. If scaring her with a trip to the police station would get him the answers, then so be it.

"You wouldn't...."

"Try me," he growled.

After a brief moment of strangled silence, the fight left her with a sigh and her shoulders slumped. She dropped heavily into the empty chair. The look of loss and sadness in her eyes almost made him take it back. But he didn't. Couldn't. He released her wrist and stepped back, watching, waiting. She dropped her chin and lowered her head in defeat.

"I really don't remember," she pleaded, staring down at her hands clenched in her lap.

"Then tell me what you *do* remember." He lowered himself into the chair across from her and waited.

She took a deep breath and nodded. "Carson and I met for dinner last night, and that's the last thing I remember before waking up flat on my back in the rain."

Jackson's hand shot out to grab hers, and she reacted with shock, jumping back in her chair and trying to yank her fingers away, but he was too quick.

"You saw Carson?" he practically shouted.

"Y...yes?"

"Last night?"

She nodded, her wide-eyed fear kicking his heart into a scattered pounding.

"I.... We had dinner. Well, I had dinner. He left. I know you two aren't talking but—"

"Casey."

"I'm still talking to him," she babbled on. "And that's the last thing I remember doing. I was talking to Carson."

"Casey," Jackson tried to interrupt.

"Well, not talking so much as listening, while he did the talking. But that's the last thing I remember. I swear, Jackson. I know you don't believe me.... Just.... Just call him. Please. He'll tell you."

"Casey!" Jackson squeezed her hand sharply. "Carson can't talk to anyone. He was in a car accident last night. He's in a coma."

Chapter Three

"Oh God," Casey whispered, blinking back tears. "A coma?"

She wanted to pull her fingers back, but they were firmly sandwiched between the press of Jackson's warm palms.

"Talk to me," he urged.

Like a breaking damn, she rushed out the details that weren't missing from her dinner with Carson. How he called her earlier in the day to beg her to meet him for dinner. His request and the package. "Then I saw him leave, and I swear, Jackson, that's the last thing I remember."

His chair scraped back, startling her.

"Where's the package?"

"My knapsack." She pointed back towards the front of the house.

When Jackson returned, he set her bag on the table and unzipped the main pocket. He reached into the bag and froze.

Oh crap. Air sucked sharply up her nose, and her hands struck out with a spasm, trapping his forearm.

She'd completely forgotten about the gun.

His eyes burned through hers.

Casey snatched her hands back and clamped them over her mouth. Horrified, she watched Jackson turn the black metal over in his hands.

"What the hell is this?" His voice was low and slow, his gaze hard.

"The other part of the story?" she whispered.

"Jesus, Casey, what the hell are you doing running around with a loaded weapon?"

"It's not mine!" She exhaled, her fingers still covering her mouth. "I...." She cleared her throat and lowered her hands. "I didn't know what else to do with it?"

Jackson slammed the magazine in place with the heel of his hand, startling her with the sudden motion. She let out a squeak and jumped in the chair.

"Where did you get it?"

"I...don't...know?"

He scowled at her, his disbelief obvious. The second time he went for the knapsack he looked before reaching inside. He extracted a small padded envelope, with no markings. "Is this it?"

Casey nodded. She couldn't seem to move her eyes away from the black barrel of the gun, watching it like a freshly squished spider, making sure it was indeed dead.

Jackson tore at the envelope and extracted a single folded piece of white paper. He tipped the envelope forward and out slid three silver keys, each with a small white tag attached.

The clatter of the keys on the tabletop drew Casey's attention away from the gun. "What are those for?"

Jackson shrugged and unfolded the paper, reading the short note aloud.

"*J—Sorry to have to do this to you, but there's no one else I trust. This is my insurance. Be careful of who you trust. There are too many coincidences. Protect her. She knows enough to make her the next target.*"

Casey took the paper from him, her lips moving as she read the letter to herself.

"Protect her?" She looked at Jackson and pointed to herself. "Me?"

"I would assume so." He stirred the keys around the table with his index finger, picking up each small tag in turn. "Pappy's tackle box. Cu'bo #16. J's secret hiding spot."

He lifted his gaze to hers, his expression intense. Questioning.

Casey shook her head. The letter, the names, they made no sense. Why would Carson send her to Jackson? Why would she need protecting? Unless....

"Jackson," she whispered. "You don't think...I mean...Carson's accident?"

He shook his head and shrugged. "I don't know. But I think it's time for the second half of that story."

Casey stared at the letter in her hands, her head filled with rhetorical questions. Carson had known something bad was going to happen to him? And maybe to her? That's why he sent her to Jackson? Now Carson was in a coma, and according to Jackson, someone had shot her?

She reached for the bandage behind her ear but pulled back.

"The only thing I remember is waking up flat on my back behind a dumpster in an alley with *that* in my hand." She paused and took a deep breath. "I tried to get my bearings but I had such a headache I...I couldn't think straight. I didn't...I didn't know where else to go." She shrugged, staring at the three keys on the table in front of her. "I waited in that old laundromat across the street until I saw you come home."

"Good Lord, you didn't break into the place, did you?"

"No I didn't break in!" she mimicked sarcastically. "I just waited in the doorway. Then you came home, and voilà," her fingers pointed into the air for a brief moment before she dropped her hands into her lap, "here I am."

"And you honestly don't remember."

Casey blinked up at him, disbelief and anger ripping past all the worry and confusion. His suspicious tone was infuriating. Blame first, ask questions later. That was the Jackson she'd come to know and hate. She cursed herself for coming. For believing he would help.

She stood with such force her chair rocked back. "You think I'm lying? With Carson in the hospital you actually think I'm cruel and shallow enough to be holding back? I love him too, you know!"

She spun on her heel, but he grabbed her upper arm, spinning her back around. "Wait."

Refusing to look up, Casey stared at the floor, blinking back tears. She wasn't going to give him the satisfaction of seeing that his lack of belief in her could still cut. How could he think...? No. With an expert mental kick, she buried the hurt. She wasn't a love-sick teenager anymore and she sure as hell didn't need anyone's approval. Especially not his.

His fingers brushed her chin, and she jerked her head away.

"That's not what I meant," he said softly.

Casey sighed. It sounded about as close to an apology as she was going to get. She lifted her head, quivering slightly to realize his mouth was only inches from hers. It would take such a tiny motion to lift her chin and complete the distance.

His grip tightened on her upper arm, breaking the spell.

She tilted her head away from temptation and looked down to where he was still clutching her upper arm—tan fingers against pale skin.

He released her and took a step back.

Oddly, she missed the contact.

"Look," he ran his hand over his hair, then crossed his arms over his chest, "this whole situation is crazy. But if something's going on, if someone's purposely done this to Carson, to you, then we need to find out what and who."

The truth of his words rolled around in her mind, and her shoulders dropped in resignation. "What do you want me to do?"

He indicated the letter sitting open on the table. "Start at the beginning. Tell me everything."

Casey stared at the scrawled message. Carson was a reporter, and a good one at that. He covered the big stories, the trials, the law, the criminals, but lately he'd been working on an investigative piece that was sure to cause some big waves across the city. He'd sworn her to secrecy...but if this story was the cause of his accident...and hers...then she couldn't keep it quiet.

"It started eight months ago," she began, switching her gaze to a spot in the middle of Jackson's chest. "Carson was following a lead about a slum landlord, and the information wasn't adding up, so he started digging around. He found a couple of blocks along the waterfront with some questionable real-estate deals. The more he dug, the more convinced he was there was something big going on. Some of the sales appeared to be completely legit. People move out for all kinds of reasons, right? But these apartments weren't being rented again."

"Not unusual."

"No," she shook her head, "but the situations are."

"What situations?"

"The apartments stayed empty. Then once everyone was gone the owners sold the entire building."

"Selling off a building doesn't sound so unusual."

"It's not the buildings, it's the people."

"I don't get it."

She pursed her lips and lifted her gaze to his. "That's because I'm not done yet."

Jackson dropped his chin, raised his eyebrows, and lowered himself into a chair, holding his hands up in surrender.

Casey joined him at the table and delved into the details.

It wasn't the building sales that scented the reporter's nose, it was the individual tenants. When a pattern started to emerge, Carson offered Casey a job helping with the research.

"He offered you a job?"

"That's what I said." She nodded.

"When did Carson offer you a job?"

"First week of January."

"That was...," he trailed off.

Casey frowned. "Yeah, yeah. Right after the *big fight*." She held her hands up and made quote symbols in the air.

Jackson scowled. "How long were you working with him?"

"I still am."

His eyes narrowed. "For six months?"

Her lips flattened into a thin line at the implied dig. She'd always been jealous of how easily people seemed to fall into careers, while she never seemed to find anything that lasted more than a few weeks. Retail clerk. Secretary. Waitress. Bartender. She'd done them all and then some, but nothing seemed to fit, so she'd kept searching. Her job-of-the-week had been a running joke for years.

With everyone except Carson.

Carson always told her she had a way with details, and in January, he swung a deal with his paper to hire her as his research assistant.

The timing of the job offer suspiciously followed Carson's big argument with Jackson, but she'd disregarded the warning flags and worked very hard to prove to Carson he'd made a good decision. She ~~knew she was the reason behind their fight. But there was no way she~~ would have let it interfere with her new job, especially after she'd discovered, to her own pleasure, she was good at it.

Very good.

And no one was going to take it away from her.

Not even Jackson Hale.

Flipping up her middle finger, she showed Jackson what he could do with his snide comments.

"Ouch." The corner of his mouth turned up. Then he held his hands up in surrender. "Okay so in January you got a job working for Carson," he prompted.

Casey chewed the inside of her cheek, realizing she had no idea where to begin. There was so much information. So many pieces. She'd spent six months digging, researching, compiling, and now there was a good chance that something she'd discovered had almost gotten Carson killed.

Almost gotten *her* killed.

By looking back through almost two years of records, city permits, various publications and other sources, she'd realized the little two-block stretch of town had impossible luck. Right after a seemingly random, ill begotten event, the individual apartment, building, or entire complex would be vacated and sold.

"Building code violations, city code violations, legal problems, arson, suicide, disappearances, and even murder. There's no way all of these things could happen to so many people, in such a small area, in a couple of years. Something is going on."

Jackson leaned forward. "You have proof of all this?"

"Yes."

"I'd call that motive."

"That's just it," she shook her head, "it isn't. I mean, it's been going on for years."

"You just said you can prove people are being murdered for their apartments."

She shook her head. "I can *prove* that people living in this two block area have *extremely* bad luck. I can only *suggest* it's more than that."

"If someone's shooting at you, it's a hell of a lot more than bad luck." Jackson scowled. "Did Carson have any idea who?"

Casey hesitated.

"No secrets, Casey," he warned.

She pursed her lips. "I...*we*...have no real proof, but one name seemed to come up more than the others."

"And?" he prompted.

"Harrison Douglas."

"Douglas." Jackson frowned. "Isn't he the guy that's on all those ads and posters?"

"That's the one." Casey nodded. "But I haven't been able to find his name attached to anything other than the sale. The deaths are all legitimate—at least, they are on paper. Heart attacks and car accidents happen all the time. For all we know, many of them are legitimate. It's when you compare the timing of the accidents against the fact that all of these people live in the same apartment building. It's mathematically improbable." She shook her head slowly. "But who's behind it? There's no way one person could be doing it all without help. It's too big. There's too much paperwork. We're talking at least two years' worth. Someone would have to be altering city paperwork and police reports."

"Well that explains Carson's warning." Jackson frowned, glancing down at the letter on the table between them.

Casey's shoulders hunched then dropped. "Last month Carson *did* call an old school buddy of his who's now a councilor—Robert Wolinski. He listened to Carson's theory and said he'd try to help."

"How?"

"He talked with other council members. Carson said it caused a bit of a stir. Buying up areas of a city block for development isn't illegal, but whatever is going on here is being done in secret, with no press releases, and no information whatsoever on the final project. It's too much."

Casey stood and refilled her glass of water. Her throat was dry, and she was mentally exhausted. The painkillers were wearing off, and her head was starting to resume its drumbeat.

She drained the glass and set the empty tumbler into the sink. "So now you know as much as I do." She turned and leaned against the counter.

Jackson shook his head and leaned back in his chair. "You dug up all that information?"

"Yes, mostly. Carson too."

"It must have been a lot of work."

"It was." She let out a huge yawn. Tipping her head back, she rolled her shoulders. "Only now I'm not so sure it was worth it."

Jackson glanced at the clock on the wall then stood. "It's after eleven. Go to bed," he ordered. "I'll take the couch. In the morning we'll follow the keys."

Casey raised her eyebrows and muffled another yawn with her

fingertips. "Normally I'd kick your butt for being so seriously out of touch with modern reality that you would give up your room instead of just putting *me* on the couch," she sighed. "But I'm too tired to care."

Jackson grinned. "*Normally*, I don't send beautiful women to my bed alone."

Casey's breath caught, and she blinked. She couldn't remember the last time she saw him truly smile. It changed his whole aura, making him look younger and even more handsome. If that was even possible.

She tried to tell herself it was just an illusion. He was still the same stubborn cement-head. Her heart fluttered for a brief moment before reality settled back in. It was Jackson Hale she was gaping at. The man who would never think of her as anything more than Meghan's trouble-making friend.

Her limbs suddenly felt leaden. The past twenty-four hours stole all her mental and emotional strength and tossed it right out the window. She let out a small, ragged sigh and closed her eyes.

"Hey now."

Jackson pulled her into his arms, and Casey stiffened with shock.

"It's going to be okay," he promised, his breath warm against the top of her head.

For a moment she refused to succumb, standing with her hands fisted at her sides, but her exhausted body mutinied towards the safety and strength of the circle of his arms. She leaned in and wrapped her arms around his torso, inhaling the mixed scent of musk and soap.

God, he felt so good.

Was it really so bad to want?

They stood in silence for a few brief moments before Jackson backed away, leaving her to stand alone once again.

"Go," he urged, his voice low and rough. "Sleep."

Fearing what she might do if she stayed, Casey turned and fled the kitchen.

Jackson was instantly awake—all his senses on overdrive. Something was wrong. His body remained still, his breathing controlled. Training and experience overrode any desire to move. He listened for any sound out of the ordinary, but the house was silent.

There. A small scraping noise coming from the front door. Someone was breaking in!

He reached under the pillow for the Beretta he'd placed there before retiring. Sliding the blanket to the floor, he slipped off the couch and stood. Sensing no other movement inside the house, he crept towards the front hallway.

He paused, listening. Two hushed voices. Harsh whispers.

Someone was making fast work of his locks.

He moved into the far corner so he would be shielded by the door when it opened. With a soft click, the handle turned and the door inched inward.

"Got it...," a man whispered to an unseen companion. "Go around back—and be quiet! We get the woman and get out."

"And the boyfriend?" A whispered question.

"Kill him."

Jackson heard a grunt of agreement then footsteps fading down the front walk. A short, stocky man wearing a black leather jacket stepped into the foyer. The intruder glanced back towards the street before easing the door closed.

As the man turned towards the inside of the house, Jackson made his move. With one swift jerk he squeezed his right arm around the man's throat, cutting off his air supply, and locked his other arm up and over the man's head. The stranger was strong, beefy, pulling and swinging. But he was no match. The struggles stopped, and Jackson lowered the unconscious man to the floor.

He searched the clothing. No ID, no paperwork. Nothing useful except for a forty-five tucked into a shoulder holster and a lock-picking kit. Jackson took the gun and the small kit and dropped them into the pocket of his jacket which was still lying across the back of the chair.

He bolted the front door and checked the street. It seemed quiet, but the shadows held too many hiding places. He double checked that his new friend was completely out before working his way to the kitchen door.

This was his domain. He knew where to walk and how to place his feet to avoid making any noise. He almost felt sorry for the poor bastard out back who was about to discover the truth.

Almost.

Jackson reached the kitchen and pulled the back door open, shadowing himself behind it.

A tall, reedy man stepped into the room, his voice low. "What took you so...."

Jackson knocked him senseless.

Shoving the door closed, Jackson stared down at the man on his kitchen floor. First Carson. Then Casey. Now thugs were breaking into his house with the sole purpose of taking Casey away. It was most definitely connected, and people were getting hurt. His instincts were telling him they had to get out before someone ended up dead.

A few minutes later he stood next to the edge of the bed,

watching the woman asleep beneath the blankets, her hair spread out across his pillow in a messy halo. He exhaled an amused snort to see how even in sleep she'd completely taken over. The far side of the bed had no blankets and no pillows. Everything was either around her, beneath her, or on the floor beside her.

The woman was a whirlwind.

Swallowing down the thoughts of where she'd be right now if she'd been in the house alone, he reached down and shook her awake. "C'mon, sleeping beauty, time to move."

She rolled out from under the covers and rubbed her eyes. "Jackson? What time is it? What are you doing? Why are you wearing a jacket?"

"Shh. We have to go."

She jerked upright, her eyes wide. "Is it Carson? Did something—"

"Carson's fine," he reassured her. "I checked right after you went to bed." He dropped an armful of clothes on her lap. "You need to get dressed. They're clean. I'll meet you downstairs."

"But—"

"No. Now, Casey," he ordered as he moved out of the room and into the hallway, "and leave the lights off."

Nearing the bottom of the stairs, Casey stumbled in shock and slid down the last two steps on her heels. If her eyes hadn't already been adjusted to the dark, she wouldn't have noticed the two men trussed up with zip ties and gagged with duct tape lying in the front foyer.

But she did.

And they were either unconscious or...dead.

"Oh my god!" she gasped. "They're not...?"

"No," Jackson replied. "They're not dead. Although the thought had crossed my mind."

"Who are they?" she whispered.

"My guess is hired goons. And we're not sticking around to find out who sent them."

"Were they trying to rob you?"

"No." Jackson pointed to her shoes lying by the front door, then to her navy windbreaker hanging on a hook inside the door. "They're dry. Put them on. We're going out the back."

Casey pulled on one shoe and hopped after him, tugging on the other. "Wait! Going where? Why are we whispering?"

Already in the kitchen, Jackson was zipping the top up on a large green gym bag. He hooked it over his shoulder and motioned for her to be silent. Casey slipped into her windbreaker, her sleep-addled brain more than willing to let her believe this was all a dream, but her body knew better.

Her chest ached from the pressure of the strangled breathing.

Too much. Too fast.

Jackson was completely in attack mode. Controlled tension radiated off him, spiking her own adrenaline higher. It was in his eyes, his stance. He watched her, his gaze direct. She forced herself to take a few deep breaths.

"Follow quickly and quietly," he ordered, his tone quiet and firm. "Do exactly as I say. No questions. No arguments."

He held his index finger in front of his lips, waiting until she nodded in silent agreement before cracking open the back door. Stepping outside, he crossed silently over the small patio and down the steps to the lawn.

Casey followed at his heels, duplicating his half crouch.

At the end of his short yard he ducked behind the tall slatted fence bordering the alley and motioned for her to do the same. He reached up to unlatch the gate. It swung out and to the right. Keeping low, he eased it open far enough to scan to the left through the opening. He shifted position and checked to the right.

Leaning back on his heels, he grabbed her hand, making her jump.

"My car is on the other side of the fence," he whispered in her ear as he pressed a key into her palm. "Follow me out and get in the driver's side."

Not waiting for acknowledgement, he stood up and jogged to his car.

Casey was tense enough to begin with, but stacked beneath Jackson's cold, locked demeanor her body pumped out the adrenaline. Her heart slammed into her rib cage with such force she had a brief vision of it exploding in her chest, leaving her dead, right there on the lawn.

She hesitated only a moment before leaping up and running through the opening. She stumbled when she came around the corner of the gate and almost smacked right into Jackson's broad backside.

If this was his car it was half dead.

In the pale glow of the streetlight the thing more closely resembled a rust pile than a working vehicle.

"Move!" he hissed.

Casey unlocked the driver's door while he stood watch. The closeness of his shoulders drowned her in shadows, and she had to feel for the slit of the lock with her fingers. As soon as she had the door open he spun and half shoved, half threw her inside. Crawling over the shifter, Casey scrambled into the passenger seat.

Jackson tossed his duffel into the back and hopped inside.

"Is this thing even going to start?" She handed him the key.

He jammed it into the ignition and shifted into neutral. Stepping on the clutch, he flicked his wrist and the car growled to life. "New engine," was all he said.

She fought to click her seatbelt into place as he backed the car out of the parking space. Shifting into first he sped down the alley, hung a right, and bounced out onto the street.

The engine let out a long, low rumble as Jackson accelerated and turned onto a side street. His head made slight movements—darting between the mirrors and the road ahead. It was well after three in the morning, so traffic was minimal.

Casey couldn't resist glancing over her shoulder—but the street behind them was dark and motionless. She watched the streetlights flash by through the passenger window, her mind skipping through questions she couldn't answer. Why were they running away in the middle of the night? Who were the two men? Agreeing with the niggling voice inside her head, she fully admitted something big just happened, and decided for the moment she was content in her ignorance.

After several dizzying turns through residential neighborhoods, Jackson pulled out onto a major street and merged onto the interstate, heading south. Her body's spiked cocktail of adrenaline and fear gradually dissipated, leaving her exhausted and spent. She stole a glance at the man beside her, taking a moment to study him unobserved and unobstructed. He gripped the wheel firmly, his movements precise and controlled as he angled them past the slower moving traffic.

When his gaze shifted towards her, Casey's heart skipped with the brief moment of panic to be caught staring. She snapped her head around, hiding the warming flush in her cheeks.

A brush of heat stroked the back of her hand, and she jerked, shocked to see Jackson's arm stretched across the console. Lifting her chin, she caught the hint of a reassuring smile when he squeezed her fingers. She didn't have a chance to respond before his hand was once again on the wheel and his concentration back to the road ahead.

Casey turned back to the window, letting the calming thrum of rubber on asphalt lull her. She tipped her head back against the seat and closed her eyes.

Once the city limits were miles behind them, Jackson went for his cell phone. Punching in a number, he held it up and waited for whoever was at the other end to pick up.

The ringing turned into a pre-recorded voice, and he cursed under his breath. Even through a machine the Colonel's voice had the power to straighten Jackson's spine. Keeping his voice low, he glanced at the woman sleeping in the passenger seat and waited for the beep.

"Boxcar, it's Ice Man. We've got a problem."

Jackson hated leaving a message, or anything else that might be traceable, but he needed to warn the Colonel. Things were getting too dangerous, and these days tapping phones was certainly not improbable. Anyone could buy anything off the Internet. High end electronics included.

Only people directly attached to his old unit knew both his nickname and his CO's, and even though they were no longer on active duty, call signs still came into play.

He knew the Colonel would understand the urgency and take appropriate action, using everything at his disposal.

Which was a hell of a lot.

As far as the outside world knew, Jackson worked for a corporate consulting firm. He wasn't sure how much Casey understood about her uncle's *business*, and he wasn't about to be the first one to break it to her. If her uncle wanted her to know CORE was really a highly restricted security firm that could work with, or without, regular law enforcement and government agencies...well...he could tell her himself.

Although Jackson had to give her some credit, Casey had been confused and terrified, but she'd followed him without question. He wasn't about to believe for a second that she obeyed him out of trust. He knew she didn't trust him at all. She was, however, certainly smart enough to understand he was on her side, whether she liked it or not.

She hadn't argued and hadn't fallen into hysterics.

Not that she was prone to any kind of emotional meltdown.

He had seen Casey in all kinds of crazy situations but never once over the years had he ever seen her completely break down. Not since the year her parents died. She somehow channeled the weaker emotions into whatever else she did.

It was too bad she always channeled herself into trouble.

Like now.

With a snort he dialed a second number.

He was going to need backup.

The phone rang twice before it was picked up with a sleepy grunt.

"It's me," he said into the receiver. "Feel like some exercise?"

"On or off the books?" came the reply, the voice instantly awake.

Jackson grinned. He'd known his partner, Lukas Trent, since his first year in the Marines, and they had become close friends over the years. When people were vaulted into the kinds of situations he and Lukas had come up against, trust in skills meant survival, and he trusted Lukas completely. With his life, and now Casey's.

"Off the books," he replied. "For now."

"Important?"

Jackson glanced sideways at the slight form beside him. "Important," he confirmed.

"I'm in."

"Meet me at the usual spot in two hours. Bring your gear."

Snapping the phone shut he returned it to his pocket.

As he drove, Jackson mulled over the events of the evening, his thoughts drifting to Carson in the hospital, then back to that fateful night half a year ago.

Carson wasn't even in town when it all fell apart. Maybe if he had been, it would never have spun so wildly out of control. But Carson *had* been out of town, and by power of elimination, Jackson was the one left bailing both Meghan and Casey out of jail.

Literally.

At the station a detective explained both women had been taken in after some bizarre attack on the bartender at a local hotspot. The bartender ended up with cracked ribs and a row of stitches under his chin.

Jackson had no desire to hear their twisted version of the story that night—or in the days following. He knew Meghan would cover for Casey. She always did.

Both women refused to talk to the police, and since the bartender wouldn't press charges, the whole matter was dropped.

But Jackson couldn't let it go.

It was his straw, his camel, his whole damn desert.

That night he'd demanded Carson put a stop to their friendship before Casey did something even more dangerous.

Only Carson had supported Casey, reminding Jackson she would never intentionally hurt anyone, especially Meghan. Then Carson accused Jackson of overacting, so Jackson did just that.

He overreacted.

Then hung up.

And that was the proverbial that.

Six months ago.

Dragging himself back to the present, Jackson glanced over at the reason behind it all—the sleeping form in the passenger seat. Slouched down against the door, her head resting in the sling of the seatbelt, she looked so young. Harmless.

He frowned and shook his head, shoving down the emotions. He wouldn't get sucked in. Not again.

Harmless, he snorted under his breath.

Harmless as a rattler.

The change in speed woke Casey. Her startled gasp shocked Jackson, and he jerked in the seat when she sat up with a gasp, struggling against the seatbelt.

"You're okay." He glanced towards her, watching her wide-eyed fear slip quickly into confusion then realization.

"I'm okay," she repeated under her breath. Brushing her hair away from her face, she settled back into the seat.

He eased the car to a stop at the bottom of an off-ramp, the left blinker ticking ominously in the silence.

"Where are we?" she asked.

"We're meeting a friend of mine." He rolled through the corner and shifted gears.

"Someone you trust?"

"With my life." He glanced over at her. "And yours."

"Ah." She nodded, turning to look out the window. "Passing me off so soon?"

Jackson sighed to feel the slice of her lack of trust. "Do you always have to do that?"

"Do what?"

"Throw everything I say back in my face?"

"Well if you'd say something nice for once in your life maybe I wouldn't have to."

Jackson knew this wasn't the time or place. He also knew he should shut up, but it was too easy to fall back into their normal pattern of hurtful attacks. The words were out before his mind could order his mouth to shut up. "Maybe if you'd act your age once in a while," he mimicked, "I'd have something nice to say."

"What the hell's that supposed to mean?" she shot back.

"You know damn well what it means." Jackson gripped the steering wheel, hanging on in desperation as six months of pressure exploded forth, and he rode it all out. "You've never taken responsibility for anything you've done, ever. All you do is get yourself into one jam after another and then expect everyone to come rushing to help you when you get in over your head!"

The minute he finished he snapped his mouth shut with a curse. *Brilliant, Jackson.* He dared to catch a glimpse of the stiff-shouldered woman glaring at him from the passenger seat. *Way to keep the peace.*

"Stop the car," Casey spat.

"What?"

"Stop the car," she commanded, undoing her seatbelt.

"Don't be stupid." Jackson clenched his jaw. "Put your seatbelt back on."

"Stop the car or I jump, I swear to God." She reached for the door handle and cracked the door open.

"Jesus, Casey, close the damn door!"

"Stop the car, Jackson!" she shouted.

She gripped the dashboard as Jackson stomped on the breaks and skidded to a stop in the loose gravel at the side of the road. As soon as the car rocked to a stabilized halt, she jumped out and walked back along the shoulder.

Jackson swore and slammed his fist down on the top of the steering wheel. He glared at the woman's form growing smaller and smaller in the side view mirror. Exhaling a loud string of curses, he shut the engine off and got out.

There were no street lights on the lonely stretch of highway, but the moon shone with enough light for him to watch her stomping angrily down the blacktop.

"Damn it, Casey! Would you get back here!" He jogged after her and grabbed her arm. "What the hell is your problem?" He swung her around to face him.

She struggled to pull her arm free, but he wasn't having any of it. He knew he was taking this too far but he couldn't stop now. This conversation had been a long time coming, and there was no place for her to run to get away from it this time. He was going to say his piece and be done with it. To hell with her.

"You don't know anything about anything!" she shouted, trying to pry his fingers loose.

"I don't know anything about what?" he growled.

"The truth!" she hissed, trying to yank her arm free.

Jackson knew if he could see clearly, her eyes would be snapping liquid fire right through him.

"Yeah, and what truth is that...?" He narrowed his eyes.

"Oh no." She shook her head violently from side to side. "Why should I tell you anything? So you can accuse me of lying? Of fantasizing? Of making up some crazy story just to get your attention? Well it won't work, Jackson. Too little, too late. You'll never believe me anyway, and I'm not going to have you phoning Meghan right now asking her if I'm telling the truth!"

"What the hell are you talking about?" Jackson released her arm, confusion abating his anger.

"I'm talking about what really happened that night at Mickey's," she exclaimed. "Isn't that what this little discussion is all about? It's *my* fault you haven't talked to Carson in six months, and now there's a chance he's going to die so you want to justify your actions? Prove to yourself that you were right all along?"

"No! Yes. I mean...." He ran his hands over his face and stared up at the star-filled sky. "Hell, I don't know anymore!"

"Yeah, well that's the kicker, isn't it?" Her voice dropped until it was almost a whisper. "You don't know, do you?"

Jackson looked down. She stood with her feet wide, shoulders back, hands fisted and ready for a fight.

Jackson almost laughed. Almost. Casey was a five foot four inch blonde spitfire, and he had no illusions she wouldn't take a swing at him. And connect. She reasoned like a feral cat. Hissing and spitting then running away. Well, he wasn't letting her run this time. Not until he knew what was going on. If someone was willing to kill for Carson's information he was going to need all his faculties.

Faculties he'd apparently lost along with his temper.

Right now he was standing in the middle of a road, transportation thirty feet behind him, in a completely open area, without one ounce of protection.

He almost groaned.

It seemed Casey Marshall not only drove him insane, she had the ability to distract him from everything he'd been trained to do.

"Look," he tried, keeping his voice neutral. "This isn't the time or the place. Get back in the car. You can hit me later."

She whispered something unintelligible.

Jackson was about to ask her to repeat herself when a pair of headlights appeared over a hill off in the distance. It would be upon them in minutes.

"C'mon, Casey. Someone's coming. Get back in the car." He paused, taking care to ease his tone. "Please."

Casey turned and looked over her shoulder at the twin specks of light. Then she whipped her head around and brushed past him, marching back to the car. She flopped down into the seat and slammed the door. She stared straight ahead, her arms crossed stiffly over her torso, refusing to acknowledge him when he got in. He started the engine and raced back onto the road leaving a shower of dirt and gravel in his wake.

Casey sat hunched against the door, staring out the side window into the darkness. It wasn't long before he heard her breathing change with a restless sleep, her posture slumping further into the edge of the door.

He shook his head at the sad realization that even in sleep she pulled away.   When had they lost even the small shred of humanity they called friendship? When had she become nothing more than a call to his anger? When had he lost sight of the cute, smiling, pigtailed nuisance who followed him everywhere? He knew she was scared. He could see it in her eyes. But instead of comforting her, he had driven her out of his car by bringing up dirt that had been buried for six months.

He mulled over what she had said about him not wanting to hear the truth about that night in the bar. Megan *had* tried to call him...but he hadn't been willing to listen. At least not then. *Was* there more to the story? Had he missed something? Something everyone knew *but* him?

Staring out through the windshield he made himself a promise.

First chance he got, he would hear the truth.

Chapter Four

Casey woke with a stiff neck, a sore back, and the beginnings of another headache. She let out a soft groan and glanced over at the *empty* driver's seat.

She jerked upright with a gasp.

He'd left her?

Oh God, she'd pissed him off, and now he was gone....

She snapped her head around in a panic until her gaze came to rest on a familiar profile lounging against the side of the car. She let out a shaking breath and tried to slow her galloping heartbeat.

He was just getting gas.

His head lifted, and he stared right at her. In the harsh overhead glare of the gas station lights he radiated anger. Danger. Casey couldn't pull her gaze away. She knew she was staring but couldn't stop herself. Part of her wanted to apologize for her earlier outburst. Part wanted to punch and kick him until he admitted he was wrong about her. And a tiny part deep inside wanted to sink back into his arms and hide, like she had in his kitchen.

The pump clicked off, and the moment snapped.

He turned and reseated the nozzle, then headed towards the small store, digging some money out of the back pocket of his jeans. Casey watched him walk. *Stride*, she corrected. Jackson Hale never 'walked' anywhere. He strode. With purpose.

After he disappeared into the convenience store, she looked around, surprised to see they were sitting at a truck stop. The parking lot was huge, with enough room to accommodate a good number of the oversized vehicles and still offer plenty of turning space. A few rigs sat off in the distance, the rumble of their idling engines thrumming through the early morning air.

Next to the gas station was a long, white building with large windows across the front. Inside, Casey saw a few people seated at tables.

Food.

Her stomach rumbled in agreement.

When Jackson returned to the car he didn't say a word. He drove straight across the lot and parked in front of the restaurant. She stared out the windshield at the red neon sign hanging above her head. *Annie's Grill.*

She turned towards him and raised an eyebrow.

"We're here." He nodded and climbed out.

"And where exactly is here?" Casey muttered to the inside of the car as she unclipped her seatbelt. Jackson opened her door and stood back to let her out.

Following behind him she suddenly wondered if he still had the Beretta tucked in the back of his jeans. His jacket covered his waistband, so she couldn't tell.

"Yes," he said over his shoulder. "It's there."

Casey stumbled, annoyed yet intrigued at how he had always been able to answer questions she never voiced aloud.

He turned and held the door open for her. She ducked in under his arm and stepped inside. The warm temperature covered her skin, and she inhaled the scent of fresh coffee.

To the right of the entrance was a large variety store. The brightly lit aisles announced everything from the basic food and household supplies to snacks, chips, and pop. Stretching out in front of her was a long hallway, signs indicating doors to bathrooms, lockers, and truck driver showers. Jackson led her to the left, guiding her beneath the high archway and into the restaurant.

A dozen people sat scattered around, some sitting alone, others clustered in pairs, their conversations low and casual. The mix of booths and regular seating staggered back along the windows to the left. To the right was a long, low counter with individual stools.

Jackson walked towards a table at the back near the fire exit. He motioned for her to sit in front of him, giving him the added advantage of being able to see the entire place with his back against the wall.

A waitress in a mint green apron came by, coffee sloshing around inside the glass decanter she carried. She looked tired but still managed a smile as she asked if they wanted coffee. Casey all but drooled.

"Please!" Casey flipped over the empty mug and slid it towards the edge of the table. Jackson did the same.

"Mmmm." Casey took a sip. It was bland and not very fresh, but it was coffee. "Thank you."

The woman smiled. "You're quite welcome, hon." She dropped the menus on the table and shuffled off to top-up her other customers while she still had a fresh pot. A few minutes later they placed their orders—French toast with a side of crispy bacon for Casey, and pancakes and sausages for Jackson.

They sat in uncomfortable silence, both pretending to be enamored with their coffee while they waited for breakfast. Casey knew he wanted answers, but there was no way she was going to get into it here. As she absently stirred her coffee, jumbled thoughts popped into her head.

He didn't want the truth, he wanted justification.

She wasn't going to be able to offer absolution.

The truth was only going to make things worse.

She struggled to push all thoughts of that night back into the hole she'd buried them in all those months ago.

It was too much, and she wasn't ready to face it yet.

Jackson straightened and nodded once in the direction of the entrance.

"What?" She spun around in her seat, welcoming a distraction.

Her attention was drawn to the man coming through the doors and into the restaurant. There was no way the approaching man was a long haul truck driver. A professional surfer, maybe. Television lifeguard. Beach volleyball player. But most definitely *not* a trucker.

He was tall and lean with a mass of unruly, sun-kissed, dark-blond hair and an I-spend-all-day-at-the-beach kind of tan. His features were classic—piercing blue eyes, a strong tapered nose, and a clean-shaven jaw. A white three-quarter sleeve shirt hung half unbuttoned over a pair of faded jeans, revealing the top of what appeared to be a very solid six pack.

The only thing that caught Casey as odd was his footwear.

Well worn, military service boots.

Ah.

Jackson nodded as the blond man slid into a seat beside him.

"Lukas Trent, at your service." The man gave Casey a lazy smile and held out his hand. She placed her hand in his, and he lifted hers to brush a small kiss across the back of her knuckles.

Casey raised an eyebrow and looked at Jackson. "Is he for real?"

"He thinks so." Jackson snorted and glared at Lukas. "You can let go of her hand now. And do up your shirt."

Lukas winked at Casey but continued to keep her fingers pressed between his. "He's just jealous. Always has been." He paused and angled his head. "And you are?"

Casey knew the minute she'd locked eyes on the boots that Jackson's *buddy* was more than just a friend. She'd bet her breakfast that Lukas also worked for the Colonel.

"Casey Marshall," she smiled widely, "at *your* service."

Lukas gave Jackson a sideways glance. "Casey *Marshall*?" he repeated.

Casey grinned and rubbed her thumb across the back of Lukas' hand. Out of the corner of her eye she noticed Jackson frown. She leaned towards Lukas, still smiling, and winked conspiratorially. "Yes,

Marshall. If you know Jackson, then you *must* have heard of Colonel Thomas Marshall?" she gushed, her voice bubbly. She wrinkled her nose. "Well, the Colonel is my Uncle...practically my daddy."

Lukas snatched his hand back in horror, and Jackson snorted.

Casey laughed, pushing back in her seat as the waitress arrived with their food order and a menu for Lukas. Without standing on ceremony, Casey dug right into her breakfast. In the few minutes it took for the waitress to come back to top up their coffee and take Lukas' order, Casey had cleaned her plate. She glanced up.

Lukas stared at her in awe, and Jackson smirked around a mouth full of pancake.

"What?" she asked, pointing back and forth between them with her fork. "I was hungry."

Lukas grinned. "I didn't say anything."

After everyone had finished eating and another round of fresh coffee topped their mugs, Lukas' expression turned serious. He dropped his elbows onto the table and leaned in. "So. What's up?"

Jackson dug into the back pocket of his jeans for Carson's letter, which he handed to Lukas.

Lukas quickly read the note and whistled softly. "Interesting." He folded the paper and handed it back.

They gave Lukas a fast, summarized version of the events of the past twenty-four hours.

"Sounds like fun. I'm in." Lukas nodded.

"In what?" Casey asked.

"In for whatever we're up to next."

Jackson snorted. "What Lukas means to say is that he's bored. And apparently we're having more fun than he is."

Lukas grinned at Casey.

"Okay." Casey shook her head slowly then turned to Jackson. "So...now what?"

He dug the three keys out of the front pocket of his jeans. "You have a pen?"

Casey dropped her chin, glanced down the front of herself, then peered at him through her bangs. "You're kidding, right?"

Jackson shook his head. "What?"

"I think she's wondering where you suspect she'd be carrying a pen," Lukas suggested.

"Precisely," Casey agreed.

"She has pockets." Jackson frowned.

"Hmm." Casey snorted, standing up. She walked over to the counter and returned with a pen and a couple of children's coloring page placemats.

Lukas grabbed one and glanced up at Casey. "What? No crayons?"

"I got you a pen too." She pointed at the second pen.

Jackson scowled and snatched the sheet of paper back. "Would you two pay attention?"

Casey slid her chair around to the side of the table as Jackson flipped over the tags on each key so they could read the notes.

Pappy's tackle box.

Cu'bo #16.

J's secret hiding spot.

Casey turned to Jackson. "You *do* know what these mean, right?"

"I'm pretty sure about two of them," he confirmed.

"Secret code?" Lukas asked.

"No, they're just things that only Carson and I would know about. I'm guessing he was worried about someone else seeing this." Jackson turned his attention to the keys. "This one is easy. It's Carson's parents' old place."

"That beautiful old Victorian over on West Gate?" Casey asked.

Jackson smirked. "Yeah. It was such a cool place for a kid. We used to spend hours trying to find secret passageways. And no," he frowned, looking at Lukas, "there weren't any secret passageways."

Lukas made a face.

"But I did find a couple of cool hiding spots I used over the years." Jackson held up the largest of the three keys. "This, I'm guessing, is a door key for that old house."

"Carson kept a key to his parents' house after they sold it?" Casey leaned forward. "I think it's changed hands at least twice. Wouldn't they have changed the locks?"

Jackson stared at the silver key in his hand. "This has to be new, because whatever he put there, he put it there recently."

Lukas picked up the other two keys. "And these?"

Jackson flipped the tags around and held up *Pappy's tackle box.* "Every summer up until high-school we used to rent a cottage up at Lake Cushman."

"Hey, I remember that place!" Casey interjected.

"The cottage two over was owned by an older man," Jackson continued. "I don't remember what his name was. Uncle Wayne thought he looked like a character from this old TV show he used to watch. *Black Sheep Squadron.* He started calling the man 'Pappy' after the main character in the show. The guy thought it was hilarious, so it stuck. That's the Pappy part. The tackle box could literally mean a tackle box. There was a small shed on the property right down by the water's edge. The key could be to the shed itself or something inside it, if it's still there. Or for something else on the property. What exactly I'm not sure, but it would be something new."

Casey read off the third location. "Cu'bo number sixteen?"

"That one has me a little stumped." Jackson shrugged and glanced at Casey. "The only thing I can think of is when Meghan was little she couldn't say school bus. It came out sounding like *coo-bow*. Hell, I still tease her about it."

"And sixteen?" Lukas and Casey asked at the same time.

"Poke, poke," Lukas began.

"You owe me a Coke...." Casey grinned, quoting the old schoolyard taunt.

Jackson gave them both a stern frowning. "A number sixteen school bus could be anywhere. But I don't think that's it. I definitely think it has to do with a bus."

He scanned the restaurant, then shook his head and looked back down at the key in his palm. "Carson would have wanted me to be able to get to the information fast. He wouldn't have spread it too far apart. We know one location is the old house, the other is the cottage. It has to be something close to either one of those, or in between."

"There are a couple of schools near the old house; maybe it's in one of the busses?" Casey asked hopefully.

"I thought about that but they're city schools." He shrugged. "They'd only have a few busses, and neither Meghan nor Carson rode the bus. It has to be something they're directly connected to. Something specific."

Lukas nodded in agreement. "Carson wanted *you* specifically to find these so it's something you'd be connected to—not just him or Meghan."

"I walked to school." Jackson shook his head.

"Maybe it's not a school bus at all," Casey said thoughtfully, pursing her lips.

"And...?" Lukas urged.

"Cu'bo." She took the key from Jackson's palm, holding the tiny card between her thumb and index finger. "Carson knew you'd remember that's what Meghan called a school bus. So we might be looking at something connected to you and Meghan, not Carson and Meghan."

"Casey, Meghan and I never did anything together," Jackson said firmly.

Lukas nudged Jackson. "Let her finish."

Casey thanked Lukas with a brief nod, then continued. "I was thinking that maybe this clue isn't for you. Maybe it's for me."

"You." Jackson scowled.

"You just said Carson was trying to tell you something about Meghan and a school bus, but you and Meghan never did anything together." She paused. "Well, Meghan and I did."

"Yes, but you never rode the bus either." Jackson sighed. "This is going nowhere. Maybe we should just start with these two and try to figure the last one out later."

"I've already figured it out," Casey insisted.

Jackson snorted. "You've already figured it out."

"Yes."

"Well, by all means, enlighten us."

Casey frowned. "Jackson, you really are a jerk, you know that?"

"My apologies. If you think you know then go right ahead."

Lukas cleared his throat.

"Do you have to be so condescending?" She crossed her arms over her chest.

"I'm not being condescending. I'm very curious to hear how you figured it all out in your sleep after I've spent the last two hours racking my brain for the answer."

"You couldn't solve a puzzle if one fell on you."

"Yes, well I was having a perfectly miserable Sunday morning all on my own until you *fell* in my front door!"

"Oh yeah, and my weekend was absolutely spectacular!" Casey huffed.

"Well maybe if you paid more attention to what was going on around you...."

She slapped her palms on the table. "You know, just once I'd like to spend five minutes with you without you treating me like an idiot."

Lukas cleared his throat. "Jackson," he muttered.

"I never said you were an idiot," Jackson continued.

"No, you just treat me like I'm completely stupid." Casey poked Jackson in the shoulder with her index finger. "Like that mysterious phone call you made in the car? You think I don't know you called Uncle Thomas? *Ice Man*?" she mimicked. "Block-head is more like it."

Jackson opened his mouth, but Lukas gave him a hard jab to the ribs.

The elbow had the desired effect. Jackson closed his mouth, took a deep breath, and turned to face Lukas. "What!" he growled.

"You asked for my help, so it starts here," Lukas stated. "Let her finish. You can argue about who solved what later. Right now you need to find all three locations. So kiss and make up and move on."

Jackson sat back in his seat and threaded his arms across his chest.

Casey glared at him a little longer before turning her head and speaking to Lukas.

"Jackson and Meghan never rode the bus, but Meghan and I did. I spent a couple of summers up at the cottage with them after my parents died. The last year we were there, right before Meghan and I started university, we signed up for a sailing camp at the resort. We spent the week out on the lake learning how to use these little one-man sailing skiffs."

She paused to take a breath.

"And?" Lukas prompted.

"They picked us up in a bus to drive us around to the docks at the other side of the lake. An old school bus that had been painted blue. Each side of the bus had huge white letters that read 'Cushman Boats'. Most of the letters had fallen off. One side had no letters at all. The other side had only four letters left...."

"The C and the U from Cushman, and the B and O from Boats," Jackson finished. "Cu'bo."

Lukas whistled softly and nodded to Casey. "Nicely done."

Jackson shifted in his seat, nodding thoughtfully.

"There's a row of lockers at the marina." Casey shrugged. "Cu'bo number sixteen."

Three pairs of eyes dropped to the key on the table.

After a moment's silence, she stood and shoved her chair back to its original side. "I need to find the ladies' room. And you're welcome."

With a disgusted snort, she turned and walked away.

Lukas leaned forward, resting his arms on the table. "You know, that was pretty good reasoning on her part."

Jackson stared at the spot where Casey had disappeared. "Yeah, it was."

"So.... Is there, ah...anything going on between you two?"

Jackson frowned at Lukas. "What are you talking about?"

"You." Lukas raised his eyebrows. "And Casey."

"No there's nothing going on," Jackson said sharply.

"Are you sure?" Lukas narrowed his eyes.

"Yes I'm sure!" Jackson scowled.

"Good." Lukas smiled.

"Good?"

"She's beautiful." Lukas grinned. "I wonder if her hair is as soft as it looks. And those eyes...she could stare right through a man with those baby blues."

"Lukas...," Jackson growled quietly.

"Hey. You said there was nothing going on," he said innocently.

"Don't even think about it."

"But you—"

"Enough."

Lukas laughed. "Fine." Then his expression turned serious. "So what's the game plan?"

Jackson scratched the stubble on the side of his face. "We need to get the info and go from there. Those guys came to my house tonight specifically looking for her. And no, she doesn't know that. I'd toss this whole thing to the police, but—"

"But Carson believed there was someone on the inside," Lukas finished.

Jackson nodded.

"The Feds?"

"I thought about it. But we have nothing. Carson had an accident. Casey doesn't remember. The guys at my place were burglars. All coincidental without hard proof. And besides, the whole situation is...," he searched for the proper words.

"Too personal?" Lukas suggested.

Jackson ground his teeth together. Someone was hurting his family. And that was not acceptable. No matter what he thought of Casey, she was his responsibility now, and he would protect her at all costs. But he needed to know what he was up against. He didn't agree with people taking the law into their own hands, but if the law was already on the wrong side, the decision was a hell of a lot easier to make.

"We're up against goons with guns and we have no information. We need to know who the players are and what's involved. If it's enough we'll contact your buddy at the FBI."

Lukas nodded in agreement.

"I left a message at the office," Jackson added, his thoughts jumping. "We'll need someone to check into the two guys trussed up in my front hallway."

"What do you want me to do?" Lukas asked.

"You sure?" Jackson turned towards his long-time friend.

"I'm sure."

Jackson grabbed one of the placemats and flipped it over to the blank side. He sketched out a rough map from their current location to the lake, drawing in the old cottage, Pappy's shed, and the docks at the resort. He handed the two smaller keys to Lukas, along with the map.

"Take these two, and we'll take the house. Get in and get out. Watch your back and don't be a hero. Whoever these guys are, they're playing for keeps."

"Roger that." Lukas stood. "What about you?"

"There are a couple of small motels up the road. We'll grab a room and hole up. There's no way we'll be able to do anything until after dark tonight anyway. We'll touch base tomorrow."

"And the Colonel?" Lukas asked as he dropped the two keys into the front pocket of his jeans and folded the map.

"His cell was off. I left a message at the house. At this point, there's not much he can do. Hopefully he'll check his messages when he gets back."

Lukas nodded and turned to leave.

"Lukas." Jackson's call turned him back. "Thanks."

"Anytime, Lieutenant." Lukas flashed him a saucy smirk before striding towards the entrance.

Jackson moved to his feet. Casey still hadn't returned. Tossing some money down on the table, he threaded his way through the tables. In the variety store across the hall he saw a flash of blonde and headed towards it. She stood in the middle of one of the aisles, reading the label on a box of toothpaste.

She brushed past him and headed towards the cash register. Dropping the toothpaste, a bottle of Tylenol, and two toothbrushes onto the counter, she handed the clerk her money. Collecting her change and the small plastic bag with the items, she turned around and looked up. "What?"

"Don't wander off," he scowled.

"I didn't wander off." Casey stepped past him and walked to the door. "Where's Lukas?"

Placing his hand on her upper arm, Jackson propelled her out the front doors and into the early morning sunshine.

"Ouch," she muttered when he opened the passenger door for her. "Guess I should have grabbed sunglasses."

Once they were back on the road, Jackson finally answered her last question.

"Lukas went to the lake with the first two keys."

"Ahh." Casey nodded. "And the third key?"

"We'll wait until tonight then head back to the city. You and I will check out the house."

"And until then?"

"Until then," he paused, "we stay off the road."

The "Good-Nite" motel was an older looking brown brick building set back from the road. A single row of beige doors stretched beneath the long overhang that ran the length of the building.

Jackson parked in front of the office and shut off the car. "Wait here," he ordered, not sparing her a glance as he climbed out of the vehicle.

Casey studied him through the large picture window that looked out from the main office. A tall, skinny young man with sandy blond hair stood behind the counter. He had to be in his early twenties at the most. Jackson was politely chatting while he filled out a registration card and placed cash on the counter. The kid smiled and nodded and at one point glanced out the window to where she sat in the car. Handing Jackson a key, the young man pointed to his right.

Jackson returned to the car and parked off to the side. He led the way to one of the middle units, a large silver number five hanging on the frame. Unlocking the door, he ushered her inside.

Casey glanced around quickly at the typical motel setup. Two double beds against the wall to the right, each covered in a dark floral print bedspread. Between them, a nightstand held a small lamp, an old digital alarm clock, a phone, and the television remote. On the opposite side of the room sat a long, low dresser and a hutch hiding the television set. The bathroom, at the back to the right, sat across from a short shelf with an empty closet rod. Cut through the bare back wall was a long, narrow window with faded yellow curtains half covering the frosted glass.

Once inside, the door locked and the curtains drawn, Jackson tossed his duffel down onto the closest bed. He shed his jacket and dropped it down beside the bag. Pulling the Beretta out of the back of his jeans he set it on the table next to the TV remote and flopped down on his back, crossed his arms under his head, and closed his eyes.

His breathing was relaxed and shallow. At first glance he looked like he was sleeping, but Casey knew better.

Wandering to the middle of the room, Casey stared at the white-washed walls, unsure of what to do with herself. She was definitely tired. And if they were going to be running around tonight she should get some rest herself. She should just give it up and go to bed.

But she was still angry. She turned to glare at the relaxed form of the man on the bed. Jackson had completely shot down her ideas before she'd even had a chance to say anything. Again. And she'd been right. Again. And then he'd gotten all pissy because she'd walked away.

He was nothing if not infuriating.

Her eyes moved to the weapon on the nightstand.

"Thinking about shooting me?" He snorted.

She jumped at the sound of his voice. His eyes were still closed. God, she hated how he could do that!

"The thought had crossed my mind," she muttered.

Kicking off her shoes, she took the small plastic bag she held to the bathroom and shoved the door closed. She sighed and stared at herself in the harsh light of the overhead fluorescents. She looked like hell. Dumping the contents of the bag onto the counter, she took two of the painkillers then brushed her teeth.

She examined the bandage behind her ear. Peeling back one of the corners she studied the long, harsh gouge in her skull.

From a bullet.

With a shake in her fingers she pressed the tape against her skin and straightened her head. Her hair fell back down around her shoulders, hiding the stark white of the bandage.

She stared at her reflection, willing her mind to remember something, *anything*, from the missing hours. She tried closing her eyes. Then she tried squinting. She tried waving her hands around in front of her face. Mental word games. Sitting on the closed lid of the toilet. Standing in the middle of the room. Massaging her temples.

Nothing worked.

It was still blank.

The memories were still gone.

When Jackson knocked on the door she just about jumped out of her skin.

"You fall in?" His voice was muffled through the wood.

She yanked the door open and almost stepped back.

Filling the doorway, with his hands resting on either side of the frame, he was an imposing figure. He watched her, waiting for her to make the first move.

"Excuse me," she challenged, tilting her head.

He waited a moment before dropping his arms and stepping back.

She walked across the room and sat on the far bed. It was bad enough they would be sharing a room, but with this proximity she doubted sleep would be an option. Her heart was doing a silly pattering dance just thinking about it.

She looked over her shoulder. He still stood next to the bathroom, his legs apart and his arms threaded across his chest. The way he frowned told her he was braced for a fight.

And she knew exactly what it was he wanted to fight about. She let out a loud, dramatic breath. "Damn it, Jackson. I'm too tired to argue. So whatever you're going to say, just say it and get it over with." She showed him her back and stared forward at the heavy drapes hanging across the front window.

When he spoke his voice was low and fast. "We need to clear something up before we go any further. You can't be jumping out of vehicles the minute the conversation moves to something you don't want to talk about."

"So now it's something I don't want to talk about?" she blurted out. "You're the one who's been playing ignorant for the last six months. Why is it so important now?"

"Because I'm going to be your shadow until we figure this out. That means we're about to spend a lot of time together. And since we can't seem to go more than two seconds without ripping into each other, we need to clear the air now. I need to know you're going to do what I say, when I say it."

"Fine," she muttered. "What and when."

"Casey, this isn't a game. These people have real guns."

"I think I've already figured that one out."

"Good. I want some answers, and we may as well start right at the beginning—Mickey's."

"I am *so* not getting into this with you now."

"Okay look." He exhaled and dropped his arms, his voice losing some of its bite. "I apologize for not listening back then. But I'm listening now. It's just you and me. You know damn well it's hanging out there and we have to deal with it so we can move on and figure out how to help Carson."

At the mention of Carson's name, Casey scowled at the curtains. She knew he was going for the guilt card, and damn him if it wasn't working. But how could telling him about that night have anything to do with Carson?

She turned her head.

He still stood in front of the bathroom, his arms hanging at his sides. His expression was closed and hard, but she saw the trace of sadness lurking in the depths of his eyes. He loved Carson too. And he had a right to know what really happened that night.

But the answer wasn't going to help him reach absolution.

The answer would hurt.

She thought back to the night at the jail.

God, she'd never been so scared before in her life. Sitting on the bench inside the station, they could hear the bartender, the bar's owner, and their lawyer in the chief's office. The threats. The lies. She never stood a chance.

And then *he'd* walked into the police station, all brooding dark fury, and she'd never been so glad to see anyone so much in her life.

Her fear had taken a back seat to her relief to know he was here. Jackson had come. Jackson would make it all right.

But then he'd turned the anger to her.

And she'd broken.

"Tell me," he asked again, snapping her back into the present.

The memory of his betrayal burned through her heart, and her shoulders dropped in defeat. "Damn it Jackson, it's not worth getting into." Her voice lowered an octave and slowed. "Just let it go."

"I can't let it go," he began. "Not anymore. If you want me to call Meghan at the hospital I will. But I'd rather hear it from you."

He extracted his cell phone from the pocket of his jacket, and she leapt up and grabbed his arm.

"Leave Meghan alone. She's got enough to deal with."

He looked at her expectantly, but she turned away. Walking over to the front window, she cracked open the drapes and peeked out at the parking lot. "Why is this so important all of a sudden?"

"You brought it up last night."

"No," she spoke to the glass, "*you* did. Accusing me of making up this whole thing with Carson. Telling me once again how worthless I am. Carson didn't call you that night just to bail us out, Jackson. He called you for your help. *We* needed your help. But lucky for us the charges were dropped and we didn't have to beg you for anything." She sighed and shook her head, fighting the pain of the memories.

She'd been so stupid to believe he'd help her that night.

So naïve.

And she was just as stupid and naïve to think he'd help her now.

She laughed at the realization, the sound sharp and bitter. "You wouldn't have helped me that night if Megan wasn't there. And I have absolutely no idea what made me think you'd help me this time." Letting the curtains drop, she turned towards the door.

Jackson stood in front of her so suddenly she hadn't seen him move.

"You came to me, remember?"

"Yeah." She nodded fiercely. "And you're never going to let me forget it, are you?"

"Nope," he acknowledged.

"Move." She glared up at him and stepped to the side, but he quickly countered.

"No."

"Damn it, Jackson," she cursed, her hands balling into fists at her sides.

"You're not leaving." He crossed his arms over his chest. "Until I'm finished."

His words fueled her anger, and she couldn't stop the flood of emotion. Her brain was crushed under the flood of raw pain that surged up through her heart.

"Finished?" she squeaked. "Finished what? Finished telling me what you think of me? Well that's old news. I already know. I think I've always known. I stopped trying to change your mind years ago. Mickey's was just the proverbial icing on the cake for you, wasn't it? Well I'm glad you didn't find out what happened. You're such a jerk you probably would have told them I deserved to be raped!"

Raped?

Oxygen exploded out of the room, leaving Jackson feeling like he was drowning.

Casey stood in front of him, her eyes wide and unblinking. She exhaled a pained squeak and clamped her hands over her mouth. Shuddering violently, she shoved her hands against his chest and used his stunned silence to push past him. Her motion snapped him out of his lost state, and he dove forward. With firm hands he strangled her arm and spun her around to face him.

She drove her palms against his ribcage, pushing back. Blue eyes bore into his, searing his brain with a tangled mix of pain and fear.

The situation was wrong, disjointed. Her words couldn't have been right. She stopped moving, and he braced for her to try to kick out. Then he realized with a sudden flash her fear might not have to do with the story. He released her and stepped back, his chest clenched with the thought that she could be afraid of *him*.

She stared up at him, her breathing harsh and fast. She bit the inside of her lip and glanced over his shoulder at the closed door.

Jackson wasn't sure he'd be able to stop her if she wanted to leave this time.

Dropping her gaze to the floor, she walked around him, giving him as wide a berth as the room would allow. She crossed the faded carpet to stand at the far side of the window. Cracking the edges of the curtains, she peeked out through the dirt-streaked glass.

Her shoulders slumped, and she sighed heavily. "Last summer when I was working at Mickey's for a couple of months, Brian was one of the regular bartenders. He was...." She shook her head and dropped her weight to lean against the window frame. "He was always coming on to me. At first it wasn't any big deal—just harmless flirting. It was annoying sure, but I just ignored him. Then it started getting...," she paused, searching for the word, raising one shoulder then dropping it, "weird. Touchy feely. I kept telling him to back off, but that just seemed to egg him on. And then...." She shook her head and sighed.

"Then?" he croaked and cleared his throat.

"A couple of times he caught me alone in the employee area and tried to put the moves on," she continued, talking at the glass, her voice just above a whisper. "One night, when we were closing up...." She hesitated, letting the curtain fall back over the window. Rolling until her back was against the wall, she tipped her head back and squeezed her eyes shut. "He locked me in the back storage room with him. He

53

was pissed off that I kept rejecting him. Kept telling me all the things he wanted to do to me. Who knows, I mean, maybe if one of the other girls hadn't come back to get something it might have turned out differently, but nothing happened, and I...I quit the next day."

"You quit."

She nodded.

"But nothing happened."

She nodded again, blinking open her eyes. Jackson saw the pain and horror swirling beneath the unshed tears, and it tore into him. She dropped her chin to stare at the floor. He stepped forward, stopping in front of her, staring down at the top of her head. What her voice lost in intensity, his blood gained twofold. He had to force himself to breathe. To wait. To listen.

"I wasn't supposed to be out with Meghan that night, you know," she finally said, speaking to her sock-covered toes. "She was meeting people from work, but they stood her up. She called me to come join her. I guess...I guess she heard from one of the waitresses that Brian wasn't working there anymore so I didn't think anything of it. She never would have phoned if she'd known."

She shuddered, and Jackson almost reached out, but he held himself off, his hands fisted at his sides.

"I didn't notice him working behind the bar. I wasn't paying attention. Never occurred to me he'd still be working there."

Jackson couldn't keep his muscles from clenching. His stomach surged. He didn't want to hear this. This wasn't what she was supposed to be saying.

"I had to go to the bathroom, and with the music and the crowd I never heard him coming."

Her voice cracked, and he couldn't stand still any longer. His arms locked around her, and he pulled her away from the wall and up against his chest. She stood stiffly before him, fighting his embrace, but he refused to let go. After a moment, the tentative touch of her palms brushed against his hips. Resting his chin on the top of her head, he mentally emptied a full clip into the phantom bartender.

"He just shoved me into the office and knocked me onto the floor," she whispered, her breath soft against the base of his throat.

Jackson growled.

The bartender is a dead man.

She wiggled, and he realized how tightly he held her. He released her and took a step back. Long blonde hair curtained her downturned face.

"Okay." He cleared his throat and swallowed. "I get it. You don't have to finish."

Her entire body stiffened, and her head snapped to the side. She lifted her head; there was no sadness to be seen, only fire and pain.

"I don't have to finish?" She lurched forward and jabbed him in the chest with her finger, her voice once again fast and angry. "Oh no. No, no. You don't get to turn it off and on, Jackson. You wanted the story so here's the story. All of it! You're the one who wanted to know what *I* did to get Meghan arrested, remember? Well here it is. What *I* did to cause it."

"I'm sorry," he apologized, guilt kicking him in the gut. "I don't...I understand now."

"No, Jackson, you don't," she hissed, her eyes shining with unshed tears. "You don't *understand* anything. Nothing I do is good enough for you and your precious family. Well they're my family too! In all the years we've known each other have you ever seen me *purposely* hurt anyone? No! But you still jumped to your high and mighty conclusions without one little detail. Well let me know when you've had enough of the details. Would you like me to *detail* how heavy Brian was when he sat on me? How scared I was? How I struggled to push him off as he was groping me? How the hand covering my mouth tasted so much like bar lime the smell of the stuff makes me want to puke now? How's that for details?"

She stood in front of him with shoulders stiff and hands balled into fists at her sides. He couldn't shake the image of her struggling under the weight of a faceless attacker from his mind.

That night he'd pushed her away.

Ignored her.

Blamed her.

Sent her home in a cab to deal with the aftermath alone.

He was no better than the scumbag who caused it.

He tightened his fingers around Brian's invisible neck.

"Casey...."

She ignored him and pressed forward, verbally forcing his six foot four inch frame back against the wall.

"Or maybe...," she swallowed then continued, "maybe you'd rather I just stick to the facts and tell you that he managed to rip my underwear off and was so busy concentrating on undoing his pants that he never heard Meghan open the door."

"Meghan?" Jackson thought he spoke but the croaking sound couldn't have been his voice.

She took several steps back and shook her head, whipping her hair across her shoulders.

"Oh, don't worry, your precious Meghan took care of him before he could get it out of his pants. She hit him with a chair then kicked him square in the face. Knocked him cold. She was awesome."

"Why didn't you tell that to the police?" he asked.

"Because the owner took his side. Because *you* took his side." She let out a sad laugh, her voice dropping to a low whisper. She stared down at her lap, her hands twisting madly around each other. "Brian is a good-looking guy. He's good for business. Women come to see good-looking men; men come to see the women. It was them against us, and hell, Jackson, you've known me since we were kids and you wouldn't even give me the time of day, so why should they?"

Jackson didn't reply.

He didn't need to.

The answer was simple.

He was a Grade A, number one, punch-me-I-deserve-it jackass.

"You should have told me." He forced his feet to move and crossed to the bed.

"Why?" She wiped at a rogue tear. "You wouldn't have done anything. If it had been Meghan...." She shook her head, squeezing her eyes closed. "You'd have probably killed him." She lifted her shoulder with a soft snort, then lowered it. "But me?"

"That's not true and you know it." He dropped to a crouch in front of her, cupping her hands between his, stopping the fierce twisting she was doing with her fingers. He stared at her downturned face, willing her to look at him. To believe him.

"It *is* true and you know it," she whispered, her eyes snapping to his. "If it had been just Meghan you would have been all over that police station until the charges were dropped no matter what anyone said." She blinked and licked her lower lip. "But because I was there you automatically blamed me. You didn't care what the truth was. You took one look at me and did your whole judge-and-jury routine." Her voice trailed off, and she dropped her gaze to her lap where his hands still clutched hers. "You've never believed me, Jackson. Or believed *in* me."

As he knelt on the floor in front of her, feeling her fingers digging into themselves despite the heavy press of his palms, Jackson turned off the terrifying mental images of what Brian could have done to her and concentrated on the words.

She was completely right.

That night, he would have turned the police station upside down for Meghan.

But her? He'd been so sure it was just another one of her dumb stunts....

He'd been wrong.

So wrong.

He'd blamed her.

It was not her fault.

But what *would* he have done if something worse had happened that night? Would he have ignored it because it wasn't Meghan? God, he hoped he was a better man than that.

He searched his memory for a time when he didn't immediately jump to conclusions about Casey, and he couldn't find anything. Had he always treated her that way?

Whenever he returned on leave or between assignments there had always been something going on involving Casey and Meghan. They were the double-mint twins of trouble. But he didn't remember Carson ever telling him anything out of the ordinary happened whenever Jackson was away. Why was it things always happened whenever he was around?

Or was it just him?

He reached up and cupped her chin, pleading with her to look at him. When her eyes met his, he saw the anger and the sadness fighting each other for control. A tear escaped and trickled down her left cheek.

He leaned forward and placed his palm against her soft skin, using his thumb to wipe away the drop. Finding his voice he managed to croak out, "Oh, Brat...." He shook his head slowly, his heart defaulting to the only nick-name he'd ever called her growing up. "I'm sorry. Please. Don't cry."

Her eyes widened. And then she did something he never expected.

She smiled.

It was sad, it was hurting, but it was a smile. And it was magic. Changed the presence of the room. Flashed. Then faded.

"I don't understand." He frowned, slowly lowering his hand from her cheek.

"No." She dropped her head again, hiding her face behind her hair. Her voice was quiet. "You don't."

"Explain it to me," he pleaded.

"I can't."

He cupped her chin again and guided her face up, forcing her to look at him. She looked worried now. Frightened.

Of me?

Thinking she was somehow afraid of him on a personal level cut more deeply than knowing he'd blamed her. He wanted to grab her. Pull her close. Convince her she had no cause to fear him. Make her see how sorry he was. He never meant to hurt her. Tell her he couldn't understand why he always reacted that way whenever he was around her.

"Please," he begged.

She narrowed her eyes, studying him. Then she blinked, and the blue color changed, darkened, and he suddenly felt very warm. Too warm.

Reaching out, he tucked a strand of hair behind her ear. Her lips parted, and she sucked in a sharp breath at his touch. Her tongue darted out and moistened her bottom lip. He couldn't tear his eyes away.

Then she lifted her chin ever so slightly and pressed her lips to his.

The instant her mouth touched his, a current slammed through his entire body. His brain tried to reason that she was just being over emotional.

She didn't have any feelings for him.

Touching her would be a huge mistake.

This was a really, *really* bad idea.

But he couldn't seem to get the memo out to the rest of his body.

Her kiss was softness and innocence. A contradiction that made him question everything. Her fingers gripped a handful of his t-shirt. His brain resigned, and lust stepped right in to fill the position.

He wove his fingers through her hair, twisting the long locks around his hand. She made a small keening noise in the back of her throat, and he almost lost it completely.

His arm hooked around her waist, drawing her closer. She slid forward off the mattress, landing in his lap. He sat back on his heels, and she dropped her knees to the floor, straddling him. His groin sought out the heat between her legs, and he heard her soft moan as she pressed against the hardness. One hand fisted in the soft blonde tangles of her hair, and the other caressed the smooth skin of her lower back where her shirt had ridden up.

God she felt so good.

He savored the feel of her body pressed up against his, her legs around his. Her heat. Skin like cool silk flexed beneath his palm. He traced the curve of her spine with the pad of his thumb, sliding his hand down to the edge of her jeans.

He slipped his fingers under her waistband, and she gasped.

Her head jerked up, breaking their kiss.

Jackson was briefly hypnotized by the dark blue intensity of her eyes. Churning, swirling. Desire and confusion. Her lips were swollen and parted as she fought for air. He knew he was breathing just as erratically because his heart danced madly behind his rib cage.

She shimmied back up onto the mattress and continued to crab crawl away until her back met the headboard. She pulled her knees to her chest and grabbed a pillow, covering herself with it like a shield.

Jackson might have smiled to see she was just as affected—if his groin wasn't so damn uncomfortable.

He stood up slowly and tried to adjust, but the way she stared wide-eyed at the bulge in his jeans wasn't making his erection any smaller.

Then her cheeks pinked, and she looked quickly away. "Oh God, I'm sorry...," she muttered, hiding her mouth behind her palm. "I don't know.... I didn't...." She squeezed her eyes shut and muffled the rest of her thought with the pillow.

Since there was only one viable option, Jackson backed towards to the bathroom. "I'm going to take a shower." He tried for calm but felt rather glad he could talk coherently at all. "Maybe you should get some rest."

Practically launching himself into the white-tiled room, he latched the door, stripped, and quickly threw himself under a spray of very, very cold water.

As he stood in the water, goose bumps breaking over his skin, he couldn't think past the single question that rotated through his mind.

What the hell had just happened?

Chapter Five

Leaning back in his obscenely expensive leather desk chair, Harrison Douglas sipped an imported single-malt and surveyed the city from his thirty-forth floor corner office. It was late afternoon, and the normal people sat in bumper-to-bumper traffic, scurrying to return to their homes in the suburban maze like little mice.

Harrison no longer had to worry about making that drive. His commute was the length of his penthouse. It never ceased to amaze him how people could spend their entire working lives complaining about having to sit in traffic every day—and not do anything about it.

Well, he had certainly done something about it.

There was no way he was going to finish his life penniless and broken the way his father had. It had been pathetic. Watching him waste away his final years, alone, in the low income accommodations of a state run facility.

There was no way Harrison was going to end up in a public anything. He was personally making sure of that.

He had drive.

Determination.

Work ethic.

But so did a hundred other people in his field.

No, it wasn't what you knew, it was *who* you knew.

And he had come to know a lot of influential people in his rise to the top. Influential people who were more than willing to trade favors and instill knowledge.

The first lesson he learned?

Money could buy more than possessions...it could buy people. If Harrison didn't have someone in his address book who could help his cause, he went out and bought someone.

It was a lesson which served him well as he rose through the ranks to become the biggest name in commercial real-estate. A name which now reached beyond the country's borders.

Three years ago he had been approached with an offer and opportunity he couldn't refuse. An international developer with a not-so-rosy reputation was looking to build a showcase piece on American soil. They were willing to pay anything to make it happen.

It was his chance to make millions with one deal. His greatest accomplishment and his final contribution to the field of real-estate.

After the sale was completed he would be a millionaire several times over. The money would fund several investment portfolios to carry him through early retirement and straight into the playboy lifestyle he deserved.

And now, he was close enough to his final goal that he could taste the champagne and caviar. Years of planning and organizing, networking and bribing, collecting and molding. Everything was finally falling into place, and the closer he got to the finish the more excited he became.

His plan was quite ingenious, really.

He had delicately calculated all the possible outcomes before putting the final pieces into motion. All the chance scenarios. All except one.

The reporter.

There were millions of dollars invested and millions more to be made, and there was no way some cockroach of a journalist was going to stop him.

In another lifetime he may have respected Carson as a man of great intelligence—a worthy opponent.

But this was not that lifetime.

So Carson Hale had been dealt with. Regrettably, his meddling also required his assistant to be similarly silenced. Unfortunately, the woman was proving to be less than cooperative with her own demise.

Harrison swung around and faced the man waiting patiently in a guest chair.

Marcus Sandiman was one of the best fixers in the country. And he was completely for hire. Harrison had been bankrolling Sandiman's retirement fund on and off over the years and had finally put him on a very expensive retainer two months ago. While it was a pricy investment, Sandiman's skills were worth every penny in Harrison's mind.

To look at Sandiman was to see a non-descript man in his late forties with dark brown hair and brown eyes. He was an average height, average build, and dressed like half the businessmen in the city. He drove a sedan, lived in a middle of the road apartment complex, and was completely unnoticeable.

Until you looked in his eyes.

And if you were one of the people unlucky enough to get a close look, you would see he was anything but ordinary.

Marcus Sandiman was a cold blooded killer.

And he loved his work.

Harrison set his glass down on the coaster next to the phone on his desk. He locked his fingers.

"Next time perhaps you should go yourself?" Harrison suggested, narrowing his gaze at the man across the desk.

Sandiman shrugged, unconcerned. "Briggs and Coombs came highly recommended. I have already expressed my...displeasure...to my source."

"Did they at least search the house?" Harrison sighed, his disappointment evident.

"Once your detective arrived and discovered the situation, they vacated." Sandiman angled his head. "It will be searched tonight."

"And the reporter?"

"His condition is," Sandiman paused, "sketchy at best. If it looks like he'll pull through, then I'll ensure he doesn't."

"We need to find the woman."

Sandiman nodded his agreement. "If I may suggest...perhaps you should call your rotund police friend."

Harrison nodded in agreement. Leaning over, he dialed a number on his speaker-phone and waited for the connection.

After the fifth ring, a click sounded and the thrumming of loud music mixed with scattered hoots and cheers.

"Trevino," came the gruff, low growled greeting.

"Lonnie. Is this a good time?"

"Yah, yeah," Lonnie muttered. "Gimme a minute...."

Harrison heard a loud scraping noise, the music and voices slowly fading into the background, then the sound of a door closing.

Harrison grimaced at the mental picture of the overweight detective getting his jollies at a strip club. It was quite pathetic, but luckily for him, everyone had their vices. Including the detective. At least Trevino could follow orders. Harrison's orders.

"Yeah, okay, what?" came the voice.

"We need your...assistance...with a certain matter. As you know, I've misplaced something and would appreciate your help in locating it."

"Your luck is getting expensive."

"Very well then, if you're too busy...."

"No," came the immediate reply. "I'll report their car stolen. Have anyone who finds it contact me. You *might* get lucky."

"Good," Harrison said briskly. "I want her found. As for the rest?"

Lonnie grunted. "That went according to plan. I'm sure you'll catch all the details later tonight."

Harrison smiled. He was fully expecting to be well entertained tonight with the eleven o'clock news. Death had a way of bringing everyone out of the woodwork. He had been hoping for more of a scandal with the addition of the woman, but he'd have to settle for one at a time. Even though a lover's-spat-murder-suicide would have been much more fun.

"I want the woman." Harrison glared at the speaker-phone. "You can deal with the man as you see fit."

"Same deal for each."

"Agreed. And Lonnie?"

"Yeah?"

"Double, if you get me the list." Harrison nodded towards Sandiman, extending the offer to him as well.

"I'll call you as soon as I know anything."

The line went dead.

Harrison sat back in his chair and caressed the smooth leather arms.

Detective Trevino was a rather disgusting man. To Harrison, who prided himself on his great physical shape for a man in his sixties, there was no excuse for the incredibly sloth-like condition of the overweight detective. He was shocked that Trevino was still employed by the police force, but luckily for Harrison, they considered him a reasonably good detective.

Trevino wasn't Harrison's only *friend* in law enforcement. But he was definitely the one more interested in doing practically anything for the money. Trevino was very good at taking care of Harrison's police business as long as he was paid on time.

Harrison made a mental note to transfer double the deposit tomorrow.

After all, he now had to cover the mysterious disappearance of both Jackson Hale and Casey Marshall.

When Casey awoke she knew instantly Jackson was gone. She didn't have to open her eyes to prove to herself he wasn't there—but she did anyway. Darkness shrouded the room, the shadows long and silent, the heavy curtains turning the last of the late afternoon sunlight into a dim yellowed glow. The only sounds were the muffled gasps of traffic on the highway outside the motel.

She had fallen asleep waiting for him to get out of his incredibly long shower. According to the clock, close to eight hours had passed—it was already late afternoon.

She looked around the room. Through the shadows she saw that his duffel bag still sat on the dresser, so wherever he wandered it couldn't have been far. She glanced at the other bed. It was rumpled, and the covers were thrown back, so he'd apparently been in it at some point.

No gun on the nightstand, though. Casey didn't know whether she should be relieved the gun was no longer there, or worried that

Jackson had felt the need to take it with him. She settled on a little of both.

Her gaze landed on a pad of paper propped up against the lamp. Clicking on the light, she picked up the note and read the short message.

Gone for supplies. Don't leave the room for any reason.

She tossed the pad back onto the nightstand and threw off the covers. Reaching her arms into the air, she did a few slow stretches and groaned as the memory of her earlier slip surfaced.

She'd obviously lost her brains as well as her memory.

Part of her was really quite glad he was gone after the insanity that had gripped her. The man was absolutely infuriating. She wondered if he'd phoned Meghan while she slept and decided she wouldn't put it past him.

What the hell had she been thinking, throwing herself at him like that? The retrospective turn of their conversation had sent her spiriting back to that age old question: Were his lips as soft as they looked?

She sighed and lightly touched her fingers to her mouth. Yes, yes they were. And the insane amount of heat that radiated off his body had gone right through her soul. It was like being molded by hot liquid. The momentum behind his kiss had left her shaken and most definitely wet in places she didn't know she could be.

She suddenly thought about taking a cold shower herself.

"Get a grip, Casey," she chastised herself. "He was so impressed he ran away. Now he probably thinks you're even more of a nutcase than he did before."

Walking over to the window, she drew back the curtains to let in what was left of the afternoon light. She glanced around the empty parking lot. Jackson's rust-bucket of a car was also missing.

As she stood staring out at the pavement, she wondered how Carson was. She really wanted to call Meghan but decided against it. The minute she heard her best friend's voice she would turn into a blithering idiot and spill everything in one long wailing sentence. She had never been able to keep anything from Meghan.

Jackson was wrong. She would *never* do anything to hurt Meghan. Ever. So calling her friend was definitely out.

Her gaze moved to the phone on the nightstand. She thought about calling Uncle Thomas. He would certainly know what to do. But then again, he would probably just tell her to listen to Jackson.

She shook her head and sighed.

Why did everything in her life always come back to Jackson Hale?

Her eyes were pulled back to the duffel bag on the dresser.

She stepped towards it, curiosity slowly taking hold.

If he went for supplies then what was in the bag? She tried to judge the contents from its shape. A change of clothes? Food? Her stomach grumbled hopefully.

The sound of a key in the lock jolted her out of her thoughts, and she spun to face the door.

Jackson shouldered his way in carrying an assortment of bags, his mind moving in a dozen different directions as he tried to ignore the sexily rumpled woman standing in the middle of the dimly lit room.

He'd tried to catch some shut eye earlier, but his mind had refused to stop replaying what it felt like kissing her breathless. So he gave up and decided a little fresh air might clear his head.

While he was out he'd gotten through to Kat at the office and filled her in on the details. She agreed to start working it from her end—background information on Harrison and a discrete search into a possible issue with the police department. She'd also keep trying to contact the Colonel and let him know his niece was in good hands.

So far so good. Now if only the aforementioned niece would stop staring at him like he was some kind of two-headed monster.

Tossing the bags down on the end of the bed, he moved over to the windows and pulled the drapes closed. Flicking on the overhead lights, he turned back to look at Casey, who still stood in the same spot, a slightly pink flush to her cheeks.

He held up a large bag with the name of a popular department store on the side. "I thought you might like a change of clothes. They should fit."

Casey reached forward and wrapped her fingers around the bag's handles. Digging inside she saw he'd purchased a pair of jeans—her size—a light gray t-shirt with something written across the front in rhinestones, a pair of sports socks, and a package of children's Hello Kitty stickers. She looked up sharply.

He feigned innocence. "What? Wrong size?"

Heat rose in her face, and she fought a sudden urge to wipe that smirk off his.

He turned back to the bed and picked up a small bag with a pharmacy logo.

"C'mon," he said, walking back towards the bathroom. "I want to check your head before we go."

"Go?" Casey placed the bag on the dresser and turned to follow him. "Already?"

"It's going to be dark soon, and it's at least a two-hour drive. I'll need time to scout the area."

He flipped on the bathroom light and dumped a small tube of antibiotic ointment, some tape, and a package of gauze pads onto the counter. Casey stepped into the room, and he pulled her closer. She tensed

"Relax," he chastised, reaching up and tilting her head. He combed her hair away from the side of her neck. "I need to take this off."

He gingerly peeled back the tape, taking time to pull out the strands of hair caught in the edges. Once the bandage had been removed, he threw it in the trash and examined the wound.

"Healing nicely," he mumbled under his breath.

Casey watched the movements and flow of the two people in the mirror reflection. The shoulder of her t-shirt had a dark spotted stain. Blood. Her blood.

She wondered why she hadn't noticed it before. Reaching up, she tried to scratch it off with her fingernail.

"Hold still," Jackson commanded.

Her gaze switched to his reflection. He concentrated on applying a thin layer of antibiotic cream to the side of her head. She studied his face, his expression, his movements.

Seeing his well-honed body, a person would know he was strong. His mannerisms and the way he carried himself showed he was intelligent. One look in his eyes when he was angry or in the zone and you saw a man who was one hundred and ten percent lethal.

But the way he held her head and lightly touched her neck was slight and gentle.

The wall she'd tried so hard to build up around her heart gave a tiny little crack. "Oh no you don't," she whispered.

"It's okay I'm done." Jackson stepped back and met her eyes through the mirror. "What's wrong?"

Her focus changed. She shook her head quickly. "Nothing."

He watched her for a moment longer, then shrugged and put the cap back on the ointment before walking out. "We should go soon."

Casey stood silently in the bathroom.

Then an arm appeared in the open doorway waggling a submarine sandwich.

She stifled a laugh when the arm, then the sandwich, disappeared.

Following the vanishing sub out into the room, she grabbed it from him and peeled back the edge of the wrapper.

"Mrfff meelf ud oom ere?" she said around a mouth full of bread.

"What?" Jackson laughed.

She finished what she was chewing. "What else did you buy?"

And immediately took another bite.

Jackson nodded to the last two bags. "Change of clothes for me. A new jacket for you since yours smells like a dumpster."

"It does not smell like a dumpster."

"It smells like a dumpster."

Casey wolfed down another mouthful. "What's in there?" She nodded towards his green duffle bag.

Jackson regarded her for a moment before answering.

"My other supplies."

"Like...?"

"Money. ID. Electronics." He paused. "Weapons."

Casey looked from Jackson to the bag, then back to Jackson.

He shrugged. "Open in case of emergency."

"Like now?"

"Like now."

They finished their meal in silence.

Chapter Six

Darkness had long settled when Jackson drove them past Carson's old house. At Casey's insistence, they had first completed a quick drive-by of Jackson's brownstone, then her downtown apartment.

Actually, she didn't just insist. They argued almost the entire drive. She had a feeling she'd finally won because he wanted to shut her up.

Casey didn't currently own a car, so she preferred to live downtown, close to the transit system. Her one-bedroom apartment sat over a hair salon which she completely loved because it gave her unlimited access to hot water and all the long steamy showers a girl could possibly want.

Everything looked normal on the outside at both locations, but Jackson flat out refused to stop no matter how much she tried to goad him into it. He'd agreed to do a drive-by, but that was all. She couldn't really find any argument with his point that neither one of them had pets; it wasn't like there were animals to worry about.

But then she'd developed such a case of nerves when they were driving past Jackson's place she almost told him to forget about her apartment, but she didn't want him to think she was giving in.

Now that they were driving past Carson's old family home, she was downright skittish.

The old Victorian stood dark and silent, set deeply into the lot, its looming position far away from the street. No lights on inside or out, and most of the windows had curtains or shades drawn. A large FOR SALE sign stood crookedly staked in the overgrown front lawn, and the bordering flowerbeds sprouted with clusters of weeds.

Casey loved growing up in this neighborhood. The street was old and established, ancient trees you couldn't wrap your arms around, massive lawns, and few fences. It had been open and carefree and filled with the silly fun and games of children. She and Meghan had spent many a day playing on the long wraparound porch.

Craning her neck to see past Jackson, she tried to catch a glimpse of the window at the back of the house where her room had been. The room she'd claimed as her own after her parents' had died and she'd moved in with her best friend's family. She'd always missed this place. Meghan's parents sold it shortly after their daughter started university. They didn't need the large space without children taking up the extra rooms.

Casey sighed. It was a house that deserved a family—children to run barefoot across the sloping front lawn, a baby in a playpen on the front porch. Laughter and memories.

Now it just looked empty and forgotten.

Her head automatically turned to look across the street at the two-storey brick house she'd spent the first fourteen years of her life in. A lot of renovations had been done to the building and yard over the years—it was almost a different place. Yet it still made her sad to see it. She didn't really remember all that much about her parents anymore. Oh, she had photos and mementos, but the memories had faded over the years into feelings that they'd loved her and she had been happy. But little else.

Jackson placed his hand on top of hers and gave it a gentle squeeze. She jumped.

"You okay?" he asked.

She shook her head with a small laugh. "Yeah, I'm good. It's just been a while since I've been down here." She sighed and turned to look out the window into the darkness. "I miss it here," she confessed.

His fingers tightened around hers briefly before he removed them to shift gears. They drove around the other side of the block where he pulled up against the curb and parked.

"So what now?" she asked after he shut off the engine.

"Now I go find the hiding spot."

"That sounds awfully simple."

"It's not. That's why you're staying here."

"But—"

"No buts, Casey. You're staying in the car. It will be a hell of a lot faster for me to get in and out without having to worry about you."

"But I—"

"Casey…," he warned. "This isn't open for discussion."

She stuck out her tongue.

"Oh, that's mature."

Opening his door, Jackson shook his head at her and stepped out onto the street. He shrugged out of his jacket and tossed it into the back. Reaching under the driver's seat, he pulled out his gun and tucked it into the back of his jeans.

"Promise me you'll stay here," he ordered, adjusting his t-shirt down over his waist to hide the gun.

She sighed.

"Promise me," he growled.

"I promise I'll stay out here." She was giving him her best frown when he closed the door.

Casey quickly leaned over and rolled down the window. "Wait!"

He turned and jogged back across the street.

"How long?"

He leaned through the window. "If I'm not back in fifteen minutes, call Lukas. His number's in my cell. Right pocket of my jacket. Speed dial six."

"But what about you?"

"Just do what I said."

"I'm not leaving you."

"Just do what I said."

She rolled her eyes. "Fine!"

He turned and crossed the street. Casey watched as he faded in and out amongst the shadows along the side of one of the houses, disappearing into the darkness behind a single car garage.

"*Stay in the car*...," she quietly mimicked.

She sighed at the argument going on inside her emotions. She was totally miffed at Jackson's annoying alpha male persona, yet at the same time, incredibly relieved he was here.

Casey didn't have a watch and didn't want to keep the car idling just for the clock, so she dug Jackson's cell phone out of his pocket. Snapping it open, she double checked the time.

Then checked again.

And again.

Fifteen minutes was going to be a really, really long time.

First she tried to think of the opening line to a song that was always on the radio lately, but she could only remember the chorus. Then she rifled through the glove box—nothing exciting there. An elderly man a couple of houses over shuffled out with his garbage. Then shuffled back up his driveway.

She checked the phone again.

A whole five minutes had passed.

She groaned.

Crawling over the shifter, she moved into the driver's seat. The window was still open, so she hung her head out slightly and peered down the street.

A large, towering pine tree blocked out most of the ambient light leaving the car in a giant shadow. There were street lights staggered up and down the block, and a few of the houses had front porch lights or garage lights on. One place still had blue-and-green Christmas bulbs dressed around the eaves.

She sat back in the seat, drumming her fingers on the steering wheel. "C'mon, Jackson, hurry up."

She stared out the window at the spot where he'd disappeared and willed him to reappear.

Sang a couple of nursery rhymes (they were the only songs her worried mind could remember).

Adjusted the zipper on her new jacket.

Rolled the window up.

Changed her mind and rolled it back down.

A dog barked nearby, so she stuck her head out of the window again, trying to gauge which direction the sound came from. After a few more sharp barks, someone off to the right yelled at 'Bear' to get in the house. The barking ceased.

Casey checked the cell phone again.

Eleven minutes.

Her heart started beating faster. He said he knew where the spots were, he just had to check them all.

Soon enough, she'd reached the fifteen minute mark, and panic bubbled to the surface.

What if something was wrong? What if there were people waiting? What happened to those men who'd broken into his house? They must have been be pretty pissed off. Did they know about Carson's list? Was this some kind of trap? What if someone had seen him and called the police?

Her heart raced faster with each unanswered question.

Suddenly the hair on the back of her neck rose. She looked around wildly. No movement on the street. Nothing had changed. Through the silence she heard the sounds of her ragged breathing. There was no one out there.

So why did she feel like someone was watching her?

She stared into the shadows near the garage where she had last seen Jackson. Maybe she was just picking up on his return.

Stillness.

Hell, even the air was dead tonight.

She shivered. The feeling that something menacing was out there wasn't going away.

She checked the time.

Sixteen minutes.

She cursed.

There was no way she was leaving, that much was certain. He'd made her vow to stay here. He didn't ask for any verbal commitment about *leaving*. So technically she wasn't breaking any promises.

Where the hell was he?

After counting one-Mississippi-two-Mississippi all the way to one hundred, she took a deep breath and climbed out of the car.

Standing beside the door, she crossed her arms in an attempt to ward off the chill but she wasn't cold from the temperature. Something wasn't right. Her entire body was covered in goose bumps.

She took a few tentative steps into the open street, hoping to hear something—anything—signaling Jackson's safe return.

The sound of an engine starting startled her, and she nearly dropped Jackson's cell phone. She spun around just as a large dark car shot away from the curb a few houses down.

Casey realized with growing horror that the car wasn't only speeding up—it was aiming right for her!

The next few seconds played out like a slow motion video replay. Frame by frame.

The taste of copper filled her mouth as adrenaline spiked her into a full-out run back towards the curb.

The car moved much too fast.

She'd gone too far into the middle of the street.

She wasn't going to make it.

Jackson rounded the corner of the garage, tucked against the weathered wooden siding, and moved towards the street. The over-taxed revving of an eight-cylinder broke the silence.

A split second of information flashed through his mind like photographs, compartmentalizing details and preserving them for later reflection.

Casey. Standing in the middle of the street, her body turned away from him. Denim-clad legs pumping, running, rushing towards the far curb.

The car. Black metal four-door, headlights off, surging out of the shadows, adjusting course to chase her down.

Him. Flying forward, pavement skimming under the toes of his boots. Arms outstretched. Hitting hard and leaping, twisting, falling.

Something slammed painfully into Casey's back, expelling all the air out of her lungs. She was propelled forward and sideways, her body spinning to the piercing screech of metal on metal before crashing backwards through a very large hedge and landing with a teeth-cracking thud on the ground.

She lay on her back straining to breathe. Her entire body rang from the force of the collision, her heart jumping and trembling inside her chest.

She was still alive, but they could come back at any moment!

Her limbs twitched as she made an effort to sit up but couldn't seem to get off the rocky ground.

She twisted, trying to roll onto her stomach, pushing against the weight pressing on her lungs. She couldn't see anything through the mess of hair tangled across her face. She swiped at it and barely managed to move enough of it around to look through.

Broken branches and bushes.

"God*damn* it, Casey, I told you to stay in the car!"

Jackson?

She suddenly noticed that it wasn't lumpy dirt she was laying on—it was a body!

She struggled to roll off him. He twisted to the side, rocking her onto the ground. With a grunt, he launched himself upright, his knees landing on either side of her torso, pinning her to the dirt. Pointing his weapon down the street after the disappearing car.

He exhaled a string of curses. "Are you okay?"

Casey nodded and then realized he wasn't even looking at her. "Yes?" she managed to croak out.

A flood of lights kicked in to their left, illuminating the yard beside them.

He hauled her to her feet. "Can you drive standard?"

"What...? I...yes...."

"Good. Drive."

She stumbled through the bushes, Jackson dragging her by the lapels of her windbreaker. He threw open the passenger door and shoved her roughly inside. She scrambled over the console while he climbed in beside her.

"Go!" he ordered, rolling down his window.

Casey stomped her foot down on the clutch and started the car. She tried shifting into first but her fingers still clutched his cell phone. She tossed it between the seats and jammed the shifter into gear.

She struggled to pull on her seatbelt between shifting. Jackson took the end and clicked it into place as she straightened onto the next street.

"Right at the next lights," he instructed as he reached into the back seat.

Casey barely slowed as she took the corner, and Jackson had to grip the headrest to keep from sliding into her.

He spun back to the front clutching a large roll of black cloth. As he unrolled it he briefly saw it was actually a long strip of black material full of thin slots. From the pockets he arranged another gun and several magazines.

She hoped to God they were full...and that he didn't really need to use them.

He slammed a magazine into place, and she jumped.

"Left at the second lights," he ordered, watching out the back window.

Traffic was light, and Casey drove as fast as she could without attracting attention. Her arms shook so violently she had a hard time directing the shifter. Both of the windows in the car were now open, and the near-death experience coupled with the wind chill cut deep into her bones.

She drove without thinking, turning when he said to turn, slowing when he said to slow, and speeding up when he urged her faster. Eventually, the city fell away behind them as they followed one of the secondary highways south.

They had been driving for close to half an hour before Jackson indicated she could pull over next to a boarded-up roadside vegetable stand.

The car skidded to a stop in the loose gravel, and she turned towards Jackson.

In the faint light of the dashboard, she saw that he was wound like a coiled spring. Tension radiated off his body in waves. A sheen of perspiration covered his arms and face. There was a long raw scratch down the side of his neck, and several smaller scratches sketched over his arms. He held tightly to the gun, a second one sitting loaded on the seat between them.

His eyes were black and void of emotion.

He looked ready to kill.

She was oh-so-very glad that he was on her side.

Her body bent with a great tremor. She glanced at her hands. Her fingers were frozen around the steering wheel so tightly her knuckles whitened. "Great...," she muttered, teeth chattering. "I can't move my fingers."

Jackson leaned over and shut off the engine.

She took her foot off the clutch, and the car lurched forward before settling in.

With a last glance down the darkened highway, he turned and set the guns on the dashboard. Sliding closer to Casey, he placed his hands on top of hers. The heat from his palms scorched the backs of her hands making her hiss.

Jackson swore softly and peeled her fingers off the wheel. Her hands now free, he clasped them together and pulled them against his chest, pressing them into the heat of his body.

"Well that was f-f-fun.... Let's not do that again any-t-time soon."

Jackson cast a worried glance at Casey. She sat straight up in the passenger seat, looking unblinking through the windshield, staring at the dotted yellow line reflected in the twin headlights.

She appeared half asleep from exhaustion, refusing to let go.

It was close to half an hour before he came across a familiar black-and-yellow sign advertising a local discount hotel chain. Five minutes later, and he half pushed, half carried her into their ground floor room.

She collapsed across the end of the closest bed and curled into a ball, asleep before Jackson had finished wrestling her out of her jacket and shoes. He pulled the sheets and blankets down on the second bed and arranged the pillows.

He stood beside her, staring down to where she huddled, her breathing not yet regulated by sleep.

When he'd come around the corner of the garage to find her standing in the path of that car, his body had reacted without hesitation. He couldn't bring himself to think of what would have happened if he had been so much as a half a second off. He'd traveled to Hell and back over the years with his unit, but nothing prepared him for the sheer terror of watching her nearly crushed to death by a ton of speeding metal.

She twitched in her sleep, her hand snapping out into a fist before tucking back in tight against her body. She looked so fragile, pale skin and tangled hair, curled into a childlike ball across the end of a queen-sized bed.

He'd always considered Casey Marshall to be all force and fury. Forever trying to prove something to the world.

But now....

Now he had to ask if that had really been him.

Was *he* the one trying to prove something when it came to Casey, and not the other way around?

Through the years, the times they had been together and hadn't stabbed out with angry words were so rare he couldn't even remember them. The second someone mentioned Casey's name he tensed. Whenever she came within any kind of personal distance he braced for a verbal showdown, and guaranteed, he'd get one. He was convinced she was his punishment for doing something heinous in a previous life.

But looking back now, he couldn't say who actually started each round. Before yesterday he would have insisted that Casey had done it all, caused it all. But now....

He felt like a total jackass for not even trying to find out what happened that night at Mickey's.

But what about all the other times?

There were too many to count.

Somewhere deep in his soul he must have known things weren't always her fault, yet every time he reacted like they were. It was pretty evident now just why she had grown to resent and despise him over the years.

Which he totally deserved.

He softly scooped her up into his arms and cradled her against his chest. A small sigh escaped her lips as she burrowed against him.

She really is just a little bit of a thing.

What that car could have done to her....

He kissed the top of her head before placing her onto the other bed, tucking her under the covers. She let out a soft murmur, pulled her knees to her chest, and rolled towards the wall.

He gave himself a mental shake.

This was going to require some serious re-evaluating.

Unfortunately, now was not the time.

Someone had gotten too close to her tonight, and he wasn't going to take any more chances.

Grabbing a chair, he wedged it between the beds next to the nightstand, effectively positioning himself between Casey and the door. With utmost efficiency, he grabbed his duffel bag and started to unpack.

Chapter Seven

Just after four in the morning, a quick rap sounded on the door. Jackson bolted out of his chair and strode to the far corner of the window. Flattening himself against the wall, he tilted his head to the side and peered out through the crack in the drapes. He had positioned the heavy material earlier to give him a decently camouflaged view of the parking lot and more importantly, the door.

The angle of the glass distorted the view, but it was enough for him to recognize Lukas.

Once inside, Lukas took one look at Jackson's dirt-smudged face and clothes, the scratches on his arms, the gun in his hand, magazines on the bed, and grinned. He dropped his duffel bag on the floor. "Had fun did we?"

"Speak for yourself," Casey muttered from under the blankets.

Jackson gave Lukas a look which told him now was not the time. Instead, he directed a question at the blankets. "You okay in there?"

"Yup."

When the blankets didn't move, Jackson turned back towards Lukas. "Success?"

Lukas reached into the top of his bag and extracted a very large padded envelope, which he handed to Jackson.

"You question my abilities? That was in the locker," he said, indicating the manila package. "And this...," he pulled a mini-cassette tape out of his back pocket, "was in the shed."

Jackson turned the tape over in his hand. It was the type used in older answering machines or small pocket recorders. While most people made the move to digital, many still preferred the old analogue technology.

The blankets on the bed moved, and a small hand appeared where a foot should have been. Casey blinked at them from half under the covers. Jackson wasn't sure how she'd managed to turn herself around, but she had obviously been sleeping upside down.

"Shut it. I have to pee." She glared, holding her hand out, palm up. "Can I have the bag of clothes?"

"It's on the counter in the bathroom. I figured you'd want to shower and change."

"Mmm." Casey smiled. "Shower."

Lukas glanced at Jackson and raised his eyebrow.

Jackson frowned. "Get a grip."

"What?" Lukas smirked innocently.

Casey scrambled out of the bed and headed to the bathroom.

"Nice hair," Jackson called.

"Up yours," came the muffled reply as the bathroom door locked shut.

While the shower ran, Jackson filled Lukas in on the evening's trouble. Lukas agreed that they must have picked up a tail when they passed by either Jackson's brownstone or Casey's apartment. Whoever it was had either been good, or very lucky, because they'd gone unnoticed. Lukas stepped out to visually sweep Jackson's GTO for any tracers, but found nothing.

Jackson was beginning to wonder just who else they were up against besides a real-estate junky. If Harrison Douglas was involved, then he was using hired guns, and they obviously knew how to play the game. But not knowing for sure who the players were made it all the more dangerous.

Jackson had already switched to using one of the fake IDs he carried in his duffel bag and paid cash for the rooms. If anyone was looking for a paper trail they wouldn't find any credit or bank card used in his name, or Casey's.

But that didn't mean they couldn't be found.

They needed to find out just what it was they were up against.

Jackson repacked his duffel bag, except for his Beretta, which he tucked in the back of his jeans. Lukas took his cue and armed himself equally.

Then they turned to the items Lukas brought back with him. The manila envelope was three inches think and weighed several pounds. Jackson tore the top and slid the contents out onto the empty bed. It was all paper—pages and pages of handwritten notes and photocopied elements. Permits and legal documents, newspaper articles, police reports, rental agreements, leases, and more. Some of the documents were dated as recently as last month, and others went as far back as three years.

Lukas looked sufficiently impressed. "That's a lot of research."

"Thank you," Casey answered, standing in the doorway of the bathroom, wearing new clothes and finger combing her damp hair.

"I like your shirt." Lukas grinned.

Jackson's mouth turned up when she glared at him. The shirt he'd purchased was a tight fitting light gray baby tee with the word *BRAT* studded across the front in silver rhinestones.

With a disgusted snort, she pushed between them and walked to the bed.

"These are mine." She pointed to the handwritten pages. "Notes I took and details from video or audio files. Dates, times, and sources. The rest is close to six months of digging. And some of these are copies of documents from Councilor Wolinski." She paused. "It's pretty much everything we could find relating to anyone who bought, sold, lived, and died across those blocks in the last three years."

Casey broke all the related pieces up into matching piles and placed them around the empty bed until the surface was buried under various sized piles of eight-by-ten copy paper. Pointing at each pile, she rattled off what each group of papers contained, from city permits to copies of police reports, insurance documents, legal documents, newspaper stories. Anything relating to sellers or owners in the two-block radius had been categorized and catalogued.

They stood quietly staring down at all the paperwork.

"This doesn't look like normal, day-to-day stuff," Lukas surmised, breaking the silence.

"No, not when you look at it like this."

"There's definitely something going on," Jackson finished.

She nodded. "Exactly. I mean, look at all this information. There's no way all these things could happen to this many people to make them move out of their apartments. Sure it's spread out over three or more years, but it's just not possible that it's all coincidental. And you'd need some pretty tough contacts to pull it off. Someone inside city hall, and someone inside the police department, for starters. But who? Aside from Harrison Douglas, who?"

"Did Carson suspect anyone?" Jackson asked.

She shrugged. "I got the impression that Councilor Wolinski was on to someone, but Carson never said anything to me." She bit her lower lip. "Is this all there is?"

Jackson showed Casey the small cassette tape. "Lukas found the paperwork and this. And," he took a USB jump drive out of his front pocket, "this was in the old house."

"A tape and a hard drive. Those aren't much help."

"Not necessarily." Lukas reached into his duffel bag and produced a small, hand-held tape recorder. "I thought we could use this."

Casey smiled. "Nicely done."

He bowed his head. "I thought so."

Jackson handed Lukas the tape. He snapped it into the small machine, rewound it, and pressed play.

Classical music.

Three sets of eyes dropped back down to the cassette player.

Lukas fast forwarded.

He pressed play again—more classical music.

Suddenly, the music cut out with an electronic chirp and voices faded in and out. The microphone was muffled, scratchy. They heard what sounded like a bus passing by.

Mumbled voices, unintelligible bits, a man speaking.

...told you before I'm not interested in selling...plans already approved and we have the permit....

A second male voice, deeper, threatening.

...no choice in the matter. Plans can be changed, Barnett. Your permit has been cancelled. You will sell the property....

You can't do that, it's illegal! You tell Douglas he's not going to get away with this....

Tell him yourself....

There was a sharp static sound as the microphone rubbed against something. Then, after a sharp squeal, the tape went back to the classical music as though nothing had happened.

Lukas rewound the tape and played the conversation again.

"Interesting," Jackson muttered.

Casey looked up. "Douglas? Harrison Douglas?"

"Most likely."

"Do you think Harrison knows about this tape?" she asked.

He nodded. "It's a safe bet."

"Shouldn't we take this to the police?"

Jackson gazed over Casey's head at Lukas. "Not yet."

Lukas' face was impassive, but Jackson knew he understood. There were too many unknown factors. What had really happened to Carson? Who was trying to kill Casey? Why did Carson suspect someone in the SPD was on Harrison's payroll?

"What about the drive?" Lukas asked.

Jackson looked down at the small rectangular object he held. It was only slightly larger than his pinky, but he knew these small portable computer drives could hold a hell of a lot of data and information.

"We need a computer."

Casey turned to Lukas.

"Sorry, sweets. No laptop." He grinned.

"It was worth a shot." She sighed. "So now what?"

Jackson frowned at the pile of paperwork. "If Carson and the councilor were trying to finger someone inside city hall, then there might be something in here that tells us who. Same for the police department."

Casey shook her head. "I've been through it over and over. I didn't notice anything."

Jackson reached over, and after a brief scan, chose two of the piles. "Police reports." He handed a stack of papers to Lukas. "See what jumps out at you. I'll do permits."

"And me?" Casey asked.

"You can be our sounding board."

Casey climbed onto the bed that wasn't covered in papers and propped herself up against the headboard. "Sound away."

After thirty minutes of watching them read in silence, Casey decided it was incredibly annoying to be forced to listen to page turning mixed with hums and haws and no indication of what they were thinking.

TV time.

She picked up the remote, and with the volume turned down low, started flipping channels.

It had just reached the top of the hour, and some of the local networks were doing the five a.m. news recap. She watched one station cycling through a 'breaking news' montage. Tiredly squinting at an overnight-house-fire-drunk-driver-morning-commuter-mess blur of stories, she was about to flip the channels when they cut to a reporter standing outside a restaurant somewhere downtown. The word LIVE flashed across the top of the screen.

Over the young, dark-haired man's shoulder, bathed in spotlight, was the side of a red brick building, its windows filled with the outline of neon beer signs. Next to the bar stretched a huge line of yellow police tape, stringing across a large opening to disappear somewhere behind the reporter.

Casey's hand froze in place—still outstretched—clutching the remote.

The alley.

Her alley!

The building. The bar. The street corner.

She crawled forward across the bed on her hands and knees, hypnotized by the image, willing the reporter to move out of the way.

Across the bottom of the screen words scrolled. *Robert Wolinski Murdered. Popular City Councilor Found Shot. Police searching for witnesses.*

If Lukas hadn't caught her she would have toppled right off the end of the bed and crashed face first onto the floor.

"Casey...!" Lukas exclaimed, his hands grabbing her hips to keep her from tumbling off the bed.

Jackson's head snapped up. He jumped up and lifted Casey off of Lukas. He tried to spin her around to face him, but she fought to keep her eyes on the screen. She wiggled around in his arms until she once again faced the television. Jackson adjusted so he had her back pinned up against his chest while she squirmed against his arms.

"No...it's...he's...that's...."

"I see it."

The network switched away from the reporter, and Casey jerked and cursed. The screen showed a packaged reel from an earlier press conference. Clutching the remote with both hands, she jabbed the numbers until she came across another network that was still on location.

"That!" She pointed at the television with the remote.

"Yes I saw. He's dead.".

"Not that! The alley. The alley!"

Jackson loosened his grip as she spun back around in his arms to face him.

"That's the alley, Jackson," she pleaded.

He looked at the television over the top of her head. She watched over her shoulder but didn't move. Her arms reached out and wrapped tightly around Jackson's waist, her fingers still strangling the remote. Lukas leaned forward and pressed the volume button.

The trio stood in silence as the reporter gave a quick summary before signing off back to the network. Councilor Wolinski had been found shot to death in an alley. Police believed he had been killed late Saturday night or early Sunday morning. Because the bar had been closed through Sunday, the body wasn't found until late Monday morning by one of the kitchen staff.

The police had no weapon and no witness.

No witnesses.

Casey shuddered. If she had been in the alley at the time someone had shot Wolinski, and if Wolinski's death was connected to Harrison Douglas, then Carson's story wasn't the only reason Harrison would want her dead.

She was the witness the police were searching for.

Chapter Eight

After thirty minutes of being grilled by Lukas and Jackson, the only thing Casey could think of was how much she would like to punch them both in the nose. She opted instead for locking herself in the bathroom.

She didn't remember anything more than she already had...which was nothing.

The only plausible explanation was that she had seen whoever shot Councilor Wolinski. And there was an even better chance that the gun she'd carried away was the murder weapon.

She was a target, a witness, and she could be arrested for withholding evidence.

It was turning out to be a fantastic week.

"Lukas is going to grab some snacks. Do you want anything?" Jackson asked through the door.

"Yes please. I'm starving," she said, turning the handle and stepping out into the main room.

"I'll hit the variety store across the street. They might have day-old coffee and stale donuts out by now." Lukas was heading out the door. "I'll see what I can scrounge up."

"If you're done pouting I'd like to take a shower."

Casey stuck her tongue out as Jackson walked past and into the bathroom.

"Just don't open the door without making sure it's Lukas. And only Lukas."

"Yeah, yeah," she muttered, rolling her eyes.

"Casey," he warned.

"I know. I know." She sighed. "I'm sorry. It's just that this is getting really...stressful." She chewed on the last word.

Jackson propped his shoulder against the doorframe.

"We'll figure it out."

She started to turn away then changed her mind. One shoulder rose slightly then dipped. She shook her head and looked up into his eyes.

He seemed so relaxed. Calm and in control. A man who adapted, adjusted, and moved on.

Her mind was splitting into personalities—wanting to go home and pretend nothing was wrong, wanting to run and hide and not look back. Wanting to be anywhere but here, and wanting only to be here.

She should be at home, sleeping in her warm bed, blissfully ignoring the world. Not hiding in a motel she couldn't find on a map with a reluctant bodyguard.

And following along with the rest of the bad karma she was up against, her bodyguard would have to be Jackson.

"Why are you helping me?" She gave herself an internal smack. That *so* did not come out right. "I mean...," she quickly started then stopped again. "Oh hell, I don't know what I mean."

"You need me."

"You hate me."

"I don't hate you." He scowled.

"You don't like me."

"The way I feel has nothing to do with the fact that you need my help."

Casey sighed. It was a reasonable answer. But somehow it wasn't the right answer anymore.

She'd pulled him in.

He was here because he had to be.

And suddenly she was fifteen years old again, climbing a tree she knew she wouldn't be able to climb back down, just to prove a point. And there he was, standing below, waiting for her to need his help.

Everything crazy she'd ever done was under watch of those hazel eyes, waiting silently for her to need his help.

Then one day they were gone, moved on.

He'd stopped coming for her.

And God, how she'd missed him.

So she brought the game to him.

Now here he was once again—rescuing her from doing something stupid.

And getting shot for witnessing a murder is pretty stupid.

Unfortunately, this stupidity wasn't a risked calculation.

What if he hadn't been home this time? What if he had turned her away? What if he wasn't there when that car had tried to run her down? Too many possibilities, too many unanswered questions.

His face blurred. She turned her head and bit her lower lip. His arms wrapped lightly around her shoulders, pulling her back against his chest. She placed her hands across his forearms and lowered her chin onto his arm.

"I will never let anything happen to you, you know that," he said gruffly, his conviction firm.

She nodded, afraid to use her voice, tears burning behind her furiously blinking eyelids. Jackson held her tightly while she reburied the frightened child.

Inhale. Exhale.

Deep slow breaths.

After a few moments she dropped her hands and raised her head.

He held her a brief second longer then lowered his arms.

Turning, she stepped away, breaking the contact of her back against the heat and strength of his chest.

"Sorry," she muttered.

He shook his head. "Don't apologize."

"You, um...you should go shower." She tried to smile but knew it didn't quite work.

"Are you okay?"

"I'm good. Crisis over." She turned and walked back toward the beds, ignoring the awkward pause before the bathroom door closed with a click.

With her hands on her hips, she surveyed the pile of papers on the bed and mentally purged all the tangled emotions with a long, drawn out sigh. She'd found a piece of herself working on all of this. Something done right. Something that didn't need anyone's help but her own.

It certainly had been a lot of work—seeing it displayed like this— but it had also been...challenging. She'd enjoyed digging through all the old newspapers, the files, the reports. It had taken a lot of time, but the days had gone fast. Carson had been incredibly impressed with everything she was able to dig up. Heck, she even impressed herself. She'd even started to think maybe she'd finally found something solid on which to hang her job-of-the-week crown.

And now?

She highly doubted that potential-witness-on-the-run-from-hired-killers was a good thing to put on a resume.

What the hell had happened to her life? It wasn't much to start with, sure, but at the very least, for the last six months, it had been semi-normal.

As she gathered up the stacks of papers and shoved them back into the envelope, she thought about calling the hospital to check on Carson. She glanced at the phone. But she wasn't family, so she would have to call Meghan's cell...and then she'd have to explain everything, and that wouldn't do either.

Casey sighed.

The phone taunted her.

She could call Uncle Thomas?

Suddenly she didn't care if he told her to stick with Jackson—she just wanted to hear his voice telling her so. He had the most powerful voice, gravelly from years of smoking cigars and issuing orders. He didn't talk to people so much as command. And he rarely had to raise his voice to do it. There was just something about his tone and presence that made everyone fall in line.

Everyone except Casey and his three daughters. They were the only ones who knew his weakness—hugs. His daughters could get away with just about anything if they could get their arms around him.

She loved him unquestionably and desperately wanted so very much to hear his voice.

The water shut off in the bathroom so she quickly dialed his number before she lost her nerve. But there was no answer.

She hung up then smashed her knee into the nightstand when the room filled with the shocking sound of ringing.

Jackson ripped the bathroom door open and strode into the main room, glaring at the phone as it chattered a second time. Casey let out a squeak and spun around, her body jerking at the sight of him coming across the room. The phone chirruped again, but she couldn't bring herself to look away from the distraction coming quickly towards her.

Jackson Hale in a pair of jeans and absolutely nothing else.

He'd barely done them up. In fact, the top button was quite assuredly undone, and as a result, the waistband rode a little lower than it normally would have. Okay a *lot* lower. His chest was bare, and oh what a chest it was. Tanned. Solid. Defined.

She wondered if it would feel as smooth to the touch as it looked.

The phone rang again. He leaned past her and snatched it up, saying nothing. She turned slowly, her gaze roaming over his broad back, and decided it was equally as magnificent as his front. She honed in on a drop of water that trailed slowly down the center of his spine. The sudden desire to lick it off made her dizzy.

"Go," he growled into the phone, then slammed it back down onto the receiver. He spun towards her, and she looked up, frozen in place as he pinned her with a stare. His hazel eyes darkened, swirled, hypnotized, then he blinked, and it was gone.

Her heart kicked up the beat before her mind admitted there was something seriously wrong.

Jackson Hale was in the zone.

"Get your shoes on." He zipped up his jeans. "Now, Casey!" he ordered, breaking her out of her trance. He turned to throw everything within reach into his duffel. He grabbed the bag and tossed it effortlessly towards the back of the room.

Panic welling in her throat, Casey scrambled towards the door and quickly pulled on her shoes, watching Jackson throw the jump drive and cassette player into the top of Lukas' bag, running with it to the back of the room. He dropped the bag onto the floor and leapt into the bathroom to grab his t-shirt. Wrapping it around the hand holding the Beretta, he stepped up to the window and smashed out the glass.

Good Lord, what's happening?

Circling his hand around the window frame, Jackson quickly brushed off the shards and hoisted himself up for a fast look out the narrow opening. Dropping down, he spun towards Casey and scooped her up, shoving her feet through the open window.

"What...?" she squealed as he pushed her through.

"Quiet," he ordered. "Lukas' truck is right outside."

The window was a good five feet off the ground, and Jackson had her half way through, feet first, before her brain kicked in and she struggled to help. She peered out into the darkness. There was indeed a huge black pickup parked right outside, its engine running. The side of the truck was almost as high as the window. Pushing off the window frame, Casey scrambled into the bed of the truck.

Jackson tossed the first duffel bag through the window, and the surprising weight of it almost knocked her over when she tried to grab it. She braced herself for the second one, which almost immediately followed the first. Then Jackson wriggled through the opening and rolled head first into the bed of the truck. As soon as he landed, he pounded his fist on the roof of the cab.

Lukas stepped on the gas, and the truck lurched forward, sending Casey staggering to the back. Jackson caught her before she toppled over the tailgate and forced her down. Lying on his back, he flung off the t-shirt and extracted his gun.

The truck bounced over a curb and slammed to a stop. Casey squeaked as the jerking motion slid her several feet forward. She struggled to sit up, but strong hands grabbed her waist and shoulders and dragged her back down.

Jackson rolled her beneath him, wrapping his free arm under her head and crushing her against his chest. He threw his right leg over hers, effectively pinning her against the cold metal.

She squirmed under his weight, mashed between the hard truck bed and his solid frame. She couldn't see much of anything with her head jammed against him. The speed of his heartbeat against her cheek made her own race faster.

She suddenly realized what he was doing, and her stomach rolled. Whatever was out there—whoever was coming—he was using his body as a shield.

She panicked. She'd asked him for help, but not this!

"Quiet," he whispered urgently, his breath coming in hot bursts along the top of her head. "Stop moving!"

She felt a change in pavement and a smooth increase in speed. The green glow from a passing intersection bathed the bed of the truck just before they angled through a wide banking turn and sped up.

The highway.

After what seemed like an eternity of her being slammed between Jackson and the truck bed, the vehicle came to a bone jarring stop. Lukas jumped out and opened the rear door. Jackson leapt up and grabbed Casey's arm, hauling her to her feet and practically throwing her over the side of the truck at Lukas. Lukas caught her, and before her feet touched the ground, swung her around and deposited her feet first into the back seat of the crew cab. Jackson jumped over the side and tossed the duffel bags in beside her.

They barely had the doors closed when Lukas spun the tires in the loose gravel. The back end of the truck slid sideways before one of the rear tires caught traction and swung them onto the pavement.

Casey didn't know whether to scream, cry like a baby, or laugh at the absurdity of what just happened.

"Anything?" Jackson asked, glancing out the back window.

Casey turned to look out the back, but all she saw was the dark highway.

"I can't be sure. There's a vehicle or two back there, but nothing close enough."

"Where to?" Jackson glanced around.

"The condo?" Lukas suggested, his hands gripping the wheel as he expertly maneuvered the truck around a narrow corner.

In the front seat, Jackson nodded his agreement, his gaze shifting to the road behind them.

"What on earth is going on?" Casey finally managed to squeak out, her voice high and loud.

"When I got to the far side of the parking lot a black sedan came in fast," Lukas started. "My instincts said move, so I did. I hopped out the side door and watched three guys walk in, pulling out badges of some sort. The energy was totally wrong. There was no way those guys were locals, or feds. I phoned you from the courtesy phone next to the pool then grabbed the truck."

Casey took a moment for his words to sink in and played out a silent conversation in her mind. Someone had found them? Men with guns? Three men? Who were they? The men from Jackson's place? Was it the same car that tried to run her down? But these guys had badges. Maybe they really were the police. But how would they have known to look for them there? Was there a bug somewhere like they always found in the movies? Should she check all her clothes and jewelry? But she wasn't wearing any jewelry! Maybe it was in Jackson's car? What made Lukas think they weren't really the police? How could he tell what room theirs was from the back?

And with that train of thought, the next question was the one she voiced out loud.

"How the hell did you tell Jackson all that in a two second phone call?"

Lukas turned his head to look at Casey, his brow furrowed. He glanced hurriedly at the road then snapped his head back around.

Then he burst out laughing.

She leaned forward between the seats and looked over at Jackson. He was grinning like an idiot.

What the hell, she fumed. "It was a perfectly valid question!" She flopped back against the seat and crossed her arms in a huff and stared out the window.

"Oh, Casey, my love, if I didn't think Jackson would kick my butt I'd kiss you," Lukas finally said, his laughter dying off into a soft chuckle.

"What? What did I say?"

"He didn't tell me all of that on the phone." Jackson snorted. "He didn't have to."

"Then what?" she asked. "Did you use some kind of secret code?" She still had no idea what was so funny.

"No." Lukas laughed again. "No secret code."

"Casey," Jackson said, trying to keep a straight face. "All he said was...." He chuckled, trying to continue.

"All I said was...," Lukas started.

"Move, now. Back window...," Jackson added.

"I'll be waiting," Lukas finished.

Then both looked at each other and the laughter began again.

At first, Casey glared at them as though they'd both lost their minds. She was being chased by hired killers, and these two were laughing it up like she'd just told them the funniest joke ever.

Casey fought a smile. There was something ridiculously silly about two grown men giggling like little boys. But she *still* didn't understand what was so funny.

So she asked them.

Jackson turned to look at her and with a wide grin asked, "Of all the questions you could have asked about this whole situation, you asked *that* one?"

Casey frowned. Yes, okay, so she had a lot of questions. Hell, she had a dozen of them right off the top of her head. But yes. After running through them all in her head, she had indeed blurted out the craziest.

She shook her head, muttering, "I've completely lost my mind."

"Anything else you want to know?" Lukas asked, snapping her a sly grin.

Jackson groaned. "Don't get her going."

"What?" Casey demanded. "I have perfectly valid questions."

"Yes, apparently you do," he teased.

Casey couldn't help but smile at the infectious grin the two men were giving her. Shaking her head, she slid back and settled into the rear seat of the truck. For the duration of the ride back to town they let the atmosphere relax. She knew Jackson and Lukas were both still diligently keeping watch, but they were trying not to let it show.

After a while, the motion of the truck lulled her into a half-aware state. That and the low, calming sound of Jackson's voice. His security and strength calmed her, and her mind drifted.

The thought that Jackson had been willing to protect her by offering himself up as a shield cut right into her soul. Yes, it had been instinct and reaction, but it still made her heart ache.

She sighed softly.

The minute she'd noticed boys, she noticed Jackson Hale, and everything else had been only a comparison. An attempted copy. She knew that now. Understood it. But was she willing to live with it? Spend the rest of what little time she had running from the truth?

It seemed like such a simple thing in the midst of everything going on around her. He was trying to protect her. Save her. Play the hero. But if anything happened to him she would never be able to live with herself.

So the question remained.

What was a girl to do?

Since she couldn't come up with a viable answer, she eventually gave up and slept.

Chapter Nine

Warm skin brushed the side of her cheek, and Casey cracked her eyes open, her sleep-addled brain thoroughly enjoying the view of Jackson's handsome face staring down at her from above.

"Honey, we're home," he whispered with a crooked grin.

Lying half across the lumpy stack of duffel bags beside her, she let out a soft grunt and rolled her head towards him. The part of her brain that was still trying to sleep couldn't seem to stop staring at his mouth. She sighed happily and closed her eyes.

"Uh-uh, sleepyhead." Jackson gently shook her shoulder. "Up and at 'em."

"Mmmm...." She pouted.

"Come on, Brat." He gave her another shake.

Lukas opened the far door and reached for the duffel bags. "You coming?"

Casey sighed and forced herself upright. Jackson backed away, giving her room to shimmy out of the back seat.

Once her feet hit the pavement, she took a few stiff steps into the laneway and threw her arms above her head in a much needed stretch. Clasping her fingers together, she pulled her arms straight up and slowly arched her back. She let out a loud groan and counted to twenty. With a fluid move, she rounded her spine and rolled forward and down to touch her toes. Damn, she really wanted a half-hour shower and her own pillow. Holding the position for a count of twenty, she inhaled and straightened, running her fingers through her hair and scratching her skull.

Hearing no noise behind her, she peered over her shoulder at the truck. Jackson and Lukas stood like statues, staring at her, looking like they had each swallowed a rather large bug.

"What?" She frowned, checking out the front of her shirt. Her clothes were on straight and everything.... "What?" she asked again.

Lukas' gaze shifted to Jackson, who appeared to be having trouble breathing. "Nothing. Nothing at all," Jackson muttered.

Lukas shouldered his duffel and turned towards Casey, pointing to a section of the underground garage behind Jackson. "Elevator's that way." Then he walked around the side of the truck and hooked his free arm around her waist, pulling her along beside him.

He tossed his bag at Jackson. "Carry that will ya?" He smirked.

Casey could swear she heard a low growl as they passed Jackson, who fell into step beside her. Lukas glanced down at her with a conspiratorial wink and an infectious grin.

It was damn lucky it was almost nine o'clock. Most of the residents had already left for work, so they had the elevator to themselves.

Jackson wasn't exactly traveling incognito.

It was bad enough *she* could barely keep her eyes off him, much less some poor unsuspecting woman on her way to the office for the day.

He was rough, sexy, and wearing nothing but a pair of form-fitting faded jeans.

She shook her head and tried to look anywhere else, but the reflective walls of the elevator made it just about impossible not to catch some hard-planed angle.

When the doors opened on the twelfth floor, she sighed with relief and followed Lukas down the hallway.

The condo had a typical city view...of the apartment building across the street. As Jackson pulled the drapes, she realized the buildings were close enough that the tenants in the other building would be able to see right inside the windows at night. Only a *little* creepy.

Standing in the middle of the living room, Casey looked around at her temporary accommodations. The condo was sparsely decorated, with lots of electronics and couch-potato collections: a large screen television, expensive stereo, huge CD collection, video game consoles, and a dual monitor computer set up in the living room. There was no artwork, and the only photos were generic-looking pet pictures in the galley kitchen, pinned to the freezer door with magnets. She had to admit she was surprised it was spotless—which made Lukas laugh.

Out of curiosity, she opened the refrigerator expecting to find a case of beer and some leftover takeout but was shocked to see it stocked to the hilt with fresh vegetables, meats, cheeses, and just about every condiment and sauce you could think of.

Jackson reached behind her and grabbed a bottle of water out of the door. "Lukas likes to cook," he said simply.

Casey watched the muscles in his throat constrict and release as he downed the water. Her lower body gave a little quiver, and she suddenly felt a little overheated. Forgetting she stood in the opening of the fridge, she tried to step away but her backside bumped the fridge door. All the jars and bottles clattered together. With an embarrassed jerk, she turned and quickly closed the door, following it with what she hoped was a nice, casual walk out the back of the galley kitchen and around the corner to the living room.

Making a beeline for the sofa, she flopped down onto the end, surprised when she sank deeply into the soft cushions. With a contented sigh, she wiggled down into the corner and propped her feet up on the coffee table. Behind her, Jackson wandered out of the kitchen and powered up the computer.

Lukas appeared from the hallway leading to the bedrooms and threw a wad of cloth at Jackson. "Put a shirt on, will ya?"

Jackson snorted and yanked the cotton t-shirt over his head. Then he pulled out the desk chair and dropped in front of the computer. "Grab the drive. It's in the front pocket of your bag."

Lukas dug out the small component and lobbed it to Jackson, who snapped it into an empty port. Stepping forward, he leaned on the back of Jackson's chair and stared at the list of items on the drive. "Carson's notes, electronic copies of documents...." He paused and pointed to something on the screen. "What about that one?"

Jackson shook his head. "It's encrypted. We need the second half."

"Second half of what?" Casey asked, peering at them over the back of the couch.

Lukas glanced over his shoulder. "There's a file here called HIT LIST but it's only part one of two. We need the second half to piece them together. Any ideas?"

Casey shook her head, rolling to a half crouch so she could lean across the back of the couch. "Carson's the computer freak. He worked from home, but seeing how he hid everything else, I doubt he would have left it there. It's probably on his work computer. Their network is pretty secure." She paused thoughtfully. "We should probably go get the most recent stuff anyway."

Jackson turned, his eyes narrowed. "Most recent?"

"He didn't hide this stuff overnight. He probably did it last week or the week before. That means anything new that came up *after* he squirreled this stuff away would have to be somewhere. The paperwork we have is a couple of weeks old. Most of the stuff I found last week was electronic. No paperwork. It's on his network drive." She made a face and angled her head. "We've been working on this story for months. No one's tried to...kill me before. It has to be something new."

"She's got a point." Lukas looked at Jackson.

"I'll go get it tonight," Casey added.

Jackson shook his head. Once. "Too dangerous."

"It was a statement, not a question." Casey frowned.

"I said no." Jackson gave her an unwavering glare.

"And just how do *you* expect to get it?" She raised an eyebrow in challenge.

"I'll go," he said firmly.

"And you'll get in, how?" The other eyebrow shot up.

"You'll give me the passwords."

Casey snorted and rolled her eyes. "I work there, remember? Security knows me. I'm allowed in."

Lukas turned to Jackson. "We can gear her up."

"I said no," Jackson growled.

Lukas crooked his eyebrow.

"Oh, for heaven's sake!" Casey muttered, spinning around and flopping onto her back on the couch. The only part of her that remained visible was her arm, which waved madly in the air. "Hello! Do you want the information or not? I'm not an idiot. I can copy a file."

"We'll be right there. We'll gear her up, and she'll be in and out, right, Casey?" Lukas directed his question to the couch.

"Quick as a bunny," she muttered. "Besides, if we go after midnight, the place will be empty anyway."

"We need the info," Lukas said pointedly.

Jackson hesitated then gave a brief nod. "Fine." He scowled. "But we're going with you."

"Wouldn't have it any other way," Casey agreed.

Jackson rolled his shoulders, working out a kink while he continued to page through the information with the computer. There was an entire folder dedicated to emails between Carson and Robert Wolinski. The Councilor had definitely been making progress. He'd referred to a compiled list of potential developers—some above board, and some with shady backgrounds—who recently expressed an interest in major real-estate deals. Was that Carson's *hit list*? Did one of the developers get wind of the investigation and decide to take matters into their own hands?

Wolinski had obviously gotten in over his head.

And as soon as the police made the connection between Carson and Wolinski, they'd come looking for Casey. She was directly connected to the research, and the first person they would want to talk to. Disappearing would make her look involved...and not in a good way. So if there was indeed someone playing both sides, then Jackson sure as hell couldn't trust the police. Not without knowing who else was involved. There were too many unanswered questions.

Casey was right.

They needed to get to Carson's computer.

After an hour of reading emails and documents, Lukas called break time, suggesting they get a little shut-eye. Sleep wasn't really necessary. He and Lukas could function for days on a few minutes of rest here and there. But for now they were relatively safe, and a few hours of solid rest would ensure they were at the top of their game.

"We need to send all of this to Kat at the office. Have her start going through it. That analytical mind of hers is bound to make some connections we're not seeing."

Lukas agreed. "I'll have her send someone to pick it up. In the meantime, why don't you put Sleeping Beauty in the guest room?"

Jackson stood with a stretch and looked down at Casey. She was fast asleep on the couch with one arm flung over her face. Stepping around the sofa, he slipped one arm under her knees and the other under her shoulders and scooped her up against his chest.

She didn't even stir.

In a small bungalow north of the city, retired Colonel Thomas Marshall gave a quick salute out the open doorway to the driver of the sedan as it backed out of his driveway. He kicked the door closed and dropped his bags onto the floor.

After having spent the weekend with his buddies, he was tired, slightly hungover, and craving coffee.

His keys landed on the table inside the entrance way, and his thumb jabbed the button on his answering machine as he walked past. A telemarketer blithered on about how he'd qualified for an all-expenses-paid cruise while he headed down the hall towards the kitchen. As he measured the coffee grains and dumped them into the fresh filter, his ex reminded him of his youngest daughter's approaching twenty-sixth birthday then gave a list of appropriate gifts he should consider buying. He punched the start button, but the third message made him pause.

It was Meghan Hale.

Her voice was strained and upset, and she was trying to find Casey, who apparently wasn't home or answering her cell. Meghan rattled off her cell number and the number of Carson's hospital room.

Carson's hospital room?

His heart skipped, stopped, and restarted with a fury over the fourth and final message.

Boxcar? It's Ice Man. We've got a problem.

The answering machine beeped in completion.

Tom grabbed the phone.

He dialed Jackson's cell.

No answer.

He dialed Casey's cell.

No answer.

Tension locked across his chest as he replayed the messages, then called Meghan's cell.

By the time he hung up, his mind was in overdrive. Carson Hale had been in an accident and was in critical condition. Casey was MIA. And a detective had come to the hospital looking to specifically question Jackson about an ongoing investigation.

Boxcar. It's Ice Man. We've got a problem.

Dialing the office, he wore a two-stride path in the front foyer until the other end picked up.

"Kat," he growled into the receiver. "What the *hell* is going on?"

Chapter Ten

The earpiece was itchy.

"Casey, quit scratching."

"It's annoying," she whispered harshly.

"Leave it," Jackson's voice crackled sharply in her ear.

Casey sighed. Two o'clock in the morning, and she was walking through the very empty lobby of a downtown office tower. The bright, harsh overhead lights made everything look surreal and washed out.

Jackson and Lukas had 'geared her up' as they put it, with a microphone and earpiece. And since she'd left her jacket back at the motel during their rapid escape, Lukas had loaned her his. She had to roll the sleeves back several times just to see the tips of her fingers, but it ultimately did the trick, giving her a collar to clip the microphone to.

If she hadn't been so nervous she would have been making spy jokes and talking into her sleeve. But she was nervous. Skittish enough that she almost asked Jackson to come with her.

Almost.

As she crossed the lobby, she tried to give herself a pep talk. She worked here, for goodness sake. It wasn't like she was stealing anything. Some of these were her files. She was allowed access to Carson's computer. This was the office, not some strange alley. She'd been here a thousand times. It was comfortable. It was just a quick trip upstairs and back. Nothing was going to happen.

She thought for certain the security guard would notice the big sign hanging over her head that said "up to something", but he barely glanced up from his *Sports Illustrated* as she hurried past the desk.

The elevator bank was at the back of the long lobby. Two covered the ground floor and higher, and a larger cargo lift on the right went down into the underground parking.

To access the elevators, she had to walk past a twenty-four-hour coffee shop. The café had doors on the street side for the general public and a large open archway leading into the tower area. They were quite a popular late-night destination, and tonight was no exception. Casey saw several clusters of people inside as she made her way past. She had to force her head from turning and seeking out Lukas, who was supposed to be sitting at a small table inside the archway. Outside in Lukas' truck, Jackson waited around the side of the building next to the loading dock, covering the back entrance in case Casey needed out in a hurry.

Taking a deep breath, she walked inside the opening elevator and jammed her thumb onto the number five. When the doors opened on the fifth floor, she stepped into the corridor, and turned towards the office entrance.

On the other side of the double glass doors would be another security guard. On-floor security was more for peace of mind than anything else, available to offer an escort down to the parking garage for the female employees who worked after hours. They pretty much kept to themselves, reading or watching the television in the reception area.

The young man's eyes lit up as she pushed through the doors. Casey almost groaned. Judging by the silence of the room, there was no one else on board tonight, and he was angling for someone to talk to. Barely twenty, he was pencil thin, with fair hair and features, sporting a rather predominant acne problem. Nodding quickly, she hurried past, hoping he would understand her silence to mean she wasn't in the mood to chat.

She threaded her way through the empty rows to Carson's desk.

"Talk to me," Jackson said.

She was so startled at hearing Jackson's voice she stumbled and nearly fell.

"Damn it, Jackson, you scared me to death!" she whispered harshly, glancing back to where the security guard stood watching her, adjusting his uniform.

"Where are you?"

"Right here." She sat at Carson's disgustingly neat desk.

"Where the hell is here?"

"Carson's desk."

"And?"

"Well give me a sec...."

"Casey...."

"What?" she whispered.

"We can't see what you're doing. You have to be a little more specific."

"Oh." She paused. "I know that!"

Someone cleared their throat. Lukas.

"Okay, okay! I'm turning on his computer."

While she waited for the machine to boot up, she took a quick look through the drawers of his desk. There was nothing unusual, but she didn't really expect to find anything anyway.

The computer flashed the welcome screen, and she reached for the keyboard, typing in Carson's username and password.

"I'm in," she whispered.

"Hurry up."

Casey frantically searched through the network drives, looking for anything referring to a list or a hit list. A few seconds later, she found it hidden in a section called "Paris Pictures". Only because she knew Carson so well did she know that the reporter had never been to Paris.

"Aha," she whispered.

Yanking the small portable drive out of Lukas' coat pocket, she plugged it into the computer and copied the file. Lukas had walked her through how to merge the files so she could see the final product.

Carson's "hit list" was a spreadsheet filled with names and addresses, phone numbers, and a long list of comments and shorthand. There had to be close to fifty names.

She hit the print button, and the machine whirred to life down the aisle. Extracting the drive from the computer, she stuffed it back into the pocket.

"Got it," she said.

"Got what?" a voice said *outside* her ear. She squeaked and almost spun backwards out of the chair. She regained her balance and looked up into the grinning face of the security guard.

"What's wrong?" Jackson asked.

"Nothing," she replied.

"You've got nothing?" the security guard asked.

"Who the hell is that?" Jackson said.

"Mark," she read off the guard's name tag.

"At your service." Mark winked.

"Who the hell is Mark?"

"Security guard," Casey answered.

"Just for now." Mark leaned forward and glanced around as though someone might be listening in. He lowered his voice and winked again. "I'm actually studying to join the police force."

"Oh, for God's sake, Casey, get rid of him!"

"Yeah," Mark said, relaxing a little too casually against the side of the cubicle. "I mean, I've always been interested in law enforcement. It's, ah, in the genes." He tipped his head closer.

She heard a snort.

Casey jumped up out of the chair and tried to squeeze through the narrow desk opening of the cubicle wall. Mark was effectively blocking her escape.

"Would you quit yakking and just get the stuff and get out of there?" Jackson hissed.

"I'm trying!"

"You're trying to join the police force too?" Mark exclaimed, a little too loudly.

"Oh for god's sake...."

"God, no!" Casey shook her head. "I mean, I'm trying...to get my stuff out of the printer. Sorry...."

She cursed Jackson seven ways to Sunday. How the hell could anyone concentrate with voices in their head?

"Oh hey, here, let me...." Mark turned towards the printer.

Casey pushed past him. "No, that's okay. I'm in a hurry. I'll just grab it and go."

She snatched the pages out of the printer, quickly folding them and jamming them into one of her jacket pockets.

"Okay, well, it was nice to meet you, but I really have to go."

"I'm working all week," Mark said hopefully.

"I'm not. Sorry." Casey backed away then turned and walked quickly through the cubicles to the reception area and out into the hallway.

Repeatedly jabbing her finger on the elevator call button, she danced from foot to foot. She was making herself nervous but couldn't help it. Her heart raced, and all she wanted was to get the hell out of there.

The elevator dinged its arrival, and she jumped. The doors slid open, and she ran in, pushing the lobby button several times. Once the elevator finally opened to the lobby, Casey let out the breath she'd held. Stepping out through the open doors, she hesitated upon seeing a man in a brown suit talking to the security guard.

He turned to face her, giving her a slow, emotionless smile. The minute she saw his face, his expression, his dead eyes, everything around her slammed to a stop.

She knew him.

The alley.

The entire lobby felt like it was shifting. Twisting and falling. Casey couldn't breathe. Couldn't move. The security guard slid under his desk, his dead eyes staring at her. Someone laughed, and her arm hurt. Then she felt pressing pain against her ribs as she stared at the open door of the parking elevator.

"Casey!"

A voice in her head. No. That wasn't right. In her ear. And outside. Calling her.

"Lukas!"

She heard him yelling her name from across the lobby as the elevator doors trapped her.

"Someone talk to me!" Jackson shouted.

The sound of Jackson's voice snapped through Casey's mind, releasing her from the grips of her frozen nightmare. Her body shuddered, swayed, then connected as she focused on the dark brown eyes of the man who was squeezing the blood out of her upper arm.

She was trapped in the elevator with a murderer.

She did the only thing she could think of.

She screamed.

"Now, now, Miss Marshall. Please be polite," the man said slowly, as though chastising a small child.

Casey gasped with a sharp jabbing pain in her side. She looked down and whimpered. The man held a very long, very lethal-looking gun, and it was jammed right into her ribcage.

He dragged her through the empty structure to the only vehicle, a large silver Buick that had been backed into one of the hundreds of empty spaces. Spinning her roughly forward, he slammed her against the driver's door. "Open it."

Casey hesitated, fear clarifying one thought. If she got into the car, she was dead.

She winced as he roughly poked the barrel into the tender flesh between her ribs.

"Open it or you die. Right here, right now."

"Hold on, Casey!" Jackson's voice cut through the fear. "*Just hold on!*"

Casey struggled to force her violently shaking hands to grasp the door handle, praying for Jackson to hurry.

A sharp clattering over by the elevators forced her captor to turn, wrenching her shoulder as he roughly snapped her around in front of him like a shield.

A shadow moved behind the elevator bank. The man's arm jerked next to her ear, and a large chunk of plaster exploded off the far wall. Realizing he was shooting at something or someone, Casey shrieked and tried to pull away but he held her fast.

Then the sound of squealing tires and a powerful engine spun him the other direction, dragging Casey around with him. Casey's legs nearly buckled to see the truck as it whipped across the upper level.

Jackson!

She gasped and looked over her shoulder. The shadow must have been Lukas!

The man in the brown suit steered her forward as he hauled open the driver's door. He angled her into the car, forcing her to bend by twisting her arm around until she gasped with pain. He released her with a hard shove, and she collided with the console between the seats.

"Let her go!" Lukas' voice shouted in her ear, its real-time echo bouncing off the cement pillars of the parking garage.

Another gunshot.

A shout.

Return fire.

Falling forward, desperation kicked in, and Casey crawled frantically across to the passenger seat. In a blind panic, she tore at the door handle. The door swung open, and she tumbled out onto the pavement, slamming hard onto her knees.

With screaming tires, Lukas' black pickup slid around the far corner and drove straight for them. Crouching on the cold cement floor, Casey screeched and covered her ears as the sharp clangs of metal hitting metal added to the cacophony of sound. Lukas' truck swerved through the empty parking spaces, narrowly avoiding a cement pillar. Then another gunshot rained chunks of cement down on top of the Buick, dusting her hair.

"Move, Casey!" Jackson's voice screamed in her ear. "Run, damn it!"

Casey's legs moved in response to the verbal command before her brain registered Jackson's words. She raced past several pillars, the truck speeding towards her from the opposite side of the aisle. One of the pillars beside her exploded chunks of cement into the air. Exhaling a scream, she stumbled. Hitting the ground hard, she turtled and covered her head.

With its engine growling, the truck whipped past her and slid sideways, Jackson maneuvering the large vehicle between her and the Buick.

From her hunched position, Casey watched the silver car in horror. It shot across the parking garage and up the ramp to the first level. Her eyes followed Lukas as he ran after the car, emptying his magazine. The back window exploded in a shower of glass, but the car disappeared around the corner of the ramp.

She turned to see Jackson running towards her, his steps crooked. In fact, everything seemed crooked. She tried to stand, but couldn't seem to get her legs to hold steady beneath her.

The last thing she remembered before the darkness was someone shouting her name.

Chapter Eleven

"Drink this."

Jackson handed Casey a tumbler topped with whisky. She sat propped up against the headboard on the bed in Lukas' spare room, her hands shaking so badly he had to help her hold the glass.

It was only through years of practice that he was able to keep from shaking himself. The whole event had scared him more than he was willing to admit. His heart had all but stopped when he heard the absolute terror in her scream. And when she dropped in the parking garage, he immediately feared she'd been shot. He only started breathing again once he realized she'd only fainted.

As he helped her sip the strong concoction, his brain shifted from anger to guilt and back again. She'd come to him for help, and since then had nearly been run down and almost kidnapped at gunpoint.

He should have been with her, not sitting outside. Hell, he should never have let her go alone in the first place! It was a stupid mistake and it wasn't going to happen again.

As of this minute, he wasn't letting her out of his sight.

And with more questions than answers, the task was not going to be easy. Who were they really up against? Who was the gunman in the Buick? Why was he taking Casey? Why not just kill her there? Would she have been a bargaining chip for Carson's information? Was Lukas now on their radar as well?

He shook his head, shifting his concentration to the woman in front of him. She hadn't said a word since the parking garage. Her normally bright eyes were dark and distant. He knew she was in shock, but the longer she remained silent the more concerned he became.

He took the empty glass out from between her white knuckles, his fingers brushing hers. Her skin felt cool beneath his, so he set the glass on the nightstand and reached for her hands, warming them between his.

She looked up, the intensity in her gaze hypnotizing him. Her expression was closed...clamped off and hidden. But the longer he stared, the more he recognized the shift in her eyes. She blinked, and the energy intensified.

Jackson couldn't stop the smile from quirking up the corner of his mouth.

It was hidden in the depths...but the traces were there, slowly swimming to the surface. Suddenly he understood. Casey wasn't withdrawing from the fear of her ordeal...she was biting back the guilt and anger at herself for falling into the trap.

"Ahh, Brat." He shook his head slowly, earning him a dark scowl and an eyebrow raise.

He should have recognized it—he'd been at the receiving end of that fireball as far back as he could remember. But this time he wasn't gearing up for a fight. He was so relieved that she was okay he completely forgot he should be totally pissed off with her for talking him into going alone. So instead of yelling he did the only thing he could do.

He kissed her.

She hesitated—if only for a moment—before leaning into him with a soft sigh, her lips pressing tentatively against his. Then she sat back slowly and placed her palms flat on his chest. Jackson braced for the shove. But it never came.

Instead, she twisted her hands into fists, filling them with his t-shirt, and pulled herself forward until her mouth was so close it almost touched his. Her breath teased across his lower lip. He was frozen. Waiting.

It was like falling into a volcano.

God, he wanted her.

But he didn't move.

Couldn't move.

Then she made the connection and all bets were off.

He could taste the sweetness of the scotch as she parted her lips beneath his, her tongue darting through to dance with his. Her hair flowed softly over his fingers as he slipped his hand around the back of her neck, his other resting against the side of her hip.

The silky heat of her skin pressed under his palm as she leaned forward, the material of her shirt sliding up. The tentative touch of her fingers on the side of his neck drove him crazy, and he almost groaned. He could think of nothing more than wanting to feel her, skin against skin—his hands were hungry, roaming under her shirt, searching for more.

She jumped to the side, and he froze, the little voice inside his head screaming at him for losing control. Her eyes were dark and heavy, but pain swirled in their depths.

She reached down and placed her hand on top of his, holding it against her side. "I'm sorry," she whispered. "I didn't mean to jump. I think...it's bruised."

They remained locked together, gazes connected, but the spell broken. Jackson swore under his breath and pulled his hands away. He tilted to the side and lifted the edge of her shirt up, cursing to see the angry bruise forming along her ribs. He probed the edges gently with his fingers, apologizing when she winced. Breathing slowly to keep his fury at her assailant at bay, he guided her shirt back down.

"I'm sorry." He pushed himself up off the bed and backed to the door, unable to see past the fact that here she was: hurt, injured, and the best he could do was paw at her like a hormonal frat boy. "I should probably go," he managed to get out. "You should get some rest."

He was nodding like an idiot as he stepped out into the hallway, closing the door. Knocking his forehead against the wood, he squeezed his eyes shut. What the hell was wrong with him? The woman had nearly been killed and here he was thinking with his pants.

Why was it no one could make him lose his bearings like Casey Marshall?

Pale and gray light came through the curtains, the overcast day calling out for her to pull the covers over her head and go back to sleep. With a loud yawn, she snuggled back into the blankets, fighting to stay asleep just a little bit longer. Her night had been restless, plagued with flashes and dreams of Wolinski's death and her ordeal in the garage. She squeezed her eyes shut and tried to block out the return of the images.

It wasn't working.

Then, of course, she had to quickly move past the images of nearly dying at the hands of a maniacal gunman to the other images of nearly dying at the hands of Jackson Hale.

She groaned and buried her face with her pillow. For years she'd dreamed of what it would be like to feel him against her, taste his lips, touch his body. She tried everything she could think of to get his attention, and then some.

After all this time, when she *finally* put him into the past, moved on, and made peace, it lasted for a whopping six months. Even her traitorous body was getting in on the act. She couldn't seem to get anywhere near him without thinking about naked bodies and what it would be like to feel his on hers.

She sure as hell didn't have much first hand knowledge, but her body seemed to understand the concept just fine. Even the act of *thinking* about him turned her lower belly to Jell-O.

Before the night at Mickey's, her only other experience had been a university frat party where she'd lost her virginity to an equally drunken fellow student named Kenny. He passed out on top of her as soon as he finished—which was pretty much immediately. There was no emotion, no passion, no fun. She dressed and left and never let it get past heavy make-out sessions again.

Oh, she'd had the offers and opportunity. But something inside her had always pushed back. She wanted the whole package, not a night of convenience.

And no matter who she met, or where she was, she couldn't escape the fact that she only wanted it with one man.

And now, here, with her world crushing in around her, she couldn't stop thinking about him.

Not anymore.

Last night, in the darkness of the room, between the brief snatches of sleep and the nightmarish memories, she actually thought of death. Of dying. Of leaving so much unfinished. There were so many things she wanted to do, to say. It came down to one chance, one night, before...well, before it was too late.

Because she knew now what she'd seen. She knew now why someone was trying to kill her. And she knew just how dangerous the situation was.

She had watched Robert Wolinski die.

The cold eyes of the man in the brown suit played out behind her closed eyelids, making her gasp. She snapped her eyes open and sat up. Her mind spun with the images and horror and she wanted it gone. Wanted her life back. She witnessed someone murdered in cold blood, and someone was trying to kill her.

She had never felt so afraid.

Jackson would do everything he could to protect her. She knew that. But she also understood with all her heart if he succeeded, they would go their separate ways, back to their lives, and maybe even back to hating each other.

But even worse was the thought that crossed her mind if Jackson failed.

She would be dead.

Jackson had been up all night, going through Carson's notes, looking for names and connections. Cross-referencing. Analyzing. Comparing. And what he and Lukas had eventually discovered was a very disturbing picture of the horrors surrounding the waterfront apartments.

Carson's hit list was a list—of witnesses.

The reporter had managed to track down the families, friends, and even a few past tenants themselves, each one offering up another piece of the puzzle.

Tenants who watched loved ones die, only to have it filed as an accident. Family members who could contradict reports and back them up with hard evidence. Original copies of paperwork which didn't match the doctored copies filed at city hall. Put it all together, and it would be the foundation for one hell of a solid court case.

Harrison Douglas would definitely want to make sure it disappeared.

Along with anyone else who knew about it, and anyone listed on it.

With a little help from Google, they knew seven people listed were already dead—and all within the last week alone. Suicide. Accidental drowning. Two car accidents. Heart attack. Mugging. Drug overdose. It would seem Carson had been accurate when he labeled it the *hit list*.

He and Lukas had discussed plans and options, and everything came back around to the same thing. The police. Several names came up consistently in the police reports in Carson's notes. But were they dirty cops? Or just the poor officers whose beat covered this very unlucky waterfront? Both men knew they couldn't take the chance without support.

Lukas had a friend at the FBI, and Jackson agreed it was time to call him. The whole situation was out of control, and the rest of the people on the list needed to be warned. So while Lukas contacted his buddy and took him copies of all the information, Jackson would get Casey out of town.

He had seriously considered sending Casey with Lukas. If not to get her immediately into FBI custody for safe keeping, then to keep her away from him. It was getting too personal. He couldn't think straight around her, and it was going to get them both killed. He had all but proven that last night by letting her go into the office alone. Lukas tried to convince him there was no way they could have known one of Harrison's men would have shown up, but it didn't matter. Jackson knew he'd made a bad call. He couldn't afford to have it happen again.

Then he went and plastered himself all over her.

Mistake number two.

Now he could barely concentrate, much less come up with a viable plan of action.

What the hell was it about Casey that made him second-guess everything?

He had no claim on her. So why was he feeling so...attached?

He sighed.

Casey Marshall was making him crazy and that was that.

When she finally made an appearance, Lukas served breakfast. Eggs, roasted potatoes, sausages, bacon, fruit, and freshly ground coffee. Casey knew she probably over complimented him, but damn the man could cook. Once the meal was finished and everyone was sufficiently full, the conversation turned back to their situation and the events of the past evening.

Inhaling sharply, she decided it was now or never. Pushing her empty plate away, she leaned forward on her elbows. "I remember what happened," she blurted out.

Jackson froze, his coffee cup halfway to his mouth. Lukas, on his way to the kitchen with empty dishes, spun on his heel and dropped back into his chair. He set the plates back on the table and regarded her expectantly.

"I saw him die," she admitted. "Brown Suit was definitely there. Carson too. And...and someone else." She shook her head, the memories superimposed over the image of Jackson's face, which watched her intently from across the table.

Jackson reached over and threaded his fingers through hers. "You need to tell us exactly what you remember. Work through it. Give us everything. No matter how small."

Casey closed her eyes, watching the memory unfold on the back of her eyelids. He held tightly to her hand, offering her his strength and a point of contact with this reality.

"It's dark. Raining. I'm hiding. I can see Carson," she said softly. "He's talking to someone in that alley. Yelling. They're fighting, but I can't quite hear what they're saying. Something about waiting."

She tipped her head, biting the inside of her cheek.

"Carson tells the other man to wait, and this car pulls up. I can see the other man's face now because of the headlights—it's Robert Wolinski. Then someone gets out of the car, maybe two people...." She hesitated, gnawing her lower lip. "The Councilor just...jumps." Her body jerked in response to the memory of the man's body folding in on itself. "He steps back, and his hands are holding his chest, and there's blood everywhere."

She opened her eyes and locked onto Jackson.

"They saw me. *He.* Saw me. The man in the brown suit. He...tried to kill me."

Lukas shook his head, his voice low and soothing. "Brown Suit couldn't have been your shooter, Casey."

"I saw him," she whispered, despair welling up into her chest that he wouldn't believe her. She spun her eyes towards Jackson.

"You said you could clearly see them both in the headlights," Jackson repeated, looking directly at her, his fingers tightly gripping hers. "They wouldn't have been able to see you to get a clear shot. You—"

"Were behind the lights, so the shot had to come from someone else," Lukas finished.

"There was someone else there?" she squeaked, gaping at Jackson in horror. "How many people are trying to kill me?"

"No one's going to kill you," he said firmly, dropping his chin to give her a pointed stare.

Casey wanted to believe him. She did. But she couldn't think over the little voice screaming in panic inside her head.

"Are you sure you don't remember who else was there?" Lukas asked.

Casey shook her head. "No?"

"Do you remember hearing anything? A gunshot?" Lukas prompted.

"I don't think so. I mean, maybe. I don't know. I don't think there was any sound when he shot Wolinski." She placed her palm over her forehead, unable to remember if she heard a gunshot. "I'm sorry...I don't remember."

"It's okay." Jackson nodded encouragingly. "You did fine."

She turned to Lukas. "Why is it so important?"

"I'm just wondering because they didn't stick around to make sure the job was finished," Lukas stated.

"Finished?" She snatched her hand back from Jackson, clutching it to the base of her throat.

Jackson frowned at Lukas. "That was subtle."

Lukas held his hands out, palms up. "I just mean they must have left in a hurry because they left you alive. Probably because of the sound of the gunshot."

"Unless they intended to come back later." Jackson frowned.

"And by then she was gone," Lukas finished.

Casey dropped her forehead onto the table and lightly banged it against the wooden surface. "This whole situation is so messed up. I don't even know what's going on anymore."

"Okay, let me try," Lukas offered. "Of the three people who had access to all this information, Carson's already in the hospital, someone has tried to kill you twice, the councilor is dead. All the paperwork points to Harrison Douglas. The goons who broke into Jackson's apartment may or may not be the same two people who showed up at the motel with Brown Suit. We have a possible connection inside the police and city hall. Brown and two, maybe even four; other people are gunning for you, and they want the list of names of people they're going to happily kill off, seven of which are dead already. And you've just discovered you're now a murder *witness*. That about cover it?"

Casey cursed and banged her forehead against the table until

Jackson slipped his hand between her head and the hard surface.

Jackson growled, and Casey lifted her head.

"What?" Lukas shrugged. "I'm just summarizing."

"You'd better call him now. The sooner the better," Jackson instructed with a scowl.

Lukas stood and grabbed his cell phone off the coffee table.

"Call who?" Casey asked, lifting her head off of Jackson's palm.

"I have a friend at the FBI," Lukas answered.

"The FBI?" She blinked. "Is that safe?"

"We need to tell someone," Jackson said quietly. "Especially now."

Casey turned back towards Jackson, almost shocked to see a flicker of worry flashing through his eyes before he closed it off. Worry. Jackson Hale *never* worried. And most certainly not for her.

Reaching across the table, he covered her hand with his. "Look. Things are heating up, and we can't stay here any longer. That list is a *death* list, Casey. The people on it are dying. Literally. There are big players out there, and we're going to need help. Lukas is going to talk to his friend, and you and I are getting out of town. We need to go someplace where we can hole up for a couple of days."

"A couple of days?"

"It's going to be a day or more before Lukas can set anything up. We can't stay here."

"Then where?"

"I'm still working on that."

Casey chewed her bottom lip while images of dingy, movie-style safe houses and one-room motels flipped through her mind, quickly followed by the known fact that the bad guys always found the murder witness at the neon-signed motel.

"What about the lodge?" She blurted out the only safe place she could think of.

"What lodge?" Lukas asked.

"Uncle Thomas has a cottage, a cabin, up in the foothills. We could ask him if we can...stay there?"

"That might not be a bad idea." Jackson nodded, standing up and sliding his duffel bag across the coffee table towards him. He dug a map out of the side pocket then grabbed a pad of paper and a pen from the desk. "Show me where it is."

Casey pointed out the location on the map and sat back while the two men covered the logistics of their next steps. They were both in the zone, talking in acronyms and short forms, arguing over one detail, disagreeing over the same point they actually agreed on, and finishing each other's sentences like an old married couple. She had absolutely no idea what they were talking about.

She was confused, scared, stressed, a murder witness, running for her life, calling the FBI, and discussing the merits of hiding out at a cottage. It was turning into the most horrifically surreal experience of her life.

Yet for some reason, something in her found the interaction between Jackson and Lukas to be downright comical, and it snowballed from there.

She started to giggle and got a glance from each, which made it funnier. The giggle became an outright laugh. Two heads turned to stare at her. Which made her laugh harder. They both stood up at the exact same time and the exact same speed then turned directly towards her. She slid down over the back of the couch onto the cushions and laughed until tears flowed down her cheeks. She was in such a state that she had trouble getting a solid breath, unable to do any more than clamp her hands over her face and stare at them through the tears. Eventually she tried to get off the couch, but managed only to tumble onto the floor and wedge herself in between the bottom of the couch and the coffee table.

Lukas ran into the kitchen saying something about a glass of water, which was apparently hilarious in some aspect because she couldn't stop laughing. The absolute panic in their actions pushed her right over the edge. She shook so hard she wasn't making any sound. All she could do was wave her hands at them trying to sign that she was just fine.

She wiggled as Jackson tried to pick her up—she was perfectly happy lying on the floor—but he lifted her to her feet anyway. Lukas stood in the doorway holding a glass of water and absolutely no clue about what to do. The what-the-hell-are-we-supposed-to-do-now look that passed between them just kept her going.

"You should...," she blurted out, before dissolving into another round. "You should see your faces!"

Jackson stood behind her and wrapped his arms around her upper body, holding her firmly against his chest.

"Casey, damn it, what the hell is wrong with you?" he growled in her ear.

That threw her right back into the silent mode again, just arm waving and tears. Except her arms were pinned under Jackson's reverse hug, so all she could do was wave her hands like a marionette. Which was also spectacularly comical.

"I don't think you're helping," Lukas chastised.

Jackson stood holding her while she laughed and cried and gasped for air, and after a good five minutes she'd finally calmed down to a moderate giggle, sniff, and shake. She knew she wasn't holding herself up, and if Jackson decided to let go she would fall flat on the floor. Eventually the urge subsided, and she turned her head and loudly kissed his forearm.

"Damn, I needed that." She angled her head and smiled up at him. He looked angry, worried, and damn sexy.

She steadied her feet beneath her, and with a residual giggle, shook her head. "I'm all better. You can let go now."

Jackson opened his arms, and she stepped out, accepting the glass of water Lukas held out. She was still grinning like an idiot but managed to drink half of it without spilling any down her chin.

She handed him back the glass.

"Sorry," she said, not really meaning it. "I couldn't help it. It was just...." She giggled, wiping furiously at her cheeks and eyes with the shoulders of her t-shirt. "It was just really funny."

"Apparently," Jackson muttered.

"And do you do that often?" Lukas asked, his eyebrow raised.

Casey smiled. "Only when overly stressed...or really drunk."

"Keep that in mind," Lukas suggested to Jackson, who nodded in agreement.

Before Casey could open her mouth, three knocks sounded at the front door in rapid succession.

Jackson shoved Casey down the hallway towards the bedrooms, then snatched his gun off the computer desk. Lukas stepped forward, gun in hand. All the humor of the previous moment lost in a heart pounding panic, Casey watched from the back bedroom as they flanked the doorway.

"Where is she?" a loud, low voice sliced into the apartment, bouncing off the walls.

Casey squealed and ran down the hallway, flinging herself full force into her uncle's outstretched arms. "What took you so long?" She smiled, relief washing over her.

"You okay?" Tom Marshall glanced down at his niece, pulling her back so he could give her a thorough once over.

She nodded. "I'm okay."

He glared over her head at the two men standing directly in front of him. "Fill me in." The no-nonsense look in his gray eyes left no room for discussion.

For the next thirty minutes he was given a complete briefing. He asked no questions, made no comments, just listened intently. When it was over, he turned towards Casey. "Let's walk."

Everyone knew that meant it was time for a private conversation. Casey followed her uncle to the back bedroom and waited while he

112

closed the door.

He stepped closer, ran a hand over his military-cropped gray hair, and shrugged. "What am I going to do with you?"

"I know, I'm sorry, but—"

"You've gotten yourself into quite a mess this time."

She shook her head. "It wasn't my—"

He held up his hand. "I'm proud of you."

"You are?" Casey was shocked. She thought for sure her uncle would be furious with the whole mess. "But...but what about the police? I didn't come forward as soon as I knew?"

He shook his head. "No, you did what you needed to do. You listened. You followed orders. And you stuck to it."

"So you're not mad at me?"

"Oh, I'm mad all right." He dropped his hands to his hips. "I'm also glad you're safe. But it's not over yet."

She sighed and sat on the edge of the bed. "I know. But what do I do?"

He sat beside her, moving his arm when she shoved it back to lean against his side. "What do you want to do?"

Casey shrugged. "I...I don't know. Part of me wants to come forward. Part of me wants to kick Harrison's butt. And...part of me wants to run as far away as I can and not look back."

He smiled and wrapped his arm around her shoulder, tugging her closer. "So who's winning?"

"Unfortunately, the part that wants to kick his butt." She rested her head on his shoulder. "But I'm scared, Uncle Thomas."

He hugged her tightly then stood up, guiding her to her feet. "These boys are the best, honey. Nothing's going to happen to you as long as you stick with them. Keep listening. Keep following orders. Everything's going to be just fine. You have my word."

With the Colonel's approval, Lukas called his friend at the FBI. It was time to take things to the next level. They had the ability to take him down themselves, but outside of law enforcement, it may not make it to trial. They could also just as easily make him disappear, but without knowing who he was working with, or what really happened to Carson, it would leave too many loose ends.

They needed someone official.

And the FBI was pretty official.

Chapter Twelve

Department store organization made absolutely no sense. Casey shook her head with a frown and tried to reason out why sunglasses would be placed next to bread and crackers. But she couldn't connect the retail dots.

Standing in the main aisle, she scanned the rows. Jackson was in the shoe section browsing for boots to replace the badly fitting pair he'd borrowed from Lukas. And after their movie-style escape from the motel, Casey had nothing but the clothes on her back, so she was going to have to start with the basics—two of everything.

They were just over an hour from her uncle's lodge, and the popular department store was their last opportunity to pick up supplies. After this, the only place to buy anything was a two-pump gas station with a pop-and-chip variety store.

She steered the cart down a side aisle. So far she'd thrown in a denim jacket, a pair of jeans, some shirts, toiletries, and underwear. Now all she needed was socks.

She passed a rack of racy-red lingerie and couldn't resist fingering the silky material. How did women actually wear this stuff to bed? It looked absolutely gorgeous. She eyed the tiny spaghetti straps and the lacy v-neck. It had to be damn uncomfortable to sleep in. The material flowing over your hips would definitely bunch up and twist as you rolled, and you'd most likely wake up in the middle of the night with the whole thing wrapped around your waist.

She personally hated sleeping in anything more than her skin.

She held it up in front of her, judging the size.

Did Jackson like red?

Sweet Lord. What on Earth am I thinking?

She flung the hanger back onto the rack.

"Definitely your color," Jackson whispered in her ear.

Her face heated. Doing her best to look nonchalant, she shoved the cart over towards the display of socks.

"Did you find your boots?" she asked, concentrating on reading the label of a package of sport socks that apparently helped lift as well as breathe.

Jackson dropped an armful of clothes into the basket and topped it off dramatically with a large beige shoebox. "Done."

She threw the socks into the cart. "Then I guess we just need to hit the grocery section and we're good to go."

Several aisles and a checkout later, they were bagged and boxed and walking out the automatic doors. The parking lot was quite full for a weekday, this being one of the few locations for miles around offering one-stop shopping. Vehicles dodged and weaved up and down the rows, following patrons who exited in the hopes of getting the next best parking spot. Cars double parked in front of the sidewalk, dropping passengers off, while others waited for pedestrians to cross in front.

Reaching the back of Lukas' truck, Jackson lifted the bags out of the cart and tossed them into the back seat of the crew cab. Casey spun the empty cart around and threaded her way over to the next row, leaving it inside one of the outside cart-return shelters.

As she headed back she noticed a man struggling to pick up several cans that rolled away between the cars. She stooped to grab can of tomato soup and crossed over to where he was bent, peering underneath a white delivery van.

"I think this is yours." She smiled and held out the can as the man straightened up. When he reached his full height, he turned towards her and sneered.

Her subconscious reacted first, and she sucked in as much oxygen as her lungs would hold in a split-second shock.

The man from the brownstone.

He leapt forward, his hands strangling her upper arms. He spun her around and jammed his hand over her mouth, trapping her scream beneath his palm.

The sliding door of the van behind her crashed open.

"Hurry up!" came the order from inside the van as she was forced roughly back towards the opening.

Forgetting anything she'd ever heard about self-defence, Casey reacted with a more primal mode of survival—leg kicking, body twisting, full-blown panic.

Her feet left the ground, and she bounded against her captor's grip like a frightened feline. Hopping left then right in an attempt to break his hold. The man spun her quickly towards his partner in the van, and she kicked her legs forward, cracking the second man across the cheekbone and sending him tumbling into the back of the empty cargo area. Because both her feet were off the ground, the man holding her stooped with the sudden weight and his hand slipped. Planting her feet on the asphalt, she bent her knees and launched herself straight up, slamming the top of her head against the bottom of his jaw. Stars exploded behind her eyes, but the terror ripping through her veins kept her standing as he staggered back, yanking her with him. His fingers dug tightly into her upper arm as he hauled her back against his chest, his left arm circling around her waist to keep her from dropping back down for another shot at his chin.

Realizing she still clutched the can of tomato soup, Casey lifted her arm up and, fueled with pure adrenaline, aimed for where she prayed the side of his head was. She connected with something hard, and a screeching howl echoed in her ear. Then her shoulder screamed in protest as she was spun around and tossed chest first into the side of the hatchback.

She whipped around, can of soup held high, and faced the back of a gray-clad torso twisting with the motion of rapid-fire punches.

Jackson dropped the tall man who'd been mauling Casey to the pavement with a crushing uppercut. His free hand immediately shot out and snagged the fat man, who tried to scramble into the front seat. He pulled the goon off balance and slammed his head against the floor of the van. A quick left and the man was unconscious.

Turning towards her, he wrapped his fingers around her wrist and dragged her through the gathering crowd of curious onlookers. Ripping the passenger door of the truck open, he shoved her inside and ran around to the front.

The truck hit the highway on two wheels.

After a speed-limit-shattering, adrenaline-spiked, twenty-minute drive, Jackson spun sideways onto the dirt road Casey's map indicated would be their turn off. It was a registered fire-lane, which loosely translated into a tire-track path crowded with tall trees and wild growth. Coming across a narrow opening off to the side, Jackson slammed into reverse and backed into the brush. Hidden amongst the trees, he shut off the engine and jumped out of the car, commanding Casey to stay put. He searched the underbody, the wheel wells, the trunk, and the engine.

His fingertips brushed against a small tracer tucked up under the frame, and he cursed himself for being cocky enough to think their pursuers wouldn't have the technical savvy to plant two GPS units. They'd found the first one before they'd left the parking garage, but hadn't swept for a second. It was an idiotic mistake, and he would have had no one to blame but himself if something had happened.

Crushing it into the gravel beneath his heel, he hopped back into the driver's seat and turned towards Casey.

She still sat stiffly in the passenger seat, a can of tomato soup clutched so tightly between the fingers of her right hand that her knuckles had long lost their color.

"C'mere, Brat," he whispered, reaching for her with his arms and his heart.

With a sob she dropped the soup onto the floorboards and flung herself across the console.

Jackson lifted her onto his lap, wrapping his arms around her. She trembled against him, chanting "don't let go, don't let go" into his chest, her arms locked in a death grip around his waist. Her legs were tucked so tightly against her chest she nearly formed a perfect ball.

He tipped her face up and pressed his lips against hers, rage and pride flowing out in his kiss. He could taste her fear, hovering just beneath the salty tang of her tears. When he'd seen her struggling—so close to being pulled into a van by hired killers—he'd nearly lost it. The distance between the truck and that cargo van had been miles of space to cover in an instant.

But she'd held her own. She'd fought back like a wildcat.

His wildcat.

Jackson broke away and tucked her head under his chin, trying to control his air intake, subliminally calming her with steady, exaggerated breathing.

He didn't know how long they sat there, locked together, slowly breathing in tandem. And he didn't care.

She was safe. She was here. She was his.

The single lane, gravel dusted road they traveled on was shaded in an overhang of tall pine trees, making it appear darker than it really was. When the lane emptied out in front of the cabin, the light from the setting sun was almost blinding.

Jackson stopped the truck in the middle of the clearing and stared at the building in front of them.

"Cabin? I thought you said it was a cabin?"

"It is." Casey straightened up in her seat and turned towards him, her expression suddenly filled with dread. "Why? What's wrong?"

"Nothing." He smiled and shook his head, staring at the sight in front of him. "It's that it's not a cabin, it's a damn chalet!"

The *cabin* was no more a cottage than his brownstone. Perched on the top of a small rise sat a very large, two-storey A-frame log home with a full-sized, wraparound porch. Silhouetted against the fading purples and pinks of the sunset, it stood tall and solitary beneath the fading sky. With the exception of a lone oak growing off to the right, the area was cleared of trees for a hundred yards around the perimeter. Only low ground cover and wild clover remained.

Parking in front, he killed the engine and climbed out. Taking a moment to stretch, he inhaled slowly, filling his nose with the sharp tang of pine and the soft, underlying hint of clover. Wind rustled across the trees, shifting the tips of the towering pines as it passed. High above, a hawk circled, his wingspan wide and still as he soared.

Jackson's boots sank in the soft dirt as he stepped forward and walked around to the front, giving the building, and the area, a more thorough once over. Extremely dense forest surrounded three of the sides, and the fourth side—the front—was a very steep rocky drop down into a valley crisscrossed with a small river.

A small rock wall stretched across the top edge of the cliff, ending only when it reached the heavy line of thick pines on either side. Planting his hands on the rough surface, Jackson carefully leaned over and stared down the rocky cliff side. The drop had to be at least a hundred feet. He straightened and looked across the valley, following the land as it rose and fell, rolling its way up into the mountains.

The view was spectacular.

With a shake of his head, he made a mental note to try to explain to his boss the difference between a cabin and retreat.

Shoving off the wall, he turned and walked back around to the front, glad to see that the only way into the area on wheels was through the single-lane road they had just traveled down. A man *could* eventually navigate through the brush, or up the rockface, but he doubted the people they were up against were that skilled. If they were, Casey would already be dead. A man who would scale a hundred foot rockface to assassinate someone wouldn't first try three bumbling attempts to grab her. No, they'd take their shot and be done with it.

The little voice inside his head reminded him of his previous mistake with the GPS tracker, and he scowled to himself, admitting he wasn't about to rule anything out.

Not if he planned to keep her alive.

And speaking of her....

Where was she?

"Casey?"

He stopped. A muffled thump and string of curses sounded from under the front steps. He moved around to the side in time to see a shapely bottom taunting him from beneath the third and forth steps.

"What are you doing?" He leaned over and took a moment to admire the snug fit of the denim as she wiggled backwards out of the narrow opening.

"Getting the spare key," she answered, brushing the dirt and cobwebs off her legs. She walked up and unlocked the large front door. Turning to the beeping panel next to the door, she quickly punched in the security code to disable the alarm system.

Jackson had to admit he was equally impressed, if not more so, with the inside of the colonel's retreat. It was a damn fine piece of craftsmanship all around.

Off to the right of the entranceway stood a large mudroom, with plenty of storage cabinets and washer-dryer combo. To the left of the foyer was a walk-in pantry with several shelving units, each overflowing with dry food and supplies.

Further inside, a huge living area and open concept kitchen were separated by a large wooden table, which was easily big enough to seat ten. The front windows ran the length of the wall and stretched floor to ceiling, offering an amazing view. To the right, across from the windows, were two large bedrooms and a full bathroom. By the kitchen, a staircase ran up to the second level loft.

The entire place was decorated with a mix of wooden furniture, throw blankets, old photos, and eclectic knickknacks.

Casey smiled. "Uncle Thomas has spent every summer up here since he got out, working on this place. Not bad, huh?"

"Not bad," Jackson agreed, sliding the patio door open and stepping out onto the deck. "How the hell did he get hydro all the way up on this ridgeline?"

Following him outside, Casey quickly explained the land was originally intended to be used as some kind of emergency lookout or fire-tower and station, so the local municipality had expended a small fortune to run power to the rise. But then something happened and the actual location for the station was moved several miles further south. The colonel's offer was accepted, and he bought himself a very elite vacation spot.

Casey sighed and leaned against the railing. "Beautiful," she whispered.

Jackson glanced sideways at her, his mind agreeing with her assessment. Unfortunately, it wasn't the deep purples streaking across the twilight sky he was looking at, but the gorgeous, sexy blonde with the soft smile and the deep blue eyes.

It wasn't much after they'd finished unloading the supplies from the truck that Casey gave up and called it a night. Her body was completely spent from a combination of the fresh mountain air and the taxing stress of the past few days. By the time they'd finished bringing everything in she couldn't take two steps without one of them being a stumble. Leaving Jackson to choose from one of the rooms on the main floor, she retreated to the second floor master bedroom, which covered the entire top floor of the A-frame.

Two of the widows from the main level extended up through the floor, reaching all the way to the roof, offering a spectacular view to any who had the pleasure of standing before them. Her uncle had always bitched about how much of a pain they were to cover over each fall with plywood, but even he had to admit it was well worth it.

From the lofty perch high above the cliff face, it was like standing on the edge of the world.

Stepping forward, she leaned against the glass and stared out across the rapidly darkening world. The valley floor was already deep in shadow, and towering over it, the mountains in the distance were outlined in a royal purple as the night chased away the last of the sunset.

Watching until she could see nothing more than silhouetted outlines, she gave in with a yawn and shed her clothes. The soft cotton sheets were cool against her bare skin, and she burrowed into the pillows. With a happy sigh she fell fast asleep.

It was pitch black and silent when Jackson's eyes snapped open. For an instant his mind struggled to pinpoint his location, and then his memory made the connection. The colonel's cottage, main floor bedroom. As he listened to the lack of sounds around him, he was unable to determine what woke him. His subconscious hadn't automatically kicked him into the zone, and he didn't sense any immediate danger, but damn it was freaky quiet.

He was trained to sleep just about anywhere: cold rain, desert heat, under a tarp right next to a landing zone. Sound and weather could be mentally ignored. But utter silence...well, that was just unusual.

It was then that he heard it.

A distant squeak.

He lifted his head off the pillow and held it midair, his ears straining to catch another instance to help confirm the direction.

A mewing sound?

He angled his head.

It was coming from the kitchen.

With the light from the three-quarter moon shining in through the giant wall of windows, he stealthily navigated his way to the kitchen, the bare tile cool against the bottom of his feet.

He willed the sound to come again so he could follow it. Nothing. He was just about to give up and go back to bed when he heard it again. In the corner near the stairs...no...it was coming from upstairs.

Casey?

He hesitated at the foot of the stairs, unable to feel any presence inside the house except their own. Unwilling to chance anything, he raised the Beretta and moved silently up the stairs.

As he climbed, he kept his footsteps steady, concentrating on the feel of the room around him. The air felt still and calm, holding no discernable trace of malice. His gut was telling him they were indeed alone, but the noise bothered him nonetheless. The heavy wooden railing blocked his view of the room until he reached the top of the stairs. Peering through the hand-carved slats, he confirmed no movement before moving up the last few steps.

He led with the barrel, tracing his eyes methodically across the room until he came to the bed. And there he paused.

It was completely empty.

The bedding was a mess, the giant comforter half shoved over the footboard and most of the pillows discarded haphazardly across the floor.

Jackson looked around a second time, seeing no trace of Casey.

Where the hell is she?

Had she gone downstairs to sleep? She'd said the room closest to the bathroom was usually hers.

But no.

He would have heard her.

Another muffled squeak split the silence, and he froze, cocking his head and honing in on the sound. It had come from the far side of the room, near the corner. Squinting, he caught a glimpse of something small and light-colored on the far side of the dresser. Behind it? No...beside it. He inched ahead, pressing his weight across the slatted wooden flooring, easing himself forward so as not to creak the wood and give away his position. Gun raised, he targeted the far side of the room.

The pink shadow shifted when he got within a few feet. He dropped to his knee and realized what he was really looking at. Pink toenails. Casey's foot.

His chest constricted, and he swore.

Stepping around the dresser he saw her cowering in the corner, lying in the fetal position on the floor, sobbing. He reached up and set the gun on top of the dresser, then scooped her up and carried her back towards the bed. She felt so light and small, her body curling into his, seeking warmth and protection.

Jackson inhaled upon feeling the incredibly cold chill of her skin against his chest. He was halfway across the room before it dawned on him that the reason her skin was so cold was because the woman was one hundred percent naked.

His body jerked, his steps faltering. Her arms looped around his neck, clinging to him with desperation. Tears dripped down onto his shoulder. Keeping his eyes up, he praised himself for not looking down. Then her breath caught, and her pebbled nipples rubbed against his chest.

Not good.

Snapping himself back into reality, he pushed forward and attempted to put her down onto the bed. Much to his internal dismay, she wouldn't let go. He tried to unclasp her hands without hurting her, but she just held on tighter. He felt the naked press of her skin against his torso, the soft mounds of her breasts pushing against his chest, the smooth skin of her thighs across his forearm.

Good Lord, if she didn't let go of him soon....

"Please...," she whispered, the tremor in her voice tearing away his defenses. "Stay."

Jackson carried on one hell of an argument inside his head as to why he should *not* leave a beautiful, naked woman, so obviously upset, alone. And, why he *should* get the hell out of there and run for his life. He wasn't sure exactly how the battle was won, but he suddenly found himself climbing into the bed with her. Laying on his side, he pulled her in against him and reached for the comforter. He tried to wedge the blanket down between their bodies, giving himself relief from the distraction of the skin-to-skin contact, but she shifted until she lay half across him, her soft sobs wrenching his heart.

He stared up at the arched ceiling, a feeling of helplessness and loss tightening across his chest. It broke him apart to see her so lost. He ached to do something, anything, to heal her pain. But what words? Her life had been turned upside down, and a few platitudes wouldn't resolve anything.

So he offered the only thing he could.

Himself.

Wrapping his arms around her, he held her until the tears faded into short soft gasps and snuffles, and eventually ended in hiccups. She soon fell silent, lying next to him, her hand splayed over his heart. Her breathing was soft and steady, but he knew she was still awake.

"I'm sorry," she whispered. "I was trying to be quiet."

"I wasn't sleeping," he lied.

She remained silent, her index finger tapping out a silent rhythm against his chest.

He placed his hand on top of hers, holding her palm over his heart. "You wanna talk about it?"

She shrugged, her eyelashes tickling his shoulder when she blinked. "It's just...this place," she admitted. "It's like...like home. Safe, you know? I just...I just...couldn't stop."

Jackson took a deep breath and exhaled slowly. He understood the dangerous game comfort zones played. You could keep your guard up as long as you were on the outside. But when you hit home, a place of sanctity and security, the barriers always came crashing down and left you an emotional mess.

"I'm here," he reminded her, turning to kiss the top of her head. "I won't let anything happen to you."

"I know," she answered, shifting against him and snuggling further into his side.

The longer they lay together, beneath the soft comforter, in a king-sized bed, alone, the more trouble Jackson had keeping his mind on the business at hand. He tried to think of baseball, football statistics, the names of his elementary school teachers, anything to help block out the fact that he had a beautiful, naked woman curled up against him.

Tried.

And failed.

He struggled to ignore the smooth, cool press of her skin, covering just about every inch of the left side of his body. He didn't want to think about the way she'd thrown her leg up over his, her left knee resting dangerously close to the swelling heat tenting his boxers. He worked on blocking out the teasing feel of her fingertips that idly traced an aimless looping pattern on his chest around his heart. And he most definitely was not trying to slip his fingers beneath the heavy weight of her breast which pressed so softly against his side.

His fingers twitched, brushing her skin, and he felt her shiver.

"Jackson." She exhaled, her low whisper breaking him into goose bumps as she lightly kissed the side of his neck. Hearing his name on her lips nearly pushed him over, but he held himself in check. Then she shifted, and her knee pressed against his groin, sending a shockwave up through his lower body.

"Casey," he croaked, his mouth suddenly dry.

She lifted her head, her hair spilling down around her head to flow across his shoulder like liquid silk. She lowered her head until her mouth hovered a breath's width above his. When she licked her lower lip, her tongue touched his, and he quivered beneath her.

"Please...," she whispered, the sadness in her voice driving right through to his soul. "Don't go."

And just like that, he knew he was lost.

With a groan of concession, he pulled her completely on top of him. He explored her mouth with his tongue, tasted the damp salt on her cheeks, kissed her nose, her chin. Pushing back the covers, he guided her upright, spreading her thighs so she straddled him. The heat and molten wetness between her legs burned through his boxers, and he groaned. His hands settled on her hips, holding her in place, his blood heating to know they were separated from skin on skin by nothing more than a thin layer of cotton. He rocked his hips, sliding forward and back against her wet folds.

From her lofty position, Casey took in the power and strength of the man sprawled out between her legs, feeling the incredibly heady rush of being able to look down on such perfection, knowing that even if only for this brief moment, he would be hers. She shuddered as his motion increased the scorching fire that ached between her legs. When his hands reached up to cup her breasts, his thumbs brushing over her pebbled nipples, she moaned and dropped her head back. Her body's rhythm automatically matched his, her hips moving in a dance so primal her inexperience mattered not. Her entire body was tight. Burning, needing. Pushing and grinding, moving with ancient rhythm.

God, she felt as though her entire being was on fire.

She looked down at where he lay between her legs, the moonlight casting spears of light and shadow over his body, and watched his muscles tremble beneath her light touch as she grazed her fingers across his abdomen. She wanted to know him everywhere. Memorize everything. He radiated power and strength. It was intoxicating enough to begin with, but tonight, here and now, it was utter abandonment.

Lifting himself up with his arms, he took one of her nipples between his teeth and rolled his tongue over the tip. Casey gasped, her hips bucking involuntarily as knots of tension twisted through her lower body. He switched back and forth, one breast to the other, hand, mouth, fingers, teeth. She groaned and slid her hands down his shoulders, clutching the smooth muscles of his forearms. His tongue continued to swirl and twist, his teeth nipping, suckling her until she wasn't sure she'd ever be able to breathe normally again.

Pressure built deep within her, and she squeezed her hips, forcing her center tightly down against his hardened erection.

Jackson let out a hiss of air between his teeth and forced her hips up. Within seconds, the offending underwear was tossed to the floor.

Resuming her position, she placed her hands on his shoulders and pushed him down onto the pillows. She leaned forward to kiss him, her happily abused nipples brushed across his chest, making her gasp in shock at the lightning sensation that rippled through her body. Jackson caught her mouth with his, stealing her breath and nipping her lower lip. Her body swayed with an ache and hunger so powerful she felt as though she was going to shatter. His hands tightened around her hips, guiding her slowly back against him. Flesh on flesh, her body shuddered as she struggled for air. Hot. God, he was so hot.

Despite the heat of her own arousal, the tip of his erection scorched her skin, and she cried out. Unable to stand the agony any longer, she released her hips, slowly impaled herself on him. He stretched her so tightly it was almost painful. She hissed in surprise, halting her downward motion. Beneath her he froze. Watching. Waiting. His hands clamped firmly on her hips, his body unmoving, while she perched above him, his member half buried inside her.

"Casey?" he whispered.

"It's okay." She nodded, fear surging through her that he might stop. She eased herself down until she firmly sat atop him, their bodies locked together.

Casey rocked to the side, repositioning, reveling in the incredible feeling of fullness. He groaned with the pleasure of the movement and closed his eyes. He released his grip on her thighs, moving his hands away to fist in the bottom sheet. She felt the shift in power and knew he was waiting for her. Her heart cried out at the precious gift. He was offering her control.

She rose ever so slightly on her knees, then slipped back down, sliding on him, riding him with a slow, deliberate motion. His hips rose in matching rhythm, increasing with speed and thrust, leading her, encouraging her. She rose and fell, her head back, the ends of her hair teasing erotically against her back. Faster, harder. She knew she was moaning, crying out, couldn't stop it, didn't want to stop it. Pressure filled her, tightness and release. Again and again her hips bucked, convulsions ripping through her lower body as the explosion stole her breath and she could do nothing but scream his name.

Beneath her his body bucked and stiffened. His hips thrusting sharply up, his hands digging into her hips, crushing her against him, filling her to a fullness she could never have imagined. He pulled her forward, laying her across his chest while they shuddered through the last of the tremors, their breaths mingling.

Jackson held her, the feeling of her rapid heartbeat kicking back against his own. To watch her astride him, a gloriously naked goddess bathed in moonlight, had taken every ounce of willpower he had not to explode the minute he slid into her. She had been incredibly tight. Too much so. When she stopped he had been very afraid that he was her first. He'd been pretty damn sure there had been no virgin barrier, but then she'd gone and taken him all in before he could stop her. He didn't have the mental processes to dwell on it at the time, but now, in the aftermath, he wondered.

Minutes passed before she moved, angling her head to a more comfortable position.

"I'm still alive, right?" she whispered, her breath cool against the side of his neck.

He smiled. "I believe so."

"You?"

"I'm not sure yet."

She nuzzled his neck, her voice so soft he wondered if she was talking to him or herself. "Is it always like that?"

"Like what?" he finally asked.

"Like...electricity. I can barely think." She lay splayed across him, her body still clenching him inside her, the tightness refusing to let him slip away. Her hand slid up the side of his neck and played gently with his hair. "I had no idea it could feel so...." Taking a deep breath, she exhaled the word "Good." The way she slowly writhed her hips back and forth already made him hard inside her. "I'm beginning to think I should have tried it again."

"Again?" he managed to croak out.

"Mmmm...." She licked the side of his jaw. "I didn't like it so much the first time."

"Didn't like what the first time?" Somewhere his brain was telling him it didn't like where this conversation was going, but he could barely breathe with the way she undulated on top of him.

"Sex, silly. If I'd have realized I could have been doing *this* the whole time...."

The incredibly arousing purring noise she was making low in her throat sent him over the edge. With a primal growl, he rolled on top of her and drove deeper. He hooked his arms under her legs and urged her to lock them around him. With her ankles looped over his back, she opened herself fully, and he claimed all, her hips rising to meet his with each thrust. Fingernails raked across his shoulder, urging him faster, harder, until finally her scream tore through his soul and he released what little he had left inside her.

He collapsed next to her, his arm flung possessively across her abdomen, his leg locked between hers. She gasped for air, her arms lying limply over her head in surrender. Judging from his raging heartbeat he was just as affected. Too exhausted to do anything more than roll onto his back, he pulled her against him.

As he lay there, staring at the jagged patterns and shadows across the walls, Jackson's mind began its slow return to reality, and he thought about what she'd told him. He couldn't wrap his head around it. Had she just admitted she'd only had sex once before? It was the only explanation for her words, yet the concept made no sense. Because if it did, then wild and crazy Casey wasn't as wild as he'd believed.

In fact, he was beginning to think he didn't have the faintest clue about her. One partner? Hell, she was practically a virgin!

But it didn't make any sense!

He'd seen her at the parties, the guys falling all over her. She flirted, she made out, and she'd even left with them, gotten into their cars. He'd watched them drive away more than once. Had it all been for show? Had she simply hid it from him like she did with the night at Mickey's?

But why hide it? Had her first experience really been that bad? The thought kicked his senses into overdrive, and he almost shook her to demand the details. Once? Had it been consensual? Was that why she never slept with anyone after? She was a beautiful woman; was Mickey's not the first time something had happened?

Jackson suddenly felt nauseous with worry and anger.

He had to know.

"You still alive?" he asked.

She nodded.

"Tell me."

"Tell you what?" she mumbled.

"The forgettable first time."

She sighed and shifted against him, her head resting on his shoulder. "Why?" Hesitation caught in her voice.

"Sizing up the competition."

She snorted. "There is absolutely no comparison to be made between you and Kenny Paulson. He was drunk, and it barely lasted two seconds before he passed out on top of me."

"Drunk?" His body tensed. "Did he...?"

"What? Oh. No." She shook her head. "Not really. I mean, I had no idea what I was actually getting myself into, but.... Well, let's just say it wasn't one of my smarter moments."

He relaxed, but only slightly, wanting very much to beat the tar out of the faceless Kenny for taking advantage of her.

"You've had *other* such moments?"

She snorted. "You have no idea."

He wished he could see her face, read her expression. Something told him he was just scratching the surface when it came to knowing the real Casey Marshall.

He felt her shiver, her skin cooling down, chilled with the open air. He hooked the blankets and covered their entwined bodies, holding her tightly until sleep came to claim her.

Chapter Thirteen

The sun was high up into the trees when Casey finally drummed up the nerve to crawl out from under the covers. She lay awake for hours, alone in the bed, trying to figure out what the hell she was going to do now.

She'd made a total mess of everything.

Last night she'd jolted awake from a horrible nightmare, alone in the darkness, and completely broke down out of fear and self-pity.

After her parents had died, she'd refused to let anyone see her really cry. She was braver than that. Stronger. Even Meghan had never been privy to more than the angry swipe of a few tears. But last night, in the shadows of the familiar room, she dreamt of death, loss, and heart breaking fear, because it wasn't Wolinski's face she saw in her nightmare. It was Jackson's.

And then he was there. Flesh and blood. Strong arms shielding her, warming her chilled body, holding her tightly while she cried. For the first time in her life she understood the concept of completion. In the depths of her soul she knew she would never touch the level of passion and all-consuming fire with any other man.

Her fall was complete.

She was utterly in love with Jackson Hale.

With clarity from the daylight, she had taken the wondrous emotions and memories of the night before and locked them away. He didn't trust her. Barely believed her. And was here only out of a sense of duty. She had no right to claim him and no hope for a future. Last night was a fluke, driven by her out-of-control emotions.

And now she was going to have to get up and face him. She would carry no regrets. But would he feel the same? With a sigh she crawled out of bed, wishing instead she could just disappear.

Jackson showered and shaved hours before he heard her walking about overhead. He wasn't sure what kind of reception he was going to get. Deciding she was probably going to head to the bathroom first, he tucked his pride between his legs and hid on the front porch. Enjoying the feel of the sun on his bare back, he tried to clear his mind.

The fact that she'd been flopping around in the bed for hours told him she was not in any hurry to come downstairs. She was either embarrassed or rightfully pissed off. He deserved the latter since he obviously had the willpower of a goldfish where she was concerned. He should have just left her alone to cry it out in her pillow.

Why was it that every time he came into contact with Casey she scrambled his system? Up until two days ago he'd been firmly seated in the idea that Casey Marshall was completely mental, had absolutely no idea how to follow instructions, and would rather argue with someone than listen to facts or reason. She never obeyed the rules, hated commitment, and thought duty was a tax you paid at the border.

And now?

Now he had no idea what to think because at some point in the past forty-eight hours, everything he'd thought to be true had been taken apart and shredded.

He shook his head and herded his thoughts back into the darkness where they belonged.

He was here because it was expected of him. He owed it to Carson. It was his duty as a friend.

It had nothing to do with Casey personally.

And it had nothing to do with the fact that she was slowly proving him wrong on all counts.

He was going to make sure she reached the FBI alive and whole and then once she was safely in their hands, he would be off the hook. All he had to do was play nicely and keep his hands off her.

Nodding silently in approval at himself for finally coming up with a viable plan of action, he settled back against the railing.

Unfortunately, the plan lasted only as long as it took her to come downstairs.

She stepped through the patio doors, blowing steam off a mug of coffee, and he just about forgot everything he'd decided about keeping his hands to himself.

The low riding jeans weren't as much of a distraction as the very snug, dangerously low-necked, light blue t-shirt she'd chosen to wear. She'd pulled her damp hair back into a rough braid, the tail slinking around her neck and dropping down over the exposed swell of her breast. His gaze continued down to where the clingy material ended above her navel, exposing a wide band of creamy skin around her midriff. His fingers twitched with an urge to run across the bared skin, while memories of her heat and wetness dropped straight out of his mind and right to his groin.

Only after he managed to snap himself away from the hypnotic pull of her belly button did he notice she seemed to be having a similar problem. She hadn't moved from the open doorway and was definitely ogling his naked chest. She looked momentarily stunned, then raised an eyebrow in defiance.

He gave her a slow smile. Angry Casey was good. Angry Casey wouldn't let him anywhere near her.

"Did you get something to eat?" he asked.

"Not yet." She took a sip of her coffee. "Figured I should get the caffeine first."

"I was about to make lunch. Want something?"

She blinked. "I don't recall ever hearing anything about you being able to cook."

He shrugged. "It's hard to ruin a sandwich. Besides," he said over his shoulder as he walked past, "if I make lunch then you have to cook dinner."

He dug the bread out of the cupboard.

"When are we supposed to hear from Lukas?" she called out.

He set down the loaf and moved back to the glass doors. "We'll have to take a drive back down to the highway and try to call him from there. There's no signal up here."

"Ahh." She nodded. "Right. No cell service." She set the mug down on the railing and pushed past him, quickly returning with a small metal object. She handed him the satellite phone and shrugged at his unvoiced question. "Uncle Thomas keeps one here. What's the saying? Always be prepared?"

"That's the Boy Scouts, not the Marines."

"You were a Boy Scout?"

"I was kicked out."

"Surprise, surprise." She shook her head and disappeared back inside.

The first call Jackson made was to the nurse's desk at the hospital. Carson's condition was now stabilized, but he was still unconscious. Then he dialed Lukas, who answered on the second ring.

"I was starting to wonder about you," Lukas said immediately. "Everything okay?"

"It was dodgy, but we're here," Jackson answered, quickly filling Lukas in on the attempted kidnapping. "I don't understand why they were trying to grab her, though. If she's witnessed the murder, they'd want her dead, not taken."

"Unless they wanted to do it somewhere else? Or maybe Harrison wants to do it himself?"

"You're not helping." Jackson definitely wasn't liking the niggling feeling that crawled up through his gut.

"Sorry, buddy."

"Any word from the FBI?"

"He wants you to come in."

"And?"

"Apparently they've been watching the situation from afar but until now have had nothing more than speculation. He wouldn't say what or who tipped them off. He wants everything, including you two. They'll put someone on Carson and run the gun against the bullets that killed Wolinski. But they want Casey—in person. They're offering protection."

Jackson snorted.

"I know," Lukas continued. "But that's the deal."

Jackson scratched the side of his jaw and turned to watch Casey who had returned to the deck. She leaned against the railing a few feet away, studying him. He tried to keep his expression neutral.

"Where and when?"

Lukas started to list off the location of a safe house, but Jackson cut him off. "No. Someplace public. Try for tomorrow night around nine o'clock. I'll call you later."

He turned to Casey. She watched him intently over the rim of her coffee mug, blue eyes guarded. He knew she'd understood they would be meeting the FBI sometime tomorrow night.

"They want to talk to us. Tomorrow night."

He walked over and took the coffee out of her hands before she cracked the mug. "Come on." He put his arm around her shoulders and led her back inside. "I owe you lunch."

From her seat at the dining room table, Casey silently watched Jackson use far too many utensils and dishes to make a normally simple peanut butter and jam sandwich. Eating steadily, she kept her mouth full to avoid any opening for conversation.

Changing her mind on what topic might be safe, she decided she didn't want to talk about Harrison, the FBI, or last night. Which, she realized, pretty much left politics and the weather. With a heavy sigh, she shoved away the empty plate.

"Ignoring it's not going to make it go away," Jackson said from the other side of the table.

She was really beginning to despise how he could figure out what she was thinking. "I don't want to talk about it."

He leaned back in his chair and hooked his hands behind his head. "Okay, what *do* you want to talk about?"

"Nothing." She stood and grabbed their empty plates.

"We're stuck here until tomorrow night," he said from his reclined position in the chair.

"Fine," she muttered, plugging the sink and adding some hot water and soap. "What do *you* want to talk about?"

"Anything?"

"Sure."

131

"Tell me about Kenny."

"W-what?" Casey retrieved the mug she'd dropped in the sink. She glanced over her shoulder, but he was still sitting with his back to her, balancing on the back legs of the chair.

"You heard me," he said.

"Why the hell do you want to know about Kenny?" She frowned, turning back to the dishes.

"You said I could ask you anything."

"I did not!" She swiped angrily at her plate with the scrub brush, then rinsed it under the hot water.

"Afraid?"

"No, I'm not afraid," she muttered, digging the silverware out from beneath the sudsy surface. "It's just...it's stupid." She scrubbed then rinsed the utensils, dropping them with a clatter into the dry rack. "Why do you want to know?"

"Because I do."

With nothing left to wash, Casey drained the sink and dried her hands. Spinning around, she braced herself against the counter and stared at the back of his head, tempted to yank on his arms and knock his sorry butt to the floor. Why on Earth would he want to know about Kenny?

Unless he didn't believe her again.

She frowned.

What is he up to?

There was only one way to find out.

"Fine." She settled on a standard rule of fair trade. "Then I get to ask *you* something."

"Fair enough," he agreed.

Casey sighed. "Kenny was a senior. His sister was in some of my classes. We met at the pub."

"And?" he prompted.

"We went out a couple of times."

"That's not the whole story."

She rolled her eyes and mimicked him silently. "Oh, for heaven's sake. We were at a frat party," she muttered. "We were making out in one of the upstairs bedrooms, and he got a little too carried away. End of story."

Jackson's hands twitched behind his head. "*He* got a little too carried away?"

Casey shrugged, then realized he couldn't see her. "Well, I didn't really get a chance to say no, if that's what you're getting at."

She sighed as the memory surfaced. Looking back, it had certainly been the stupidest night of her life. Kenny had been pretty persistent with his slobbery kisses and hands up her skirt, but it had never occurred to her he wanted...well, that. She'd never had anyone sit down and give her the 'boys are scum' conversation. Chalk it up to naïvety, stupidity, and the surprising shock that a jock like him would be interested in a nobody like her.

She had honestly never expected what he was really about to do until he'd yanked her underwear aside and pushed himself into her. With the shock and pain she'd pulled her knees to her chest and shoved him off. If he hadn't been so drunk, she probably wouldn't have been able to move him so easily. But he was, and she had. He extracted himself, made a mess all over the inside of her leg, and then passed out on top of her.

It had been such a waste of her virginity, and it wasn't until years later that she truly realized what she'd lost. Not that she'd let anyone get close enough to do anything about it even if she had kept it.

Until last night.

Casey didn't realize she was staring up at the ceiling until Jackson's face loomed into view. She blinked and readjusted her focus from the rooftop to his hazel eyes.

"The *whole* story," he demanded, his voice low.

Deciding there was no way he could possibly think any *less* of her, she gave up and told him, leaving out the minor details, but giving him the general gist.

The muscle in his jaw flexed as he clenched his teeth.

"Does that answer your question?" she asked as she finished.

He nodded. Once.

"Good, my turn," she said, flipping the dishrag she was strangling into the sink. She stepped around him and flopped down into one of the big armchairs in the corner of the living room. He remained standing in the kitchen, his arms crossed.

Two can play this little game. "Why did you *really* demand Carson kick me out of Meghan's life?"

His eyes narrowed. "Because you're nothing but trouble."

"Oh. Well, that certainly explains a lot," she muttered.

"My turn." He walked over and dropped down onto the couch, propping his bare feet on the coffee table. "Tell me something else I don't know."

She burst out laughing. "You're kidding, right?"

"Nope."

"Good Lord, I have absolutely no idea where to even start. Can't you be more specific?"

He shook his head. "Just pick something."

She pursed her lips and chewed thoughtfully on the inside of her cheek. He'd finally admitted he thought she was trouble. He wanted her to leave Meghan alone because everything was her fault.

And so what if he knew the truth?

Did it really matter? Did any of it? Why would he care if she had measured everyone in her life against him? It was her life, wasn't it? So what if most of her stunts had been for the sole purpose of getting his attention? That she'd chased after him for years and he'd never even noticed? What's the worst that could happen? He would tell Meghan? She already knew. Half their trouble had been her idea anyway.

Yes, indeed.

Meghan's idea.

She smiled.

He looked suspicious.

"So you say I'm trouble and Carson should keep me away from Meghan, right?"

Jackson nodded. "Basically."

She licked her lips.

Oh, this should be good.

"Do you remember the Halloween party?"

His brow furrowed. "The one where you called us from the bathroom?"

"*That* was all your sweet little Meghan's idea." She nodded, then laughed at his wary expression. She knew he would never believe this one. It was funny now, but at the time, they had been scared witless. She flung her legs over the arm of the chair, sank back into the cushions, and told him the *real* story.

Three years ago, Meghan had invited her to some crazy, leather only Halloween party in an old converted church. Unbeknownst to Casey, Meghan was going to come up with some stranded-and-can't-get-a-ride-back excuse in the hopes that Jackson would come and stage another rescue—on Casey's behalf.

Unfortunately, it didn't quite work out that way.

At the stroke of midnight, with a deafening thud and a cheer from the crowd, the huge front doors were closed and locked up with a giant beam just like a medieval castle. The lights dimmed, the rave music kicked in, and they watched in shock as couples and triples started going at it.

Raw, naked sex.

Meghan's friend then happily explained that the wristbands they were given at the start of the night were doubled up with men inside the club. The men who had been hitting on them all night were trying to find their matching wristband, and therefore their matching woman, with an expectation of reward—sex.

When the two women tried to leave, the bouncers fiercely told them no one could leave until morning, no matter what. So they locked themselves in a bathroom stall, sharing one because the other stalls were occupied with couples who were obviously enjoying the festivities.

The bathroom was in the basement, and the windows were too high to climb out—the best they could do was crack one open in the hopes that the cold air would deter the naked coupling. It was almost an hour later before they worked up the courage to brave the dark hallway to the payphone.

"Then you know the rest from there." Casey dabbed the tears from her laughter as she finished telling the story.

Jackson, however, didn't look at all amused. In fact, his eyes narrowed with fury.

"Jesus, Casey, that's not funny."

Casey sobered at his angry tone. "Oh, for goodness sake, Boy Scout. Lighten up. And like I said, it wasn't even my idea to begin with. In fact, half the ideas weren't mine to begin with."

"Why the hell didn't you say something that night?" Jackson asked, his voice low and angry. "Do you have any idea how stupid that was? What could have happened?"

"In case you couldn't tell," she scowled back, "and obviously you were too pissed off at me—again—to notice, we were freaked out enough and just wanted to get the hell out of there! Why embarrass ourselves further by telling you it was some kind of...crazy sex party!"

He stared at her intently. "Meghan's idea?"

"Yes! I don't know where you ever got the idea that everything was, is, my fault. What did I ever do to you? Even that stupid hiking trip was her fault!"

"Hiking trip?"

"The one where she called in the search party?" She nodded furiously as Jackson's face reflected his memory recall.

Casey rolled her eyes at him. "Yeah, I'm prone to wandering off in the woods by myself. That's me, Little Red Riding Hood," she scoffed. "She ditched me."

"She ditched you."

"That's what I said."

"In the middle of nowhere."

Casey sighed. "She goes hiking there all the time. I'd never been to that park before. We had a big fight. She took off. I pouted. After a while I realized I didn't see what direction she went. I tried to follow but.... Eventually I gave up and figured I'd better stay put and wait for her to come back."

Casey had always known Meghan was devious, but that stunt was one of her worst. It wasn't until later Meghan had confessed to Casey she'd picked the fight and left her on purpose so she could tell Jackson where to find her and send the other volunteers looking somewhere else.

"And she did it on purpose too," Casey muttered, her eyes narrowing. "I still owe her for that one."

"Did what on purpose?"

"Picked a fight. Left me there."

"Your best friend picked a fight with you, on purpose, so she could leave you stranded in the woods?" Jackson repeated what she'd said as though talking to a small child.

Casey sighed, frustrated with his inability to see the truth. "Yes. That's what I said."

"Why the hell would she do it on purpose?"

She chewed the inside of her cheek.

"Why?" he asked again.

"Because she knew you were home," she finally admitted.

"What does that have to do with anything?"

"It has everything to do with it. She wouldn't have done it if you weren't home."

"What did I have to do with it?"

"If you weren't home, you wouldn't have found me."

"No, but I'm sure one of the other trained volunteers would have."

Casey shook her head at his obvious confusion. For a man who could plan with military precision, he was completely dense.

"Jackson, she wouldn't have ditched me if you weren't home to come find me. She was trying to get your attention."

"Why was she trying to get my attention?"

"Must you repeat everything I say in the form of a question?"

"You're not making any sense!"

"I'm making perfect sense! I.... You.... Argh!" Casey couldn't stop the anger from cracking her voice. Launching herself out of the chair, she stomped towards the kitchen. She should never have bothered trying to tell him anything. He was convinced she was trouble, and nothing she could ever say would change his low opinion of her.

Jackson stepped in front of her. "I what?"

"You're completely pig-headed, that's what!"

"And you aren't? You can't even answer a simple question."

"What question?"

"Why was Meghan trying to get my attention?"

"What does it matter to you?" She tried to push past him, but he grabbed her arm, holding her firmly in place.

136

"You brought it up."

"You made me."

"I didn't make you do anything. Now tell me, why was Meghan trying to get my attention?"

"For me!" she yelled, yanking her arm away. "She did it for me. Okay? Happy now? God, you're such an ass."

Casey stomped up the stairs to the loft and flopped face down onto the bed. The man was an egotistical, self centered, pain in the ass, and she hated him. Grabbing a pillow, she pulled it over the back of her head, holding it tightly with two hands while she jammed her face into the comforter and screamed her head off. Once finished, she entertained the idea of leaving the pillow there, and wouldn't that teach him a lesson if she suffocated while screaming at him? She was saved the decision when the pillow was snatched off her.

"Feel better?"

"Go away." She cursed into the blanket, refusing to lift her head from the bedding.

"No."

"Fine. Then I will." She scrambled backwards, but Jackson was faster. He grabbed her hips and easily flipped her over onto her back.

He stood at the end of the bed, staring down at where she lay sprawled out on her back in the tangled sheets. When she tried to sit up, he pushed her back down.

"What the hell do you think you're doing?" she hissed.

"Trying to carry on a civil conversation."

"I don't want to talk to you." She moved to sit up again.

He crawled on top of her, grabbed her wrists, and pinned them to the bed beside her head.

She swore and struggled. "Let me up!"

"Not until you calm down and we discuss this like adults."

"You're not an adult, you're a childish, self-centered, know-it-all, and I hate you. Now let me go!"

Lying on the bed beneath him, Casey was having a difficult time breathing. She stopped struggling and couldn't tear her eyes away. He looked like a predator. Pounced on fresh kill. Hungry. Very, very hungry. And she was that kill.

Her heart started beating erratically.

"Do you have any idea what you do to me?" he whispered fiercely.

"Yes," she answered, nodding slowly, her eyes wild and dark. "The same thing you do to me."

With her confession, he dropped down on top of her, capturing her mouth to his.

There wasn't much time after that for civil conversation.

They made slow, passionate love on the bed, where he fulfilled his promise to lick that Hello Kitty tattoo, along with just about every other inch of skin across her body. Fast and furious sex on the floor with the afternoon sun streaming down around them through the windows. Then an extremely sensual session in the shower which lasted longer than their hot water.

The sun was almost below the horizon when Casey stirred from her second nap. Securely spooned against him, she reveled in the weight of Jackson's arm across her chest, his hand possessively cupping her breast. She sighed and snuggled closer.

This...she could definitely get used to.

"If you don't stop moving...," he muttered softly into her ear, his warm breath sending a shiver of goose bumps across the side of her body. "We're never going to get out of bed."

Casey laughed and shoved his arm away, then slid out from beneath him and scrambled off the bed. With a languid stretch, she bent and scooped up his discarded t-shirt, giving him a full on view of her naked backside. Pulling it on, she turned back towards the bed.

"Better?"

"Oh no. That won't do at all." He sat up on the edge of the bed and dragged her to stand between his legs. "Since you truly have no idea about the inner workings of the male libido, I'll explain."

He ran his hands up the back of her thighs, caressing, trailing his fingers over her bare cheeks and up under the shirt to the middle of her back. His eyes were level with her nipples, which had hardened and now very prominently showed through the thin cotton.

"You see...men have this thing for beautiful," he pulled her closer, "sexy," he skimmed his hands around to cup her breasts, flicking his thumbs over her nipples, "wanton women," he fell back down across the bed, dragging her down on top of him, "wearing their t-shirts."

She laughed and squirmed against him. "I take it we're not going to make supper yet?"

Chapter Fourteen

Harrison Douglas was becoming very aggravated with the lack of progress his employees were making. Sandiman, being the best money could buy, had missed his quarry on more than one occasion. The hired help hadn't been able to hit her with the broad side of a sedan and had then muffed a snatch-and-grab outside the city.

To say Harrison was not pleased was an understatement.

Detective Trevino had reported Jackson's vehicle stolen, and luckily it turned up in a motel parking lot outside the city. Unluckily, the motel manager wasn't alive to confirm that their quarry was indeed a patron, and not just abandoning his car in the parking lot.

But Lonnie, bless his greedy little heart, was being quite inventive in trying to pin the hotel murder on Mr. Hale, as well as steering the investigation into the councilor's murder towards Ms. Marshall.

At least that part was marginally entertaining.

Yet they still had not recovered the list.

And it needed to be found. Quickly.

Not entirely comfortable with trusting his life's work to everyone else, Harrison had been doing a little research of his own. He hadn't risen so fast to the top without the occasional need for deviance.

He glanced at the name and address written on the notepad next to his telephone. Yes. Why not add more fuel to the fire? He dialed the phone and rotated slowly in his chair. "I have an assignment for you."

He admired himself in the reflection of the large windows while details were discussed and a price was agreed. He was paying Sandiman and Trevino quite handily. But they were not his only employees.

It was always good to have a backup plan.

Standing in the dark interior of the living room, Jackson stared out through the balcony doors to where Casey lay on her back in the darkness, wrapped in a large blanket, staring up at the vast expanse of sky.

He had been reluctant to join her. He had talked to Lukas, and the meeting was confirmed for tomorrow night. She was happy in her ignorance, content to just be. If he mentioned the meeting she would be forced back, and he wanted her to have at least a few more hours before reality returned.

For both of them.

Once the FBI stepped in, she would no longer need him. And he did not want to think about leaving her with someone else. In fact, he didn't want to think about leaving her at all.

She'd asked him to join her, but he'd declined. He made the excuses of not seeing the attraction in purposely lying on the cold ground in the dark. He had certainly done it more than a few times over the years. Although there was a big difference between cold dirt and half a dozen fellow marines, and a cold deck with a half-dressed, sexy woman.

His body shuddered.

Okay, so there was no comparison.

He slid the door open and stepped out. "That offer still stand?"

She smiled and pulled back the blanket.

Jackson lay on his back beside her, adjusted the comforter, and shifted her head onto his shoulder. "So what's the purpose of this little experiment?"

"It's tradition," she said simply, her voice a soft whisper, as though she was afraid to break the spell of the midnight sky. "I do this every time I come here. It's so easy to become lost. I mean, look at it. I can't understand how anyone could see all those planets and stars and still say we're the only planet with life. There's just something about it that makes me feel…," she paused, searching for the right word, "whole. Like I'm part of something. Like there's some kind of reason behind everything."

"And is silence required in your meditations on the universe?"

"No." She laughed. "Talking is allowed."

"Good, because I have a question."

She tensed. "Not this again?"

"I'm serious," he said softly, kissing her forehead.

"Okay." She sighed.

"And no ripping my head off. I want an honest answer."

Casey lifted her head and looked down at him. He wasn't sure she would agree, not with what happened earlier, but she nodded.

"You really had a thing for me?" he asked the second permission was given.

"That's your question?"

"Yup."

She sighed. "Yes, I really had a thing for you."

"You got lost in the woods so I'd have to find you?"

"No, Meghan left me in the woods…so you'd have to find me."

He shook his head slowly. "How the hell did she know I'd be the one to find you? There were twenty park rangers and volunteers looking. That was a pretty risky move."

Casey laughed. "So modest." She patted him on the cheek. "You weren't exactly just another volunteer, Ice Man," she teased. "Didn't you find it odd that you were the *only* person searching in that area?"

"No," he said slowly. "Maybe. Well, yes. I guess a little."

"She told you exactly where she dumped me. She told the others I was somewhere else."

"What if I hadn't been there? Or if I'd been busy or something?"

"Busy or something?" She giggled. "There would have been no way your macho pride would have left the search party to random volunteers. You could never have resisted an opportunity to tell me off, either. And besides, if you didn't show, she would have just come and got me herself."

"She...." Jackson paused, her explanation turning a lock that had been long sealed. All the questions and odd elements fell away, revealing the truth. "That sneaky little bitch. I'm so going to get her for that."

"Stand in line." Casey smiled. She settled back down beside him, resting her head on his shoulder.

"And the other times?"

"Such as?"

"When your car broke down outside the biker bar?"

"Hey! That was totally valid. It really broke down."

"Getting locked into the junk yard with the drooling Doberman?"

"Meghan."

"Doing the dine-and-dash at the strip joint?"

"Meghan wanted to see what the fuss was all about. I thought she had her wallet!" The bouncers were about to make them pay for their meal with a stage performance when Jackson had finally arrived to cover their bill.

He snorted. "Twisting your ankle skiing?"

"My idea." She winced. "I have absolutely no idea how to ski."

"You don't?"

"Nope. I thought you could stay over instead of driving right back to town."

"Getting locked on the roof of the library after hours?"

She giggled. "You remember that?"

"I remember having to climb up four floors of roof access ladder because you're afraid of heights." He grinned up at the sky.

"I'm not afraid of heights."

"You're not?"

She shook her head. "I knew you would insist on going down the ladder first—that whole catch-me-if-I-fall macho thing. I wanted to climb down above you wearing no underwear."

His body twitched. "You what?"

She turned her head to whisper softly in his ear, accenting each word slowly, the heat of her breath cutting through the chill of the night air. "I wanted to climb down that long, long ladder, wearing a too-short-to-be-legal mini-skirt, with impossible-to-walk-in silver-spiked heels, and absolutely no underwear whatsoever."

"You did that on purpose?" he croaked.

"Oh yes."

She rolled her head back and let out a dramatic sigh. "I went to all that work, timing and planning, and you didn't even notice."

"Oh, I noticed."

"You did? But you spent the entire climb down yelling at me? You didn't even stutter. Just started into your usual tirade about responsibility and rule breaking to the point where I blocked you out."

"That's because I was going mental trying to keep my eyes off your naked ass and wondering just who the hell you were meeting up there in the first place."

"Oh," she whispered.

"Yeah. Oh."

They lay in silence, staring up into the starlit sky.

She shivered.

"Cold?" he asked.

"Yes. Time to go in, I think."

"So why did you do it?" he asked, once they were back inside. He turned on one of the small table lamps beside the couch.

"Do what?" She winced at the influx of light.

"All of it."

Standing in the middle of the open room, wearing nothing but his t-shirt, she gave him a half smile, but he saw it didn't quite reach her eyes. He inched closer, watching the emotions swirling across her face as she eyed him with a mix of hurt and wariness. And he honestly couldn't blame her for either. Because both the hurt and her worry over his true intentions were one-hundred-percent his fault.

Hands down.

He moved closer, stopping just shy of touching her.

She stared up at him, fear and worry of the unknown plainly reflected in her expression. She took a deep breath and held it, trapping her bottom lip between her teeth. Stepping forward, she lightly placed her palm against his cheek, exhaling a shaky breath.

"Please," she whispered. "Tonight might be all I have left."

"Casey, no one is...." He growled, but she lifted herself up, quickly cutting off his argument with a soft, tentative kiss.

"Take me to bed," she pleaded against his mouth. "Make love to me, Jackson. Make me forget."

With a groan of defeat, Jackson scooped her up and carried her upstairs.

Chapter Fifteen

It was a tense ride into the city. Neither Jackson nor Casey felt much like talking. The closer to the city limits they traveled, the tenser she became, and the way she wrung her hands was starting to drive him nuts. He reached over and placed his hand on top of hers.

"We're almost there. It's going to be okay, you know. Lukas trusts this guy."

"I know." She nodded. "I mean, I think so. I just…. What will I do if they don't believe me? What if they think I killed him?"

"Casey, they're not going to think you killed him."

"How can you be so sure? I picked up the gun. It has my fingerprints on it, doesn't it?"

"They're not going to arrest you."

Casey exhaled slowly, refusing to let go of his hand.

The fact that Jackson drove three times around the block to scope out the area before he parked didn't help her nervous condition. But he finally parked, and they walked down the street towards their destination—a large Italian restaurant.

The inside would have normally been warm and inviting, but tonight Casey couldn't shake the feeling of dread that washed over her as she walked in the door. The only thing that kept her feet moving forward was the feel of Jackson's strong, warm hand moving against the small of her back. She faltered in the entrance way, wanting nothing more than to turn and run.

"Relax, before you hyperventilate and pass out." Jackson glanced down at her. "It's going to be fine, Casey. You have to trust me."

She took several deep breaths and tried to slow her pounding heart. She nodded. "I'm okay."

He clasped her hand and gave it a reassuring squeeze before leading her through the sea of tables to Lukas. Lukas stood up when they arrived and pulled out Casey's chair, placing her between himself and Jackson, and across from the purpose of their meeting. The FBI agent. It was incredibly nerve racking.

Lukas made the introductions. "Jackson Hale, Casey Marshall, I'd like you to meet an old family friend, Special Agent William Daye."

"Agent Daye," Jackson acknowledged.

Daye held his hand to Casey but had to settle for a nod when she refused to release Jackson's fingers.

William Daye was an intelligent-looking man in his forties with scholarly glasses and a dark navy suit. He had cropped, sandy-colored hair that was graying at the temples, and light brown eyes. His expression was serious, but permanent laugh lines around his eyes showed the man wasn't always all business.

A waitress came by with menus, but Daye waved her off. "Okay, let's get right to the point. We've been watching Harrison Douglas for some time now. His banking practices caught our eye, and with all the added checks and balances in place since nine-eleven it's a lot easier for us to flag strange currency transactions. We've never been able to prove he isn't on the level. He's a real-estate broker, and large payments aren't unusual. We would never have gone any further without cause, or connected him to anything of this magnitude without your help, Ms. Marshall."

Casey stared dumbly.

"The gun you found was the same gun that killed Councilor Wolinski," Daye continued. "We've also connected it with an unsolved murder last year. The victim lived in an apartment in everyone's favorite neighborhood. After his death, and with no living relatives, the condo was snapped up by Douglas."

"Good Lord," Casey squeaked.

"We're also tracking down the people from that hit-list in the hopes of keeping them from falling victim to the next accident."

Casey nodded.

"What about the other two?" Jackson asked.

Daye nodded, slid a folder across the table to Jackson. "We can confirm that the two people who broke into your house, Mr. Hale, and subsequently tried to kidnap you, Ms. Marshall, also killed the manager at your motel."

"Killed the manager?" She turned to stare wide-eyed at Jackson. "What do you mean they killed the manager?"

"He's dead?" Jackson blinked.

Daye nodded. "We believe they were after information on which room you were staying in. You were lucky you left when you did."

Jackson flipped open the folder, angling them so Casey could see. The first two sheets were the mug shots and rap sheets. He nodded at the images of the two men who'd broken into the brownstone. The same two men who'd tried to grab her in the parking lot.

Jackson read their names aloud. "Briggs and Coombs." Then he nodded. "That's them all right."

Casey gasped at the third picture. It was a slightly fuzzy photo of Brown Suit getting into his car. She looked up at Agent Daye.

"Marcus Sandiman. Gun for hire." Daye nodded towards the photo. "He's always one step ahead of us. Thanks to you three, we can positively ID Sandiman as one of the three at the motel and the man from the parking garage. Unfortunately, the murder of Councilor

Wolinski is still hanging out there. We have no evidence other than the gun, and the only fingerprints on the weapon happen to be yours." He looked pointedly from Jackson to Casey. "We're hoping that's where you'll come in, Ms. Marshall."

"Me?" Casey croaked.

"There's no security footage from either location, so your testimony is going to be exactly what we need to put him away for good."

"But I.... I don't remember all of it."

"That's okay. We have a lot of medical experts that can help clarify the rest of the pieces."

"Medical?" She shuddered, a trembling hand flying to the base of her throat.

Daye caught the attention of one of the waitresses and asked for a glass of water. When it arrived, Casey had to use both hands to hold the glass steady. The room felt a little too warm, so she shrugged out of her jacket and let it fall across the back of the chair. The cooler air chilled her bare arms and helped clear her mind.

Jackson placed his hand on top of hers, and she squeezed his fingers between hers.

"What about Carson?" she managed to ask.

"We've got a man on him, twenty-four-seven."

"And his theory about a leak with the local police?" Jackson leaned forward.

Daye looked pointedly at Casey. "We've narrowed it down, but nothing we can prove. Yet."

"So what now?" Jackson drew his attention back.

"Now we take Ms. Marshall to a safe house for the night. We'll move her tomorrow to a secure medical location and see if we can piece together the rest of what she saw. She'll be out of harm's way until they're rounded up. We've already issued a warrant for Harrison Douglas, but he's disappeared."

"What about Jackson?" Casey asked.

"Actually, Ms. Marshall, we don't believe Mr. Hale is in any mortal danger on his own. It's *you* they seem to be specifically targeting. Although...," he looked at Jackson, "it might be a good idea to lay low until this blows over. Just in case."

Casey nodded, quickly grasping at what was being said. Jackson was in no danger on his own. They were only after her. So it would also reason that Jackson was *only* in danger if he was near her. If he could walk away and keep out of sight, he would be safe. If he remained with her, he would be just as much of a target as she was. Or worse, he'd be hurt—or killed—trying to protect her. He'd already shown her he was willing to go that far.

She could never forgive herself if anything happened to him.

If he thought she needed him, wanted him, he would stay. And he'd be a target.

She couldn't let that happen.

She looked up, suddenly realizing that everyone at the table was staring at her. Daye looked calm, as though this kind of thing was completely normal. Lukas looked concerned, and Jackson looked...well, Jackson looked like he was about to pick her up like a knighted hero and drag her to safety.

She trembled.

Jackson.

God, how she loved him.

She would not survive if anything happened to him because of what she'd done. Because of her. She'd done so much to him, caused him enough pain over the years, she couldn't take the chance that helping her would get him killed. He had to go home. To be safe. To leave and not look back.

There was only one thing that Jackson Hale despised enough to make him walk away.

Her.

Crazy Casey.

"Can I talk to you?" She tried to keep her voice light.

He nodded and stood, offering her his hand.

Daye checked his watch. "Make it quick."

They walked out to the empty reception area by the main entrance. There were several large couches set against the wall to handle the overflow of customers during peak times. People could sit comfortably and wait for their reservation to be called.

Casey walked over to the far corner but was too anxious to sit. Jackson stood silently, waiting.

"What's wrong?"

She spun around to face him. "I...I didn't want to say goodbye in front of everyone else."

"Goodbye?" His brow creased.

"And thank you," she blurted out, going for a smile.

"I'm not going anywhere."

"No. Please. Listen." Her tone was too loud. She took a deep breath and lowered her voice. "You've fulfilled your promise. You delivered me to the FBI. There's nothing more you can do, you said so yourself."

"That doesn't mean I'm going to leave you alone."

"The FBI is here for me, not you."

"I'm going with you."

"No, you're not."

"Casey," he growled.

She saw the wariness in his eyes and tried very hard to contain the fear in hers.

"I'm trying to tell you that you're free to go now. The FBI is going to take care of things. You and my uncle both agreed that the final course of action was calling the FBI. And here we are. I can't even begin to thank you enough for everything, but I don't need you to baby-sit anymore."

"Baby-sit?" His voice was low. Controlled.

"Look, I'm sorry I dragged you into this. You're a great friend, and for a while there you made me forget the whole someone-trying-to-kill-me thing. If I knew this was how to get your attention, I might have tried to have someone kill me years ago." Her stomach rolled at the look of hurt that briefly flashed behind his hazel eyes before they frosted over. "All I want to do is just get this all over with as fast as possible and move on. Put everything behind me and just get back to my life."

Forgive me, Jackson.

"What are you saying?"

"Nothing. Just.... Goodbye. Thanks." She shrugged and smiled.

"So that's it?"

She nodded and tried to look as casual as possible, even though her heart hammered so fast he had to be hearing it. "That's it."

"You just want to put everything behind you." He stepped back.

"More than anything."

When he crossed his arms in front of his chest, she knew she almost had him. The doubt was there, skittering beneath the surface. One more good push and he'd be gone.

Gone from here.

Gone from the danger.

Gone from her life.

Taking a deep breath, she swallowed the bile burning the back of her throat and tried for what she hoped was a casual laugh.

"I have to say I'm pretty sure this tops anything Meghan could have ever come up with, huh?"

The hard look in his eyes carved through her soul.

"Well, guess I'd better go." She rushed past him and headed back towards the dining area. She stopped and half turned, taking one last look at the man she loved. "Thanks again for all your help." She turned and hurried back to the table, blinking away the burn that stung her eyes.

She had just thrown away any chance, no matter how slim it may have been, of a future with this man.

Her heart shattered in her chest, leaving a hole she knew she would never, ever fill.

Lukas watched her approach, his eyes narrowed. "Everything okay?"

She nodded and sat down heavily, tucking her shaking hands under her legs to keep them from being seen.

"Where's Jackson going?" Lukas asked, staring over her shoulder towards the entrance. She refused to look.

"He's going home."

Lukas gave her a controlled look. "Home."

Her stomach pushed its contents up into her throat, and she gagged, slapping her hand over her mouth. "I need to go to the ladies' room."

Daye indicated the sign for the restrooms off to the right. She walked quickly. Increasing speed, she approached the hallway until she was practically running. Slamming the bathroom door open, she ran into an empty stall and cried through the dry heaves. When nothing exited, she collapsed against the cold metal wall, clamping her hand over her mouth to hold back the sobs.

She was a fool.

A complete fool.

He would never give her a second chance.

Never.

Taking a deep breath, she left the stall and moved to the sinks. Blowing her nose with a paper towel, she splashed cold water on her face while her reflection stared back at her with broken-hearted agony.

When the bathroom door opened, hope and expectation briefly exploded. *He's come back.*

But disappointment settled into its new home in her stomach to see that it was just one of the waitresses.

"Are you Casey?" the woman asked politely.

Casey nodded.

"I'm supposed to give this to you," she said with a wink, holding out a small square of paper.

Casey unfolded the note. Something dropped to the tiles. The waitress bent to pick it up while Casey read the brief message.

Meghan's come to play. Go out through the kitchen. Tell no one or she dies.

Her knees gave out, and she crashed to the floor.

"Oh my gosh, are you all right?" The waitress bent down to help her to her feet.

Casey crumpled up the piece of paper and steadied herself against the sink. The room spun as she fought for control. *Meghan. They have Meghan.*

"Oh God," she said.

The waitress turned to leave. "You don't look too good. I'll go get some help."

"No!" Casey shouted. The startled woman spun around and stopped. "I'm okay. I'm fine, really. It just surprised me."

The waitress looked unsure. She held up a small silver chain. "This fell out when you opened it. It's pretty." Casey held out her hand in horror. A delicate, slightly crooked, half moon pendant dangled in the air, spinning hypnotically. She would recognize Meghan's favorite piece of jewelry anywhere.

Casey had a brief stint working in a jewelry shop a few years ago and was able to acquire the expensive silver pendant because it had been damaged. It had been Meghan's twenty-fifth birthday present, and her friend rarely took it off. Meghan had fallen in love with the little bend in the rounded side of the moon, claiming it looked exactly like miniature teeth marks.

If someone had the pendant, then someone had Meghan.

She tried to step forward, towards the door, but her feet held fast.

She had to go.

She had to tell someone.

They'd kill Meghan.

Jackson would know what to do.

Jackson wasn't here.

Her fingers curled around the pendant, tangling the chain into a ball in the palm of her hand. Jamming the heel of her hand against her forehead, she stared at her reflection, begging herself for clarity.

She needed to tell Lukas.

But if they were watching?

Oh God....

"I need you to do me a favor." She turned towards the woman. "Could you...could you please deliver a message for me? On paper. Maybe one of your receipts? Make it look like you're dropping the bill off to someone?"

The woman suddenly grinned. "Oh, I get it, honey! You've got man issues with a capital M!"

Casey nodded furiously. "Yes. Yes! Exactly. I uh...I need to get a message to my date."

"Well sure, sweets." She held out a pen and her order book.

Casey took them and quickly scribbled a note, describing Lukas to the woman who nodded appreciatively. "I know the one you mean. He's a hunk! Back section. He's there with an older gentleman right now?"

Casey nodded and handed back the receipt pad. "Please," she begged. "You can't let anyone see it's a note. They have to think it's a bill."

The woman nodded, tucking the paper into the front pocket of her apron. "No worries, honey. I'm a professional."

As soon as the waitress left, Casey counted to ten and opened the bathroom door. At the end of the hallway was the entrance to the kitchen. She quickly checked both directions, but the hallway was currently vacant.

Peering through the slotted windows in the double swinging doors, she watched cooks and waitresses prepping plates for the customers in the chrome-and-white kitchen. The door to the back was just a few steps from the doorway, propped open to let the cool night air into the overly warm room.

They would be waiting for her. She couldn't go. She had to go. *Meghan.* With a deep breath, she swung through the door, brushed past a busboy, and stepped out into the night.

Chapter Sixteen

Jackson swung the truck around in a U-turn and sped up the block.

She'd played him. Again.

He'd fallen for it. Again.

Get back to her life, she'd said.

Fine, Casey.

You can have your damn life.

He would gladly get the hell out of her way.

He screeched to a halt beside the stop sign he almost missed. Shaking his head, he afforded a little more concentration to the act of driving without wrecking Lukas' truck.

The woman had really taken him for a ride this time. His first instinct had been to dump her off at the police station, and that's exactly what he should have done.

Instead, he'd acted like a complete idiot and had gotten involved.

To think he had actually questioned himself! Believed he was in the wrong and had treated her badly. He'd felt sorry for her. Worried about her. Hell, he'd even apologized! She must have absolutely loved that. He could almost hear her laughing. She'd played him her whole life. Why would now be any different?

So what if she'd sent him away instead of vice versa. Big deal. He'd had women call it off before. It was easier than trying to come up with excuses himself. He'd ended plenty of relationships, and it had always left him feeling lighter. So why did he now feel like someone was crushing his lungs? It wasn't like he was losing a major piece of his anatomy.

It was just Casey, for God's sake!

His heart jumped around in his chest, waving the answer like a white flag.

He tried desperately to ignore it.

He was in love with her.

He had always been in love with her.

And it wasn't going away.

Casey stumbled out the back of the restaurant into an alley that stretched the length of the block. Her body trembled as she recognized the man leaning against the front of a large black car next to the brick wall of the building. Coombs. From a closer view she saw that he was only slightly taller than she was, but almost twice as wide. His nose looked like it had been broken several times and then reattached off-center.

A large purple bruise formed across the side of his jaw. At the spot where she'd connected when she'd kicked him into the back of his panel van.

He crooked his finger, beckoning her over, but she couldn't seem to make her legs move. He frowned and stepped closer, snatching at her upper arm and squeezing until she gasped and winced.

"No one here to help you this time, darlin'." He laughed, yanking her roughly towards his car. "Now don't try anything stupid." Opening the passenger door, he shoved her down into the seat. He leaned forward to leer at her and let his leather jacket fall open, giving her a straight-on view of the gun hanging under his arm. "I owe you one. So don't give me any more reasons shoot you." He slammed the door shut and walked slowly around to the driver's side.

"What have you done with Meghan?" she asked as he settled himself into the driver's seat.

"You'll find out soon enough," he said cryptically.

The car shot down the alley towards a darkened side street. For a brief moment, before they launched out of the alley, Casey swore she saw someone standing in the shadows by the edge of the building. But when she turned there was nothing there.

Her fingernails dug into the arm rest on the side of the door, and she huddled against it, trying to keep as far away from her driver as possible.

The faster the pavement passed, the more she knew she was about to die.

The waitress dropped the bill in front of Lukas with a wink and sauntered off.

Daye raised his eyebrow. "A bill for a glass of water?"

Lukas flipped over the paper and froze.

They have Meghan. Tell Jackson I'm sorry.

He slid the note quickly across the table to Daye.

"Check the bathroom," Daye ordered quietly. "But she's probably gone. She didn't come this way, so she must have gone through the kitchen. I'll bring the car around back."

A woman coming out of the bathroom told Lukas there was no one else inside, but he dashed in anyway. The stalls were empty. He caught sight of a crumpled piece of paper under the row of sinks and dove for it. Opening it up, he quickly read the note, then dashed into the kitchen. Hurried questions fired at the kitchen staff confirmed a pretty blonde wearing a short-sleeved shirt had indeed gone out the back door.

Lukas ran outside, but the only vehicle present was Daye's sedan.

He jumped into the passenger side and handed over the crumpled paper. "We have to find her."

Daye unclipped the cell phone off his belt and started punching numbers. "Damn it!" the agent muttered. "How did they know she was here?"

"No idea," Lukas answered, grabbing for his own cell. "But I'm damn well going to find out."

Jackson swore as his phone rang for the third time. He'd ignored the first two calls, but Lukas obviously wasn't going to let it go until he answered. He snatched the phone off the dash and ripped it open. "What!"

"Where the hell are you?"

"Halfway back to your place to return your truck, then I'm going home."

"Where? What? Why the hell...never mind. Don't answer that. Just turn around and get back here."

"Not going to happen."

"Damn it, Jackson, Casey's gone."

Jackson swerved back into his lane to avoid the parked car he almost rear-ended. "What do you mean she's gone?"

"I mean, she's gone."

"You let her go?"

"We didn't let her go anywhere—she took off. Left us a note and disappeared."

"She left you a note?"

"She turned herself over to them."

"She what!" Jackson shouted.

"They took Meghan," Lukas answered.

An ice-cold current shocked down through Jackson's body.

He threw the phone into the passenger seat and with a quick glance in the mirror slid the truck around in a perfect one-eighty.

It was the longest ten minutes of his life.

Slamming to a stop in the alley, he leapt out of the truck and jumped into the back of Daye's sedan.

Daye stomped hard on the accelerator. Jackson leaned into the front, jammed himself between the seats, and clamped his hand down onto Lukas' shoulder. "How could you let her go?"

Lukas spun around. "She said she had to go to the bathroom!"

Daye reached into his pocket and handed Jackson the crumpled note and the bill. "They got to her while she was in the ladies' room. This was on the floor. She somehow had one of the waitresses deliver the message. Pretty smart actually."

Jackson skimmed the papers and handed them back to Agent Daye. "Do we know if Meghan's even missing?"

Daye nodded. "She left the hospital several hours ago, but her car is still in the parking lot."

Jackson swore. "Where are we going?"

"My people are already set up at the safe house. We'll regroup there."

"We should go back and start asking some questions! Someone may have seen who she left with!"

Daye shook his head. "My partner's working through the staff right now. You two need to move on to the next step. You know almost as much as she does. We need to figure out where he might be holding them."

By the time they squealed into the driveway of an average-looking residential bungalow fifteen minutes later, Jackson was so tense he was ready to explode.

Daye quickly walked up the driveway, entering the house through the side door.

Jackson moved to follow, but Lukas held him back, stepping into his face. "What's wrong with you?"

"Nothing. I'm fine."

"*Fine* doesn't leave a man behind."

"Excuse me?" Jackson's spine straightened. He stepped closer to Lukas, who held his ground.

"You heard me."

"I handed her off. She wasn't my responsibility anymore." Jackson knew it was a cheap lie, but couldn't stop himself from saying it.

"Responsibility?" Lukas gaped. "Saving an innocent life isn't your responsibility? What the hell has gotten into you?"

"The deal was I turn her over to the FBI! She was *supposed* to be under their protection!"

"Jesus, Jackson. She wasn't in a safe house with armed agents. It was a public restaurant. Anything could have happened. Anything *did* happen!"

"Look." Jackson stepped toe to toe with Lukas. "She told me to get lost, so I obliged her." The minute he voiced the words he knew they sounded completely childish and idiotic, but he was too far gone to stop.

Lukas shook his head and barked out a laugh. He leaned closer and spoke slowly, accenting each word. "You have always been a seriously dumb mother when it comes to that woman."

Jackson ground his teeth and started to retort, but Lukas kept going, pushing right into Jackson's personal space.

"Didn't you hear a thing Daye was saying to her?" Lukas growled. "How *you* were safe to go home because *she* wasn't going with you? The man's a great agent, but he sucks at the people skills. He pretty much told her you would be risking your life if you stuck with her. So she told you off in some idiotic attempt to save your worthless hide." Lukas shook his head in disgust. "I should have offered to shoot you myself and save her the heartache."

"She—"

"Sucked you right in and you ran home to your mommy like a little girl," Lukas finished.

Jackson stepped back.

"Do you want her back alive?" Lukas walked forward until the toes of his boots connected with Jackson's.

"What?"

"Do you want her back alive?" he repeated slowly.

"Yes, Goddamn it!"

"Then stop thinking with your dick and start using your head." Lukas double-tapped Jackson's temple with his index finger, then shoved him back before spinning and heading up the driveway.

Jackson dropped his head back and stared blindly up into the darkness.

"Fuck!" He cursed his stupidity to the sky. He'd blown it. Completely and unequivocally blown it. She'd ripped down years of training, and years of control, and turned him into a babbling, senseless idiot.

She had known exactly how to push him. Make him think it was all just another game. That he'd been right not to trust her. She knew it would piss him off and he would treat her like he always had, believing the worst and leaving her to fend for herself.

You've never believed me Jackson. Or believed in me.

The light breeze whispered her words, tormenting him with their truth.

Casey was out there, alone, unprotected.

And it was all his fault.

If anything happens to her....

"Are you coming, or what?" Lukas demanded from the doorway.

Jackson jogged up the driveway and into the house.

Chapter Seventeen

Casey hugged the passenger door, afraid to move, afraid to look.

Each time they halted with traffic, stopped at a red light, or slowed to turn, Coombs reached inside his jacket and glared at her, daring her to give him an excuse. Her body didn't need the visual reminder. She was frozen in place, glued to the back of the seat. Her lungs struggled to fill through rapid, shallow breathing, and she was getting lightheaded.

The lights around her blurred together. Headlights. Intersections. Street lights. Neon and marquees. Flashing and blinking. Calling out.

Flashes of Robert Wolinski clutching his chest, hands covered in blood, mixed with thoughts of her friend. They wouldn't have hurt her—they needed her. Meghan was fine. Alive.

It's me they want.

Her eyes darted quickly between the driver's side of the car and the streets flying by.

She saw everything, but noticed nothing.

What would Harrison do when he got what he wanted? What did he want? Did he want the tape? The files? Did he know she didn't have anything? Would he expect her to go get it? Or would he just kill her?

Shot like Wolinski?

Accidental death like the tenants?

Car accident like Carson?

Her mind clicked through the scenarios, changing channels.

Harrison had gone after Meghan. Would he go after Jackson too? Her vision locked into the side-view mirror, desperately praying for a big black truck.

He wouldn't be there.

He'd gone away.

She'd sent him away.

Her throat closed, and she struggled to swallow.

She was alone.

There would be no rescue.

The lights faded away, and the streets darkened. She sat forward, finally taking notice. They had turned into an old industrial neighborhood filled with abandoned buildings and vacant factories. Many of the streetlights were broken or half working. There was no one around, no one she could try to use to get help, and no way anyone would possibly know where she was.

Coombs slowed the car and turned in through an open gate,

traveling down the length of a tall, windowless, red brick building. The car squeezed past a loading dock and stopped in front of a set of rusty double doors.

Casey could taste bile in the back of her throat.

Her escort turned and gave her a knowing smile. "No funny stuff, you hear?"

She nodded quickly. "Please. Just take me to Meghan."

"Take me to Meghan," he mimicked, then sneered. "Get out. Slowly."

With an unsteady breath, she climbed out of the car. Coombs walked around to her side, the corner of his mouth raised, showing his teeth. She staggered backwards against the side of the building. His hand snapped out and slammed into the metal door beside her head. He leaned closer, his breath hot on her cheek.

Turning her head away, she held her breath but didn't move. Coombs snorted and tugged open the door. Grabbing her arm, he twisted her around and shoved her inside.

The core of the building was massive and echoed like an airplane hangar—completely hollow and several stories high. Long metal beams dropped down along the sides, supporting a yellow catwalk that edged around the outside high above her head. It connected to the main floor with a staggered staircase.

Scattered lights along the walls illuminated sections of the bare cement floor with circles of dull yellow light.

The pressure on her arm increased as she was hauled across the open space. Each forward step pulled the blood from her brain like a riptide, and she stumbled. Coombs left no room for recovery, his force the only thing keeping her upright.

A long bank of offices loomed out of the shadows along the back wall, darkness haunting behind the open doorways. All the doors stood open, but only one bled light, yawning like the hungry mouth of a backlit monster.

Coombs shoved her through the open doorway and jerked her to a stop.

Inside the sparsely furnished office sat a desk, a filing cabinet, and two chairs. One of which was occupied.

"Oh God, Casey!"

Casey broke free of the arm that held her and rushed across the room.

Megan sat on the edge of a chair, her wrists bound behind her. She stared wide-eyed at Casey, her skin pale and drawn. Her hair, wavy and unruly to begin with, had almost completely pulled free of its French braid, and dried mud had ruined the once sharp business suit.

"Meghan, I'm so sorry." Casey sobbed, losing her battle with her composure. Throwing her arms around her friend's shoulders, she let the tears burn down her cheeks to soak into the shoulder of Meghan's jacket.

Casey sat back on her heels and placed her palms on either side of Meghan's face. "Are you okay?"

Meghan nodded, but her green eyes weren't looking at Casey—they stared wildly over Casey's shoulders.

"How touching," came a man's low voice and snickering laugh.

Casey jumped up and spun around, her eyes darting to the two men standing against the wall. The tall, gangly, ferret-faced man from the parking lot—Briggs—growled at her and stepped forward. She automatically retreated, banging into Meghan. An arm shot out, holding Briggs in place.

The man in the brown suit.

Sandiman.

Casey's breath caught and refused to come out.

Sandiman winked and gave her a slow smile. "We're so glad you could join us. I'm sorry to see you've left your friends behind, though. I was looking forward to a rematch."

"I c-came," Casey stammered. "You have me, now let her go."

He shook his head, his smile fading. "While I would love to be so accommodating, I'm afraid it doesn't quite work that way."

"What...what do you mean?" Casey couldn't look away from his eyes. His face, his body...he looked so...normal. Harmless. But his eyes...his eyes were cold. Dead.

"You've already seen too much, I'm afraid." Sandiman looked past Casey to Meghan.

Casey shook her head. "She didn't see anything! And neither did I!"

Sandiman laughed. "Dear, dear, dear. I know you were there."

"But...I don't remember anything! Nothing about what happened. I'm...I'm no threat. I mean, I can't say anything if I don't remember, right? Just let us go. We won't tell anyone. Please." Casey knew pleading was useless, but she couldn't stop herself. Meghan nodded furiously beside her.

"Well that is unfortunate, but I'm afraid it wouldn't make any difference. Neither one of you will be leaving here."

The words washed over her, but his tone drove right through.

"Tie her up," he ordered.

As Briggs stepped forward and snatched a section of rope off the desk, Casey tried to back away, but Coombs reached for her and jerked her arms roughly behind her back.

159

Rope cut into her wrist, and she cried out. Briggs snickered.

Coombs dragged the second chair over and forced her into the seat.

The three men stood in a half circle around her, their expressions mixed with death and enjoyment. Briggs stepped forward, and her body stiffened. She tried to retreat, but she had nowhere to go.

With calculated coldness, he swung his arm, the back of his hand splintering across the side of her face. Her body slammed back into the chair, and pain exploded through her head.

She struggled to focus.

Tasted blood.

He leaned forward again, and she whimpered.

"Enough," came the brisk order.

With Briggs and Coombs standing on either side of the chairs, Sandiman leaned in and smiled.

Casey shuddered and begged herself to look away, but the absolute cold of his gaze was horrifyingly hypnotizing.

"I must step out for a few minutes. I do hope you'll be comfortable while I'm gone." The calm, intimate tone of his voice made her stomach roll. "I won't be long. So I suggest you say your goodbyes quickly."

He stood and turned towards the open doorway. "Come with me."

Briggs and Coombs followed, snapping the light off and closing the door, leaving the women in darkness.

The ropes bit into her wrists as Casey struggled to move her hands. She twisted her head and gingerly rubbed her face against her shoulder, sponging off the blood that trickled down the side of her mouth.

"Are you okay?" Meghan whispered.

Casey swallowed blood. Her tongue found the split on the inside of her bottom lip, and she winced. "Yeah," she muttered.

"Case, what the hell is going on?"

Casey leaned towards her friend, landing her ear against Meghan's shoulder. "Megs, I'm so sorry. This is all my fault."

Meghan sniffed, sucked in a lung full of air, then let it out slowly. "This is bad, isn't it?"

"The worst kind of bad."

"Okay. Okay. We can't panic. We have to stay calm. No freaking out. Calm and cool. Just breathe. Air in. Air out. It's not like we haven't been in tricky spots before. I mean, we should be able to figure this one out, right? As long as we stay together. We'll get out of here. Get to a phone. Find—"

"Megs, you're babbling again." Casey loved her friend with all her heart and thought she was one of the strongest people she had ever met. But when Meghan was stressed, she babbled with the speed of an auctioneer. And right now, there was no time for babbling.

"Stand up and turn around," Casey whispered. "Let's see if we can get our hands free."

They slid up off the chairs and staggered back to back. Ripping fingernails and rubbing their skin raw, Casey quietly gave Meghan a brief rundown on Harrison Douglas, Jackson, Lukas, and the FBI.

"So it takes a near-death experience to get Jackson's attention?" Megan whispered harshly. "Talk about a hard sell!"

Casey almost smiled. Leave it to Meghan to skip over the whole *we're-going-to-die* scenario and hone right in on the fact that Casey had finally spent time alone with Jackson.

Then Casey thought of the last words out of her mouth, the hurtful and spiteful conversation, and the smile disappeared beneath the threat of tears.

"Wait." Megan jumped and twisted her wrists. "I think I've almost got it."

Casey stood still while Meghan wiggled and pulled. With a soft cry of victory the pressure released, and Meghan's rope made a soft plop as it dropped onto the carpet. She turned and worked at Casey's bonds.

As soon as her hands were free, Casey swiped the tears from her cheeks, then found Meghan in the darkness. She threw her arms around her friend, crushing her in a tight hug. "I'm so sorry for all of this...and I know this is a really horrible thing to say, but...I'm glad you're here."

Meghan squeezed back, clinging tightly, and whispered, "We're going to be okay. This isn't the worst place we've gotten out of, right? We've had lots of practice. We're practically experts by now. We can do this."

"Thanks, Megs." Casey straightened and gently rubbed the raw skin on her wrists. She felt for Meghan's fingers, turning them upwards. With her other hand she dug into the front pocket of her jeans and pulled out the pendant she'd been given in the bathroom of the restaurant.

"Here." She pressed the charm into Meghan's palm. "We're going to need all the luck we can get."

Meghan sniffed and folded her fingers around the charm. "So now what do we do?"

"We get the hell out of here."

Chapter Eighteen

Jackson and Lukas stood shoulder to shoulder with three FBI agents circled around a small dining room table stacked with files, paperwork, and several laptops. A giant printed map of the two-block, lake-front area covered the wall behind the table, marked with colored dots, small handwritten notes, and highlighted squares and arrows.

"There are no security cameras in the back of the restaurant," Agent Janssen began. "And so far no one's admitting to seeing anything out of the ordinary other than Ms. Marshall sneaking out the kitchen door."

A tall, reedy woman with extremely short black hair and hawk-like features, Agent Janssen spoke with the sharp, brisk tone of someone whose decisions were never questioned. She didn't wait for questions before continuing.

"The description of the man delivering the note could fit Coombs, but we're waiting on confirmation. We're also looking into security footage from the hospital parking lot, but the cameras cover the entrance, not the parking lot. Ms. Hale's car was parked at the back of the lot, so we have nothing digital. If someone grabbed her, they wouldn't have done it near the front doors."

"*If* someone grabbed her?" Jackson shot back. "Two minutes ago you said you were certain she *had* been."

Daye shot his hand up before Agent Janssen could fire off her retort. "We're going on the belief that Ms. Hale has been taken to draw out Ms. Marshall. What we don't know is where they are, or who tipped them off."

Jackson fought the urge to punch someone. Anyone. This was getting them nowhere. The city was huge, the possibilities endless, and they had no idea where to start.

Their only saving grace was that Harrison needed them alive to trade.

Correction.

Harrison needed *one* of them alive.

He almost slammed his fist through the table.

"He will take them to a location he has control of." Agent Samuels stepped forward. He spoke with intelligence and conviction and the barest hint of a north-eastern accent. Jackson had immediately liked him. No nonsense with a touch of piss-me-off-and-I-break-you.

"He's a real-estate broker. He has his fingers in half the city." Samuels looked pointedly at Jackson. "We're just going to have to wait until he tries to contact you."

Jackson shook his head. "We're not waiting around. The man is killing people over condos, for God's sake. He may very well choose to make an example out of one of them, and I can't take that chance."

"What's this building here?" Lukas had been quietly flipping through a folder filled with layout maps of the city. It included floor plans and locations of all the buildings that Harrison was currently buying or selling outside the affected waterfront area. Samuels had been in the process of cataloguing when they'd arrived and interrupted.

Samuels stepped beside Lukas. "St. Augustus. Old church building. It's being retro-fitted for a new dance club."

Lukas flipped to the next page. "This one?"

They went back and forth for a few minutes, with Samuels explaining what each building was, its location, and if it was currently occupied or under construction. Agent Janssen received a phone call and stepped out of the room for privacy.

"Look," Daye said, turning to Jackson. "There's no way we can cover all the properties. Douglas has a city's worth of locations at his fingertips."

"I'm not just going to stand around here waiting," Jackson growled. He was starting to feel claustrophobic. He needed to be doing, moving, searching, *anything* but standing around discussing the size of the city!

His heart twisted with guilt.

With only a few harsh words Casey had sent him right over the edge. He'd reacted without cause, ignoring what his heart had been trying to tell him, immediately falling back into the safe pattern of believing the worst.

He'd listened to *what* she'd said, but not *how*. The way she stood wringing her hands, the higher than normal pitch in her voice, how her eyes never really met his.

She had been terrified and pushed him away, thinking only of his safety.

And he'd turned away with no thought to hers.

Abandoned her.

Left her to fend for herself against who knew what.

For the first time in his life, when it truly mattered, he wasn't going to be there to rescue her.

He dragged his hand down over his face. He couldn't lose her. Not now. There was so much he needed to tell her. To explain. She needed to hear it. Believe in it. Believe in him.

Forgive him.

Lukas yanked his cell phone out of his pocket. He had it set to silent mode, but the mere act of grabbing it was as subtle as waving a red flag. Everyone turned.

Lukas looked at the incoming number and shook his head at Daye, killing off the notion that it was the kidnappers.

He jammed the phone to his ear, his voice softening. "Hi, Kitten...give me a sec...." He shrugged in apology to the agents, moving to step outside.

The minute Lukas said *kitten*, Jackson knew it was Kat calling from the office. He tuned out the rest of the room and zoned in on Lukas, who walked calmly past the table, cell phone in hand.

Daye and Samuels glanced briefly at him before returning to their discussion on the logistics of searching the buildings on the waterfront. Janssen hadn't yet returned.

If Jackson hadn't been staring directly at Lukas, he wouldn't have noticed his friend palming Daye's car keys from the side table. Jackson followed, his stride slow and casual. He glanced quickly over his shoulder, but he was ignored. Following after Lukas, he moved to the side door and stepped out onto the driveway.

As soon as his feet hit the asphalt, Lukas broke into a run and made a beeline for Daye's car. Jackson followed, jumping into the passenger seat without thinking twice.

Lukas snapped the phone closed and stuffed it into his pocket. "We know where she is."

Jackson's head snapped around. "What?"

The sedan backed quickly out of the driveway and sped down the street. "The colonel had Ghost following Casey. She's at a factory in the old industrial park. He can confirm at least one gunman."

"What the hell?"

"We can ask Zack when we see him." Lukas slid the car around a corner and out onto the main street. "He's waiting for us."

Zack Dunnigan—also known as Ghost—was a specter. His uncanny ability to blend in and follow had saved their hides more times than Jackson could count. As a CORE Security specialist, Zack was their go-to guy when it came to getting into tricky locations, and subsequently, getting out.

Jackson immediately decided he didn't really care *how* the colonel had added a tail, when he'd done it, or why, because Zack had eyes on Casey.

Jackson wasn't about to jinx it with questions.

"You never saw him?" he finally asked, glancing at Lukas.

Lukas scowled. "Does anyone?"

Jackson tilted his head in agreement. "Where's your gear?" He changed the subject, realizing they were going up against armed gunmen with nothing but a pair of Berettas.

Lukas snorted. "In the trunk."

"Of an FBI agent's car? That's wise?"

"What?" Lukas raised an eyebrow. "I have a permit."

"Speaking of which, shouldn't we tell Daye we borrowed his car?"

"That's up to you." Lukas shrugged. "If you're worried you're too old and rusty to handle a couple of hired thugs and rescue your girl, go ahead. Or maybe you'd rather the FBI and SWAT screamed in with sirens blaring?"

Jackson raised his eyebrow. "Old and rusty?"

Lukas grinned.

While they headed back to the restaurant to collect Lukas' truck and Jackson's duffel bag of goodies, Jackson worked on blocking out the thoughts spiraling through his mind.

He had the guns and ammo...but what he didn't have was time.

Jackson wasn't a religious man, but on this night he said a silent prayer they would arrive in time.

Hang on, Casey. I'm coming.

Inside the warehouse, Casey and Meghan frantically tried to decide what to do next.

With her ear to the door, Casey clearly heard Briggs and Coombs arguing over pizza toppings. Backing slowly away, she eased her way across the room and back to the desk where Meghan waited.

"They're still there," she whispered.

"Okay." Meghan exhaled. "We need to get out of here before the boogey man comes back."

Casey agreed. She was spiked with adrenaline, and her mind spun. They needed to stay calm if they were going to get out of here alive, but she was so far from it, she couldn't stop her hands from shaking.

"Okay. Okay," she chanted, repeatedly clenching her hands into fists then releasing them. "We can't go out the door. There's no windows. And breaking through the drywall would be *way* too loud."

"You want to break through the drywall?"

"No."

Silence.

"Can we crawl out through the air ducts like they do in the movies?" Meghan sounded almost hopeful.

Casey blinked and looked up, knowing she wasn't going to see anything more than dark shadows. "No air ducts." She sighed then squinted. "If this is one of those drop ceilings, maybe we can get up to that walkway?"

"Walkway?"

She nodded furiously, hope welling up into her chest. "There's a huge catwalk up there. If we could get onto the roof...." She trailed off, not sure what the next step would be. Deciding that any freedom was worth the chance, she reached for Meghan, clasping her friend on the arm. "God, Megs, I don't know. But if we can get out of this room...maybe...."

"We have to do something," Meghan agreed, her voice trembling. "God, Case. This is for real this time, isn't it?"

"Oh yeah."

"There's no one coming, is there...?" Megan asked softly.

Casey knew her friend meant Jackson. She couldn't answer. Her voice wouldn't confirm what her heart already knew.

No. There will be no one coming. Not anymore.

She took a deep breath. "Help me move this desk against the wall."

Inch by inch, shuffling their feet to make as little noise as possible, they moved the large desk against the back corner wall. Casey slowly climbed onto the desk and stretched up until her hands touched the ceiling.

Placing her palms flat against the roof she gently pushed upwards.

"Yes!" she whispered harshly.

Using the tips of her fingers, she slowly guided the tile up and out of the way. With the small amount of ambient light streaming down through the hole she was now able to make out the desk she stood on and Meghan's hopeful face staring up at her.

"Now what?" Meghan whispered.

Casey stood on her toes and peered over the edge. Each office had a drop ceiling, so they wouldn't be able to stand on the roof tiles. But the walls looked sturdy enough, especially if they could use the reinforced corners. The slats of the walkway loomed several feet above her head. If they could get out and onto the edge of the wall, they might be able to pull themselves up.

After that?

She looked around, trying to find something, anything to help them escape.

There. On the catwalk to the right. A door. Hopefully leading to the roof. And if they were lucky, a fire escape.

Casey ducked back down and motioned for Meghan to hand her the guest chair. Once they had it in place, Meghan kicked of her heels and yanked off her stockings, then joined Casey on top of the desk.

Easing herself up onto the seat of the chair, Casey held her arms out for balance as she straightened up through the hole. From this vantage point she now saw all but the immediate area in front of the offices. There was no movement, so she took a closer look at the catwalk.

The rest of the walkway, away from the offices, had large beams dropping down to the cement floor, but here the beams had been removed and the walkway shored up with braces to accommodate the office spacing beneath.

It would be like climbing a perfectly symmetrical tree.

No sweat, she tried to tell herself, but her pounding heart wasn't really listening.

Carefully stretching up, she reached for the nearest brace to pull herself up. Holding her breath, she wriggled and hauled herself up out of the hole. Using the beam to support her weight, she balanced along the top of the wall, being careful not to knock any of the other tiles loose.

Re-adjusting, she set her right foot gingerly on the dividing wall between the two offices. She jammed the toe of her left shoe into a gap on the catwalk brace.

She took a deep breath, said a silent prayer to whoever might be listening, and lifted herself off the edge.

Twisting and pulling, muscles screaming, she swung, swore, and snaked her way up the network of beams, through the railings, and onto the catwalk.

She lay on her stomach, panting through her mouth, looking down at Meghan, who watched her through the slits in the floorboards. Leaning her head and shoulders through the railing, she stuck out her hand and beckoned.

Casey held her breath the entire time Meghan repeated the climb. Once she reached the edge of the catwalk, Casey guided Meghan's leg over the railing and pulled her forward.

They toppled backwards onto the catwalk and lay clinging to each other. Casey saw Meghan's infectious grin and couldn't stop her own from forming.

We did it!

Then the front door slammed open like a gunshot.

Casey almost screamed but managed to slap both hands over her mouth before she made a sound. Meghan bit down on the heel of her hand. They pressed themselves against the walkway and stared in horror at the entrance.

Marcus Sandiman had returned.

And he was not alone.

A tall, smartly dressed man walked briskly in front, strutting with purpose and poise as though the world was his to play with.

Harrison Douglas.

A third man followed Sandiman in, and Casey was glad she'd already had her mouth covered. He was short and extremely overweight, making his walk more of a practiced wobble. As he hurried to catch up to Sandiman and Harrison, everything snapped into place inside Casey's missing memories.

I'd followed Carson. Hid in the alley. Overheard his argument. Headlights cut through the darkness. Sandiman shot the councilor. The fat man laughed. Harrison sat quietly in the back of the car. Smiling. Approving. Turning...to look right at her.

She'd seen it all. Seen *them* all.

And they knew.

It wasn't about Carson anymore.

It was about her.

As soon as that office door opened their escape would be discovered—it would be game over. Permanently. They had to move now.

She grabbed Meghan's hand and pointed to the door. She leaned forward and whispered in her ear, "As soon as they're out of sight we go."

Meghan nodded furiously, her gaze moving to the door at the far end of the catwalk.

It was so far away.

They'd never make it.

They had to make it.

Seconds passed into a lifetime as they held their breath and waited. When the last man finally cleared the lip of the office they tiptoed down the walkway. Casey prayed that they wouldn't look right in the office. *Please, not yet. Just a few more seconds.* They were almost at the corner. The doorway was halfway down the next wall.

A flood of light burst up through the hole in the ceiling like a spotlight.

Someone shouted.

They ran.

With Meghan in front, they rounded the corner at full speed, scrambling across the walkway, no longer taking care in how much noise they made. A huge chunk of glass above them exploded outward.

They both screamed. Ducked. And continued to run. Another gunshot followed with an almost instantly piercing metallic ringing.

Casey stumbled and almost fell. Chunks of brick and mortar rained down around them. Meghan screamed as shards scored her skin.

They were almost at the door.... The walkway vibrated violently. Someone ran up the staircase in front of them! Grabbing a handful of

Meghan's suit jacket, Casey threw her weight into the metal bar across the door, slamming it open and tumbling out and onto the roof, pulling Meghan with her.

The women scrambled to their feet and frantically ran forward. Meghan whimpered as the rough gravel surface cut into her bare feet, but she didn't stop.

The roof was scattered with large venting and air conditioning units, the first of which they quickly dove behind.

The door crashed open with a terrifying bang.

Time was up.

Chapter Nineteen

A massive, multi-level warehouse taunted Jackson from across the street. Lukas whistled softly. The building was huge.

The front section facing the street was a single-storey office area with large boarded-up windows. The next area was a storey higher and contained loading docks on the west side. The rest of the building, the longest and biggest chunk, ran a good five to six stories straight up and took up half a city block. It was ringed with checkerboard factory windows just above the second floor. A caged ladder towards the back was the only visible way to reach the tallest part of the structure from the outside.

Crouched behind a large gatehouse across the street they heard a soft whistle a fraction of a section before Zack Dunnigan dropped down beside them.

"Damn it, Ghost, you're lucky we didn't shoot you," Lukas chastised.

"Well that would likely have ruined my day, now wouldn't it?" Zack said with a smile, clapping both men on the shoulder. Dressed head to toe in black, a knit cap covered his blond hair. He held a black sniper rifle comfortably in his right hand. Lukas handed him a spare com system.

"What, no Kevlar?"

"Sorry, Ghost." Jackson smiled, eyeing the vests both he and Lukas sported. "Guess you'd better not let anyone shoot you."

"So my momma always told me." Zack grinned.

"Okay. What do we have?" Jackson dropped the banter and turned back towards the building.

"She went inside twenty-five minutes ago with her driver. Short and wide. Black leather jacket."

"Coombs." Lukas nodded.

"One man left shortly after, took the car."

"Short with a brown suit, or tall and skinny?" Jackson asked, trying to peg the players.

"Brown suit with attitude."

"Sandiman." Jackson didn't know whether he should be extremely worried that Sandiman left *after* Casey arrived, or be relieved that he wasn't alone in there with her now.

"It's been quiet since," Zack added.

Together, the trio quickly sketched out a plan.

Zack had already circled the building, mapping out the access points. The only ground level entrances were the loading docks, the front office area, and a couple of exit-only fire doors along the far side. The fire doors would require explosives, so that left the office area and the loading docks for a silent entry.

Meghan had been missing for a few hours, so there was a solid chance she was already inside, likely with Briggs and Coombs. They had two gunmen and two captives, with Sandiman and Harrison as potential wildcards.

The property to the west contained piles of rubble left over from a demolished building. A tall chain-link fence surrounded it. With the help of some bolt cutters, Lukas would come through directly across from the loading docks.

Jackson would scale the single floor office section and work his way up to the second floor windows, leaving Zack, their shooter, with the five-floor climb up to the highest level.

Everyone quickly moved into position, sticking to the edges and shadows.

"On my way up," Zack's voice finally signaled the go.

Jackson pressed against the side of the building, half hidden behind an overgrown cedar. He was about to step around the corner when Lukas called a halt.

A dark sedan turned the corner up the block near Lukas and accelerated towards their location. Retreating to the shadows, Jackson watched the vehicle slow, turn, and disappear down the side of the building.

"Showtime," he announced into the com.

"Roger that," came both replies.

With a quick glance, Jackson made sure the front was clear before rounding the corner and jumping up onto the windowsill. Between the rough brick, the aluminum frame, and the hydro post attached to the corner, he quickly scaled the roof and dropped flat onto the surface.

"I'm up."

The loose gravel forced Jackson to take extra care with his footing. He noted the rusted metal ladder leading up to the second level and headed towards it. Stepping cautiously, he reached the base of the ladder and waited.

"I'm in." Lukas' whisper announced he was entering the loading docks.

"Ghost?" Jackson waited for Zack to confirm his position. But before Zack could answer, the night echoed with a gunshot and a scream.

Jackson swore and crouched down, eyes searching, gun ready.

Casey!

Two rapid gunshots.

Glass exploding.

Another scream.

Then silence.

Zack's voice cracked in Jackson's ear.

"Relax, Lieutenant, she's still alive. Second level. Twelve o'clock. Both women are hiding behind a large AC unit. I count four guns. You're good to go."

Jackson climbed the rusted ladder, praying it held his weight.

He couldn't lose her, not now, not this close.

Harrison Douglas stepped casually into the bright spot of light from the security sensor over the door. The brilliance illuminated half a dozen large metal air conditioning units and stabbed long dark shadows across the gravel surface.

Sandiman waved Coombs and Briggs to opposite sides of the roof to surround the women.

Harrison smiled to himself, pleased to know he was finally going to be able to put this little detour behind him. "There truly is nowhere for you to go," he called out, addressing the two women. "Why don't you just come out and we'll discuss this like adults."

He watched with feigned interest as Sandiman herded Coombs and Briggs around one of the large metal boxes. The two women darted out, but Briggs and Coombs blocked their escape, weapons raised.

Harrison smiled.

Guns made such fine stop signs.

Briggs twisted the reporter's assistant's arm around behind her back, and she cried out. The redhead struggled, but Coombs held her fast, dragging her out of the shadows.

At last.

"Give it up, Harrison," the blond squeaked as Briggs dragged her closer. "You'll never get away with this. The FBI knows everything."

Harrison threw his head back and laughed. Sandiman stood beside him with a knowing smile. He saw confusion in her eyes now. Such pretty eyes too. Such a waste....

Oh well.

"Oh, my dear. How you underestimate me." He straightened the cuffs on his sleeves, taking care that they both showed the same amount of shirtsleeve. "I've *already* gotten away with it." He paused to give her one of his most practiced smiles. "Now that I have you, that is."

"What...what are you talking about?"

He rocked back and forth gently on his heels. "You've cost me an

172

awful lot of money this past week. But in the end, it was money well spent. You see," he paused, tilting his head slightly, "it helps to have friends in high places. A little Federal birdy assures me the story will never see the light of *day*."

Harrison laughed as she made the connection.

"Agent Daye?" she gasped.

He shook his head and gave his nose a quick little wrinkle. "Oh no, dear. He's too much of a goody-goody. But you're close." Snapping his wrist forward, he glanced at his watch. "It saddens me to have to be the one to bring such bad news." He shook his head sadly and dropped his arm. "But right now, all your evidence is going up in flames. Literally. Along with that annoying boyfriend of yours and his equally bothersome friend."

He laughed to see the fear and despair so clearly present on her face.

"You're lying! He wasn't there! It's lies!" She jumped forward, nearly pulling free of Briggs. The skinny little weasel almost lost his grip. Harrison gave him a thorough frowning.

"Oh no, my dear." He returned his attention to the woman once Briggs regained control. "I'm being quite honest. The safe house you were supposed to be staying at seems to have caught fire. And unfortunately, your...male friends were most indeed inside." He paused then smiled slowly. "Quite tragic, I'm afraid."

Casey's knees wobbled, and she would have fallen if not for the fact that Briggs' painful grip actually held her upright.

It can't be true.

She'd sent him away to keep him safe.

She'd sent him to his *death*?

He wasn't supposed to be there!

"What kind of monster are you?" she whispered in horror.

"I'm just cleaning up your little mess." Harrison shrugged and held his hands up, palms wide. "You see, I know all about your evidence. With the audio tape now gone, the paperwork destroyed, and you, the only eye-witness soon to be out of the way, there's no case." He moved closer. "Everything they could possibly come up with now would be purely circumstantial. My lawyers would have me out before breakfast. And my plane will leave immediately after," he finished, stopping directly in front of her.

Casey struggled to breathe as her world crumbled to pieces at her feet.

Jackson's dead.

And it was my fault.

"You bastard!" she screamed at Harrison, stumbling forward through the tears.

Briggs yanked her back, but she spun and jammed her knee up into his groin. He let go of her arm, and she twisted back, leaping at Harrison, shrieking.

From the corner of her eye she saw Sandiman stepping back, his gun raised, aiming directly at her heart.

She didn't care. Her heart was already dead.

Her eyes saw only Harrison. Rage and hate, clawing his face. Screaming. Cursing.

Sandiman stepped back and raised his gun, but before he could shoot, a loud pop sounded and he stumbled forward, a look of shock and surprise on his face. His arms drooped, and he sank slowly to his knees before tumbling face first into the gravel. This time the one screaming was Meghan.

Harrison backhanded Casey, sending her sprawling backwards. The world spun, and she landed hard. But adrenaline and despair gave her fuel, and she staggered to her feet, using her hands to push herself forwards, aiming directly for the man who'd taken everything. Her mind and body had only one thought. One memory.

Jackson.

Chapter Twenty

Across the rooftop, Jackson watched the scene play out in front of him, the images jumbled as he ran full speed towards the melee.

Casey barely reached her feet when Briggs, doing an all out dash for the doorway, slammed into her back, propelling them both forward and into Harrison, who tripped over Sandiman's body and fell backwards. Continuing their forward movement, Casey and Briggs crashed down on top of Harrison in a pile of arms and legs. A loud explosion sounded, and Casey screamed.

The image and sound of her falling forward into a loaded gun slammed through Jackson, and he froze, her name trapped on his lips. His heart stopped beating for a moment, and everything spun out of control, weaving together in silence and flashes like photographs.

A burning pain in his left shoulder. Coombs stepping out of the shadows, gun aimed. Meghan's elbow flying upwards, smashing into Coombs' nose. The gun dropping into the gravel. Meghan leaping onto Coombs in a bizarre, whirling piggy back.

Then, with an ear shattering jet of noise, reality slammed down around him, and his body was once again at his control.

He stepped forward and slugged Coombs square in the gut. The man doubled over nearly sending Meghan face first into the gravel, but Jackson grabbed her and spun her down and onto her feet. With a quick uppercut he finished Coombs off, and the man crumpled to the ground.

He spun around. Briggs. Eyes up and dead to the world, a huge bleeding hole in his abdomen. Not Casey! But where was she? Where was Harrison?

He searched frantically around the rooftop but couldn't see her. She was gone. He needed to get her...find her...but he couldn't leave Meghan to do it.

Damn it!

"Zack, get down to the front," he ordered, turning to Meghan, who sat in a heap in the gravel staring wide-eyed at the bloodied bodies of Briggs and Sandiman. "I'm sending Megan over."

"Roger that."

Jackson grabbed her and pulled her quickly to her feet, dragging her back behind the AC unit and out of sight of the doorway. He put his hands on either side of her face and forced her to look at him. "Meghan, I need you to listen to me. Are you with me?"

She nodded.

He ripped at the Velcro holding his vest in place. A stabbing pain shot through the left side of his torso, and he clenched his teeth with a hiss.

He yanked the vest down over her head and secured it.

"When I say go, I want you to run as fast as you can straight to the back wall." He pointed behind him. "There's a ladder hanging over the right side. Climb down and go to the very front of the building. Zack Dunnigan will meet you there. Make sure he tells you his name before you leave the rooftop okay? Zack Dunnigan."

She nodded again.

"Say his name."

"Zack D-Dunnigan."

"Good girl."

"Jackson," she cried softly as he stepped away. "Please don't let him hurt Casey."

He nodded and looked around the edge of the unit. He gave her a gentle shove. "Go." With a quick shot, Jackson took out the security light over the doorway, the explosion camouflaging Meghan's frantic footsteps over the rough gravel.

Once she was out of sight, Jackson chanced a look at his shoulder. Coombs had gotten him good. Right along the border of the vest. It was a through and through and bleeding too fast. He was already starting to feel a little lightheaded.

He shook his head and shoved the pain down. Control. He needed control.

Muffled swearing sounded in his ear while he surveyed the rooftop, looking for any sign of Casey or Harrison.

"Six, where the hell are you?" he spoke quietly.

More cursing.

The area around the doorway was empty, and they hadn't gone past him. That left only inside. With a quick check, Jackson stepped through the door and onto the catwalk, noting the staircase to his left. Glancing over the railing, he saw the bare factory floor.

A loud thud came from the area directly below the staircase. Jackson aimed through the slats. Lukas.

"Six, what the hell are you doing?" he whispered, quickly descending the stairs.

Lukas leaned against the side of the archway into the loading docks, panting, clutching his side. He had a split lip, and his left eye was already starting to bruise. "Lord, that guy was heavy." He panted. "It was like trying to choke a walrus."

Jackson peered at the large fat man lying unconscious on the floor. Lukas shook his head, then winced, gingerly touching his eye. "Sorry I'm late. I've been dancing with the detective the entire time."

He looked at Jackson's shoulder, the steady flow of blood dripping down his arm and onto the floor. "Looks like that hurts. Where's your vest?"

"Gave it to Meghan. Did Casey and Harrison come this way?"

Lukas shook his head. "No. No one's come down except you."

Jackson cursed.

They *had* gotten by him.

They were still on the roof.

Harrison pulled the trigger, and Casey stopped breathing. A burning pain zipped across her ribcage. Hot, wet liquid seeped through her shirt and down her side. She couldn't move.

It was over. There was nothing left. She'd lost everything. She closed her eyes and waited for the end. But something was wrong. She hurt too much to be dead. Her head still rang from Harrison's punch, and her side was on fire.

Suddenly the weight lifted, and she was being dragged to her feet and shoved into the darkness away from the doorway. She stumbled and twisted, her wide eyes drawn immediately to Briggs, who lay on his back staring blankly into the night sky.

Harrison clamped his hand over her mouth and pulled her against him. They leaned back against one of the outside vents, deep in shadow, only a few feet from the edge of the roof.

Casey's body jerked at the sound of another gunshot, and the rooftop plunged into darkness. Harrison's hand crushed tighter against her mouth, muffling her whimper as the barrel of his gun jammed against the underside of her jaw. Someone ran off to her left, and there was slow, calculated movement to the right in the soft gravel. Footsteps clanged inside on the walkway then faded, leaving her suffocating in the silence.

Harrison released his grip on her mouth and thrust her forward, his fingers biting deeply into her arm. "Move," he hissed. "Make a noise and I'll shoot you here and now."

The dull rungs of a ladder took form out of the darkness. It shot up and crested over the roof high above. Harrison spun her around to face the ladder, the gun barrel cracking into the back of her skull. "Up," he ordered. "And no tricks."

Casey quickly climbed, hoping for a chance, anything, to break away. Her arms burned by the time she reached the top, the height dizzying. She heard Harrison directly below her so she crawled over the top and rushed away from the edge, staggering to a stop with a frightened sob when she realized she had nowhere to go.

The roof surface on this level was a smooth blacktop with no vents or structures except for a small six-inch brick border circling the outside edge.

She could clearly see the lights of the downtown towers in the distance. It was such an ordinary thing to be looking at the city after dark. A few stars visible against the light of the city, an almost full moon rising through the low clouds. It was like being caught on the outside, watching time pass, the world existing around her, without actually being part of the picture herself.

Her gaze locked on the distinctive rounded rungs from the top of another ladder in the shadows in the far corner. She lurched forward again then slammed her feet in place when a gunshot echoed behind her.

She spun around to face Harrison as he stepped over the edge of the ladder, his gun aimed directly at her. His loafers were silent on the blacktop as he moved closer.

"That was a warning," he sneered. "Move and the next one won't be a miss."

Case couldn't look away. A hysterical giggle tickled the back of her throat as a wondrous sound reached her ears.

Sirens.

Casey said a silent prayer to the heavens that the police were actually on their way here, to this building. Maybe if she could keep him talking, keep him distracted....

"What do you want with me?" Her voice shook.

He laughed, the sound cold and bitter. "Want? What do I want? I want you to die so I can catch my flight. You see, I've decided to finish my contract remotely. Telecommute, if you will. You've just caused me great distress in having to move to my backup plan, but I'll survive. You, however, won't." He paused. Smiled. "I'm just sorry I wasn't able to kill you the first time."

Casey's legs weakened. "The first time?"

"In the alley." He shrugged. "I do have to confess, I'm a pretty good shot. But the shadows *were* a bit distracting. Then you had the gall to go and wander off before Lonnie could finish the job."

"Lonnie?" she squeaked, turning her head.

The sirens were definitely getting louder.

"Detective Trevino." Harrison raised one shoulder then lowered it slowly. "He's been awfully helpful. He's waiting downstairs. In the event that the police do catch up with me he'll be the one to drive me downtown, with a detour to my plane, of course. And I'm sure he'll be very creative in coming up with the reason for my escape and why you shot two men before jumping to your death."

"Why...I what?"

He nodded. "Don't worry. I'm sure all the evidence he plants will be more than sufficient to close the case on your murder suicide."

"My...what?" she squeaked again, her brain unable to process the horror of what he was telling her. "Why...why are you doing this? Why are you telling me this?"

"Because what you know no longer matters." He smiled. "My job here is done. The buildings have been cleared, and now...well, now it's time to move on. Bigger and better and all that."

"But all those people," she whispered, her hand clutching the base of her throat. "How could you do that to all those people? Over a building!"

"Money." He nodded matter-of-factly. "Now that the deal is almost complete I have a disgustingly large bonus coming. And I'm certainly not going to let anyone keep me from millions of dollars." His gaze narrowed, the smile turning quickly into a sneer. "Not that idiot reporter, and certainly not you."

"You can't get away with this." She shook her head furiously, the echoing of the sirens calling to her like a beacon. She took a step back, attempting to put space between them.

"Oh, my dear." Harrison laughed, stepping forward, keeping pace with her attempted retreat. "I already have. I only wish I could let you die a slow and painful death for all the trouble you've caused me. But that isn't in the plan."

"You didn't destroy the evidence," she blurted out. "And...and Carson is still alive."

He snorted. "I can assure you, the house and all its evidence is sufficiently destroyed. And the reporter? Well, he'll be taken care of soon enough. I have a lot of friends willing to help out...for the right amount."

"But the FBI only had copies." She scrambled to come up with another excuse. "We kept the originals."

Harrison laughed. "Copies of fake reports and doctored paperwork? My legal team would eat it for lunch."

"No! You don't think we'd be stupid enough to turn over the tape or the list without making copies first? Carson knew you had someone on the inside."

Harrison stopped moving, considering her words. He shook his head slowly and smiled. "Your attempt to keep me talking is a valiant effort. But it's the witness the jury really likes. Evidence can be manipulated. But with no witness...."

He inched closer.

Casey's heel connected with the low wall skirting the edge, and she gasped, almost lost her balance. She looked down, the dark sedan she had arrived in parked far below. Her vision swam, and she fought to steady herself.

There was nowhere left to go but down.

Chapter Twenty-One

Jackson turned away from Lukas and ran back up the stairs. Halfway up he stumbled, his legs momentarily forgetting their function, but Lukas braced him and shoved him forward.

"You're not going to get very far with that shoulder," Lukas warned, pushing when Jackson staggered again at the top of the stairs.

Lukas tucked his gun into the back of his jeans and angled Jackson towards the wall, away from the stairwell. He yanked Jackson's shirt over his head, tearing the material in half, quickly looping a strip over Jackson's shoulder and around under his arm until the wound was almost covered. He took the second piece and threaded it through the first, stretching it across Jackson's chest, around his back, and securing with a tight knot.

"That should hold temporarily."

Jackson shook his head, trying to clear the cobwebs. He needed to find Casey. "Let's go."

Lukas took the lead, moving past Jackson to the closed door. Cracking it open, he checked the immediate vicinity before running onto the roof in a half crouch, gun in hand. Jackson took a deep, steadying breath and held the door open.

Lukas looked up and pointed to the right. "They're up top. Ladder's over there."

They hugged the side of the wall and made their way to the bottom of the ladder. Jackson placed his foot on the first rung. Lukas grabbed his wrist. Jackson paused. Lukas touched his finger to his ear. Jackson heard them too. Sirens.

He nodded.

He tried to move his shoulder—it burned but the dressing was holding. Hooking his elbow around the rung for better grip, he advanced slowly higher, Lukas right below him. Jackson tried to keep his breathing steady so he wouldn't be winded when he reached the top, but he was sucking air like a recruit when he halted directly below the lip.

After few steadying breaths he peered over the edge. He could clearly see Casey and Harrison stepping across the rooftop in a bizarre shuffling dance. She inched backwards, fighting a slow battle for distance. Harrison herded her towards the edge of the deadly drop to the asphalt below.

Their voices carried across the rooftop.

Casey's foot struck the edge of the roofing, and she swayed. He almost cried out, but she caught her balance and steadied. His heart raced. He needed to get to her. He couldn't take a chance on shooting Harrison; the man was standing too close. If he dropped in the wrong direction he would take Casey over the edge with him.

He needed to draw Harrison away.

Jackson drew in a breath and exhaled slowly.

Concentrate!

He slowly eased himself over the edge of the roof and crawled forward, praising the builders for not installing the loose gravel on this section.

He fought to keep himself as small as possible, worming his way closer, trying to position himself behind Harrison. Praying Casey would keep talking, keep him distracted.

Lukas crested the top and slid down over the edge, flattening himself against the rooftop. Jackson motioned for him to remain in position.

If Jackson could force Harrison to spin or step to the side, Lukas could take him out without Casey directly in the way.

Harrison reached for Casey, and Jackson knew his time was up. He rose to his feet, and the world spun, forcing him to fight to stay upright. His heart pounded, and he raised his weapon. "Back off, Harrison," he ordered.

Jackson's gaze never left Harrison's eyes. He couldn't afford to look at Casey. Couldn't think about the gun pressed against her ribs. Briggs' blood staining her shirt and the huge tear in the side. Clotted cuts on her cheek and arms.

He had to concentrate. For both their sakes. Harrison wasn't a trained professional, he would telegraph his move. It would give Jackson that split second of time he needed.

The world spun again, and Jackson staggered to the side, regained his footing, repositioned himself, and trained his weapon on Harrison.

Harrison laughed. "Well, well. Isn't this fun!"

Casey let out a whimper, and Jackson held firm, refusing to look, knowing the distraction could get her killed. "Drop it, Harrison. The police are on their way."

The sirens now approached through the neighborhood.

"No, the police are going to help him!" Casey warned then cried out when Harrison twisted her arm.

"Your detective is taking a nap on the loading dock." Jackson shook his head. "Sandiman and Briggs are dead. Coombs is out of commission. There's no way off this roof that doesn't involve you getting dead, Harrison. So let her go."

Harrison's eyes narrowed.

182

Jackson stepped forward as Harrison's arm swung like a marionette, pivoting back and forth between Casey's ribcage and Jackson himself.

"I said let her go, Harrison. It's over. You've lost. There's no one left to help you now."

Jackson saw Harrison was starting to get upset. He needed to push him harder, trick him into moving away from Casey. Red-and-blue lights started to reflect across the nearby buildings, and the real-estate mogul twitched.

Jackson took a deep breath and hoped to God he was pushing the right buttons. "Everything you've planned? Gone. Your hired help? Dead. All that hard work? Finished. There's nothing left to go back to. You've *failed*, Harrison. Failed. Now drop the gun."

"I'll be out by morning," Harrison said firmly, but his hands shook, the gun flitting between Casey's ribs and Jackson's torso.

"No one's going to help you now, Douglas," Jackson said firmly. "You're tainted. Your flunkies are dead, and your cop's going to jail. So how 'bout you let her go and maybe we'll see about getting you a half decent meal before your execution."

Harrison's rage roared to the surface. The barrel of the gun wavered dangerously.

"The reporter's alive, Douglas. We have tape. We have evidence. We have enough to keep you from ever seeing the light of day again." Jackson took a deep breath, fighting the tilting dizziness fuzzing the edges of his mind. "You're going down, Douglas. And the fall is going to be hard and fast. I guarantee it. Now let...her...go!"

Harrison's face darkened with fury. Spittle flew from his lips as he sputtered, twisting her arm and yanking her around. "You stupid bitch! This is all your fault!"

Jackson shouted at Lukas as the gun made its final pivot, arcing away from Jackson to aim at Casey. He leapt forward, but he was too far away. Too slow.

Lukas fired, and Harrison slammed forward, stumbling against her, spinning her towards the edge of the roof, arms outstretched.

She had nothing to hold on to.

No way to stop the momentum.

And she dropped sideways over the edge.

Jackson's voice came from far under his soul.

He dove the last few feet, reaching, grasping, aiming for her arms, desperately scraping for a hold as Harrison followed her over. Jackson landed on his chest and slid forward, his arms outstretched, fire scorching his shoulder as he snatched at her wrist—the last part of her body to disappear over the edge.

His fingers caught, slipped, tightened.

Held.

The weight dragged him forward, slamming his good shoulder into the brick ledge. He looked over the drop.

Casey screamed, dangling over the precipice, her entire body hanging by the wrist that he clutched so desperately. And Harrison Douglas held onto her legs. Giggling. Laughing. Life flowing out through the hole in his back.

Harrison was dying.

But not fast enough.

He was going to take Casey down with him.

Jackson's upper body strained with the double weight.

He held on to her wrist, watching her other hand claw desperately at the wall, her fingertips raw as she tore at the brick.

She dropped lower, her arm slipping through the blood that coated his hands, and she screamed again.

Jackson groaned, willing everything he had to come forward. To hold her. He stared down into her face. Tears of fear and failure trailed down her cheeks.

She knew.

She knew he was losing her.

He couldn't hold onto both of them.

She screamed his name as she dropped even further, her wrist sliding through his clasped fingers.

Jackson struggled to hold her, the pull of their weight dragging him forward. His shoulders screamed as they were pulled over the edge, the bricks carving into his chest. He saw the realization in her eyes. The love. The pain. "You can't hold us both," she sobbed.

Harrison giggled, and anger surged through Jackson.

"You're not going to fall!" he ordered, but she dropped lower with a scream, her thumb jammed down against his palms.

She tried to swing her free arm up, grasping. Desperate to find a hold. Jackson howled in agony. "God, Casey, no!"

Everything he knew, his life, his training, his beliefs, all came down to this tiny fraction of time.

He wasn't going to be able to save what mattered most.

She was the woman he loved.

And he was about to watch her die.

His soul screamed her name as her thumb popped out of his grip, leaving him frantically clasping her fingers.

It wasn't going to be enough.

A lone gunshot.

Lukas.

Harrison's body tumbled backwards to land with a sickening thud on the pavement in a blue-and-red strobe.

Lukas dropped his gun and dove at the edge, snagging Casey's free arm and hauling her up and onto the safety of the roof where she collapsed in Jackson's arms, sobbing uncontrollably.

Jackson closed his eyes, his heart gladdened to feel her breath, her tears. He'd done it. He didn't lose her.

He shuddered.

Damn, it was cold.

He tried to pull her close, but his arms were heavy. Too heavy to hold on to her anymore, and they fell limply to the rooftop.

She grabbed his face in both hands. "Don't you dare leave me, Jackson Hale!" she sobbed. "I love you, you idiot! You stay awake! Do you hear me? You can't leave me! I love you!"

Jackson fought to open his eyes, to see her hovering above him. Beautiful. A golden haloed angel. His angel. He lifted his arm, but it felt like lead weighted it down. He touched her cheek. Wiped away a tear with his thumb. She was still alive. He didn't fail.

He wanted to tell her he loved her. To tell her it would be okay. She would be okay. He opened his mouth, but the sound wouldn't come out. So he gently pulled her head closer and placed his lips softly against hers. Tasted the tears, the softness, the future.

Then blackness.

Chapter Twenty-Two

Six weeks had passed since the night on the rooftop, and Casey still couldn't sleep. Between the nightmares and the changes she struggled through, some nights she lay in bed unable to remember what she'd done that very day. All physical traces of the rooftop healed perfectly—it was the psychological trauma she was still having trouble with.

After that night, the police and newspapers had gone wild. The *Development Murders* made front page news for two weeks. Coombs and Detective Trevino outdid each other in an attempt to come clean and cut a deal. Meghan, Casey, and Lukas had all added their statements, confessions, and information to the pool. And with Carson recovering faster each day, he wrote follow-ups on his laptop from the hospital bed.

Agent Daye had his hands full with his own team—and Agent Janssen. Apparently Agnes Janssen and Marcus Sandiman had been an item for several years, which explained his ability to keep one step ahead of law enforcement. Janssen swore all the way to prison that she'd been a victim and hadn't known who he really was. But after Daye had proven she'd taken a phone call from one of Harrison's buildings the night Jackson and Lukas had been in the safe house, believing that phone call had been the order to start the fire, she clammed up and demanded her lawyer.

If Jackson and Lukas hadn't made off with the car while Janssen was in the basement rigging the fire, Daye and Samuels wouldn't have rushed outside after them and escaped the subsequent explosion.

So Lukas was forgiven for his transgressions.

It was over.

Everyone was moving on.

Well, almost everyone.

Sitting at the dining room table in her uncle's bungalow, Casey played with her herbal tea, swirling the spoon around and around in the mug.

She'd returned to her apartment, but the solitude had eaten away at her until she could no longer stand it. So Meghan had offered up the spare room in her condo, and after days of internal deliberation, Casey had accepted. Her belongings were boxed and stored and ready for the movers who would be coming in two days. Tonight Meghan was having the room painted, so Casey was hiding out at her uncle's.

Her uncle sat down beside her, dropping an open bag of oatmeal cookies onto the table. He leaned forward, covering her hand with his, stopping the random clinking of her spoon against the porcelain.

"If you're going to get up at two in the morning to make tea," he snorted, "you should at least have cookies."

She smiled sheepishly and glanced over at him. "Sorry. I didn't mean to wake you. I guess I'm just a little distracted."

He shrugged. "I'll sleep when I'm dead. You want to talk about it?"

Casey shook her head and stared into her tea. She was so not ready to have *that* conversation.

"Look, Case," he ran a hand over his cropped hair, "you've been through a lot. You're going to be carrying it around for a while. You should talk to someone."

She tilted her head and twitched up the corner of her mouth. "I can't *stop* talking about it. Between the police, the FBI, the District Attorney, the media—"

"Now you know that's not what I'm saying," he muttered. "I'm talking about Jacks—"

Casey flipped her hand into the air, cutting him off before he could finish the name.

She didn't want to think about him.

She didn't want to hear about him.

She didn't want to talk about him.

Jackson Hale was a stubborn, childish, pain in the ass, and she hated his guts.

Jackson was airlifted to the hospital that night to spend hours in surgery repairing his shoulder. He'd lost a lot of blood, but the doctors were confident he'd make a full recovery.

When Casey heard he was finally allowed to see visitors, she rushed to the hospital, only to discover he'd checked himself out and disappeared. No goodbye, no see you later, nothing.

That was six weeks ago today.

Bastard.

She pretended to concentrate on sipping her tepid tea.

Tom dug a cookie out of the bag with a resigned sigh. "I know you're worried about him, Case. But he's a big boy. He'll be fine."

"I'm not worried about him." She frowned.

Tom bit into the cookie and chewed silently, telling her without so much as a blink that he knew she was lying.

"Okay." She caved. "So I'm worried about him. I just wish someone would tell me where he is. I mean, is it too much to ask for a postcard? An email? A text message, for God's sake? I just want to know if he's okay."

Tom fished a piece of dough out of his teeth with his tongue. "No, you want to find him so you can kick his butt."

Casey coughed and sputtered, the tea stinging the inside of her nose. "I'm sorry?"

He rubbed her lightly on the back.

"Honey, I have four grown daughters, including you. This is not the first time you, or your sisters, have spent days and weeks moping around the house, sleepless and stressing. Men are jerks. They're dumb as a ditch when it comes to women, myself included. I'd bust his butt for you, but you wouldn't get the satisfaction you need."

Casey snorted with the mental picture of her uncle going around with Jackson. He may be retired, but the Colonel was still in shape. She could definitely picture him putting all those years of hand-to-hand combat training to use.

"I'd have to find him first," she muttered, scowling at her spoon as she spun it around in her fingers. "But since he sold his brownstone and disappeared, I'm guessing he doesn't want to be found."

Setting the spoon on the table, she gulped the last of the cold tea and set the mug onto the placemat. "I just...I just don't know what to do," she admitted softly.

Tom dropped his arm around her shoulder. Casey leaned into the crook of his arm, her fingers pressed against her eyes, pushing the tears back.

Tom kissed the top of her head. "What you need to do is get some sleep."

"I know." She laughed softly and kissed his cheek. "And I'm sorry I woke you up. Again."

He shrugged and stood. "Go to bed," he ordered over his shoulder as he headed down the hallway.

"Yes, sir," she called after him.

His bedroom door at the end of the hall closed with a click. Casey stared down into the empty mug cupped between her fingers, her uncle's words echoing inside her head.

He's a big boy. He'll be fine.

Everyone could tell her that Jackson was a big boy. He could take care of himself. But that wasn't the question she needed answers to.

She *knew* he could take care of himself.

The question was, if Jackson was off taking care of himself, then who would take care of his child?

Casey dropped her hands to her abdomen, pressing them protectively over the tiny life that lived inside her.

She hadn't even had the guts to tell Uncle Thomas, hoping to leave that conversation to the last possible moment. Not that she was afraid...not really...she just couldn't face what was sure to be his disappointment.

And his fury.

Because once he knew, the colonel wouldn't be offering to kick Jackson's hide for her, he'd be offering to shoot the yellow bastard on sight.

In his room Tom picked up his cell phone and dialed a number, speaking two words into the receiver before hanging up.

"Time's up."

Standing in her box-strewn apartment, Casey surveyed the randomly placed towers of possessions and wondered if she was making a mistake. If she'd made the decision too quickly.

Every time she'd tried to remind Meghan that a pregnant roommate was not a good flag to wave in front of potential boyfriends, Meghan would turn around and remind Casey of the two recent instances when she'd fainted for overdoing it.

Her doctor said there was nothing wrong, she just needed to calm down, remember to eat regularly, and take it easy. But Casey had no idea how she was supposed to do that when her life was such a mess. She couldn't concentrate and barely remembered to eat. Everything was spiraling out of control, and the thought of being alone was even worse for her psyche than the lingering nightmares. She could sleep just fine if there was someone else around, but the nights when she was alone, her thoughts and memories overtook her common sense.

The only bright light through all of it had been her new job. The newspaper had been so pleased with all the work she had done for Carson, they had offered her a full time position, with benefits. She had readily accepted, knowing they probably did it out of guilt for her nearly getting killed over what was one of their biggest selling stories, but she didn't care. She was going to need the stability.

And the family benefits package.

The week-by-week pregnancy book she and Meghan—her sworn and volunteered Lamaze coach—had started reading showed sketches of what the baby would look like at each stage of the pregnancy. One of the images made her laugh so hard at its bizarre nutty shape that she and Meghan had taken to calling the baby Peanut. She even started talking to Peanut when alone. It made things feel slightly less solitary.

Standing in front of the window, she stared vacantly out into the night, her hands subconsciously holding her abdomen.

She had no idea how she was going to make it through the next eight months, but she and Peanut had come to an agreement. He, or she, would face life head on. They would survive.

She turned and stretched, glancing at the alarm clock sitting on the floor.

Meghan would be by shortly to pick her up and take her back to Uncle Thomas' bungalow.

"Well, Peanut." She sighed softly. "I guess it's time to go. We've got a big day tomorrow, huh?"

On cue, a light tapping resounded from the front door. She adjusted her paint-stained t-shirt and ratty gym shorts and stepped around the boxes.

She quickly removed the chain and yanked the door open, turning her back on her best friend. "Hey, Megs, I'm ready. I just need to grab my knapsack."

"Sweetie, please forgive me," Meghan said, her voice coming from the landing. "I tried to say no, but you know how he is."

Casey leaned down and grabbed her bag from behind the door.

"What are you talking about? How who is?"

She straightened up, turning back towards the doorway. Her heart skipped when she realized Meghan wasn't alone.

Jackson.

Dear God.

She blinked.

And slammed the door.

Meghan jammed her palm against it, pushing it back open. "Casey, wait."

Casey's body shook. He looked so...alive. Lean and handsome and incredibly sexy standing there in faded jeans and a dark green t-shirt. Her brain alternated between wanting to scream obscenities and shove him down the stairs—and a desire to throw herself into his arms.

"An hour," Meghan pleaded. "Just give him an hour."

His body was tense and controlled. Casey saw the wariness in his eyes, the confusion, and the sadness. The look of absolute misery storming deep in his eyes made her own burn.

"I...I can't." She fled down the hall to the bedroom, nearly knocking over a stack of boxes.

"Case, wait." Meghan followed her into the bedroom.

"What the hell is going on? Six weeks of nothing and he shows up now?" Casey rapidly paced across the hardwood floor in front of the bare windows, one of the few spots that wasn't covered with movable items. "I can't see him now! He can't be here. Meghan, this isn't fair."

Megan grabbed her friend by the shoulders and thrust a plastic bag into her arms. "I brought you something to wear. Just get dressed. Please!"

Casey wasn't sure she was going to be able to stand up long enough to make any changes to her wardrobe. She sank onto a box and lowered her head to her knees, breathing in and out slowly.

"No passing out!" Meghan warned, rubbing her back lightly.

Casey shook her head and looked up. "Please, Megs. Why is he here?"

Meghan kneeled down on the floor beside her, clasping her best friend's hand in hers. "Honey, you have to trust me. Please. Just go with him."

Casey's eyes burned. "Why?" she whispered softly.

"That's what you need to find out."

She almost said no. It had been too much. She couldn't do it again. Not now. Especially now. Going through the aftermath of the warehouse alone. Jerking out of nightmares while she slept in the hard plastic chairs of the hospital waiting room. The complete joy when his mother had called her to pass on the good news—he was going to be just fine. The unbearable rift in her soul when she discovered he was gone. The news of the baby she'd shouldered alone.

Yet he was here. Now.

Waiting.

"Oh, God, what do I do?" she wailed, burying her face in her hands.

Meghan threw her arms around her and rocked her slowly back and forth. "Oh, sweetie. I know you're going through too much right now. I wish I knew what to tell you. But you have to do this by yourself."

"What do I tell him?"

"Trust your heart."

"I don't think I can."

Meghan laughed softly. "Your heart has been chasing after that man your entire life. You have to give him a chance. You owe it to Peanut."

When Casey finally opened the door, Jackson was standing in the exact same spot. He hadn't budged.

"One hour," she said softly, not trusting her voice.

Meghan ushered her out the door. "Go."

Jackson stepped back, giving Casey room on the landing. She was afraid to let her skin make contact with any part of his anatomy, so she hugged the wall and stepped quickly down the stairs.

She rushed out the front door and into the crush of the Friday night downtown scene. The heat had broken with the setting sun drawing people outside and into the lights and music. Restaurant patios played competing music, and laughter and conversation filled the air. Patrons coming and going, couples and singles, old and young, filled the sidewalks.

A light touch on her bare elbow made her jump.

"I'm over there."

Jackson pointed to the large black SUV in the paid parking lot up the street. She fiddled with the spaghetti straps on Meghan's blue sundress and stepped forward, concentrating on keeping her feet steady in the beige wedge sandals Meghan had ripped out of a packed box.

They rode in silence, driving all the way out of the downtown core before she finally managed to find her voice.

"Where are we going?"

"There's something I need to show you."

She continued to stare out the passenger window, refusing to look at him. Sitting this close, she could simply reach out her arm and her fingers would find warmth, heat. The pull was dizzying. Her fingernails bit into her palm as she willed her body to behave.

No. She was not going to fall back in.

Tomorrow she was starting over—a new place to live and a new life. A master reset.

Sudden lack of motion made her look around in surprise. Jackson had parked and shut off the engine, and she had absolutely no idea where they were. His keys swung hypnotically in the ignition before he grabbed them.

She leaned forward and looked out the windshield.

The old Victorian.

She gave Jackson a questioning glance, but his back was turned as he climbed out. She yanked the door handle and stepped out onto the stone driveway.

The house felt completely different. It had changed aesthetically, the atmosphere completely unlike the rundown condition she had last seen it in.

It was beautiful.

The lawn was well manicured and green, rolling down away from the house to the sidewalk. Fresh marigolds lined driveway and walkways, separated in sections by tiny solar lanterns that pooled their light onto the flagstone. Even the area around the giant oak in the front yard was circled in tiny flowers.

The front porch reflected a recent coat of paint, and hanging baskets dropped from under the eaves, swaying in the evening breeze. Padded furniture and small tables decorated the deck, and a large swing seat called to her from under its awning.

She stepped closer then stopped.

Jackson stood beside her.

"What are we doing here?" she asked without looking at him, choosing instead to admire the new windows and the large double-paned glass doors. The hallway light was on, backlighting the beautiful stained-glass etchings.

She watched Jackson slowly walk up the front steps, make his way over to the swing, and lower himself casually onto the cushions, rocking the chair gently.

She moved forward. Stopped. Started again.

He patted the area beside him lightly.

It was hard to keep your distance in a narrow porch swing with such luxuriously soft cushions. Her body shifted on its own, sinking into the chair, her bare leg brushing against the rough material of his jeans. She could feel the heat of his body through the denim and tried to adjust her position, but the seat held her fast.

She sighed and resigned herself to the close proximity. "Why are we here, Jackson?"

He didn't answer right away.

She spared him a quick glance.

Lounging with his arm slung over the back of the swing, he had the appearance of a relaxed man, someone without a cause or care. Despite the outward appearance of calm, Casey could tell he was incredibly tense. In the dark shadows of the porch he looked imposing.

"I need you to let me say what I need to say," he began. "Without interrupting. Then when I'm done, if you still want to leave, I'll take you back."

"I don't—"

"Without interrupting." He paused. "Please?"

Her mouth snapped shut.

"That night I thought I was going to lose you. I wasn't going to be able to hold on. Everything I ever did in my whole life came down to that one moment, and it wasn't going to be good enough."

He held up his hand when she opened her mouth to speak. She closed it again.

"I had to rethink everything. What I thought I knew, I didn't." He shrugged. "I couldn't step forward without making sense of everything behind me. You're an enigma, Casey. A crazy puzzle. I've spent my life thinking you were someone else."

He paused, swallowed, continued.

"I'm sorry I left without saying anything. I know I hurt you, and it wasn't my intention. I tried to call you. No," he said, acknowledging the look of frustration and disbelief on her face, "I really tried. I wanted to tell you everything. How much I needed you, missed you, wanted to see you. But it wouldn't have been right. I wasn't finished, and I wanted it to be perfect."

"Wanted what to be perfect?" she blurted out.

"This." He indicated the house.

She frowned and followed his hand but didn't see anything. "I don't understand."

"It's mine."

"What is?"

"This house. I bought it."

"You *bought* it?"

He nodded.

Casey was completely perplexed. She couldn't seem to connect the dots. "Why?"

"For you," he answered simply.

She snapped her mouth shut as soon as she realized it hung open. "For me?" she said, incredulous.

"For you."

"But...I can't afford a house!"

He smiled slowly. Her body quivered, remembering the last time he smiled like that, and their completely naked bodies.

"I'm not asking you to buy it."

She felt like one of those silly bobble-headed dolls, her head nodding back and forth. "I...then...what? I don't understand."

He leaned closer, reaching up to tuck her hair behind her ear, his fingers lingering slightly longer than necessary. "I'm not asking you to buy it. I'm asking you to move in with me."

Casey shivered at his touch.

"Move in with you?" she whispered.

He nodded.

She blinked.

And shot to her feet, fighting her way out of the cushions, nearly falling when the swing bounced backwards with a jolt.

"You want me to move in with you?" she cried out, her voice high and shrill. "After everything you've put me through, you show up, unannounced, after weeks of silence, wondering if you were dead or alive, and out of the blue you ask me to move in with you?"

Jackson stood up and reached for her.

"*No!*" she shouted, smacking his hand then jabbing her index finger at his evil and demented heart. "You take off, tell no one what you're doing, return from God knows where six weeks later with not so much as a *hey, how are you*, and drag me out here, for this?"

"Pretty much." He shrugged.

"I.... You.... This is...." She took a step back, accenting each

194

word with a wave of her finger.

He stepped forward slowly, matching her inch for inch. "Yes?" he raised his eyebrow.

"This is ludicrous. You can't just waltz back into my life after running away like that! God!" She flung her hands up into the air. "Did you even think for a minute that maybe I'd moved on? Found someone else? Someone who doesn't run away from his responsibilities?"

She didn't notice she had backpedaled across the entire porch until her backside collided with the opposite railing.

"Someone else?" he repeated, stopping the barest of inches away, his voice a low growl

"Well...no...but you didn't even bother to find out, did you?" Her voice trailed off. She stared straight ahead, trying to concentrate on the stitching around the neck of his t-shirt. Casey's heart beat furiously. He wanted her to move in with him? He had missed her? He needed her? But did he love her? Was he offering her the future? The whole package? Now and forever?

Would he still want her when he found out about the baby?

Would he want the baby?

Would he?

Her head spun making the world tilt.

"Oh, God, I need to sit down." She struggled to brush past Jackson's solid form, but her legs gave out. With a curse he scooped her up and held her tightly against his chest, the abrupt motion making her stomach swirl. "Don't move so fast!" she ordered, slapping her hand over her eyes, blocking out the swimming porch lights.

When the world returned it thundered back in audio first. It was like waking up after falling asleep in front of the television. Noises infiltrate the dream and the conscious state fights to sort out the reality of each sound. A ticking clock, spinning blades of a fan, rustling of an abrasive material.

Her eyes weren't ready. Something cold touched her forehead, and she heard a small sigh.

"Come on, Brat. Please, baby. Open your eyes."

Her eyes drifted closed several times before they stayed open long enough to focus on the hazel eyes that hovered just above hers, deep with worry and concern.

She lay on a couch in what she guessed was the main living room, from what she could see of it around Jackson's troubled expression.

"Oh, damn," she muttered and closed her eyes again. "This is starting to get really freaking annoying."

He flipped the damp cloth over, renewing the cool sensation on her forehead. With a feather-light touch he brushed the hair back from her face.

"Oh, Casey. I'm sorry. It wasn't supposed to happen like this."

She snorted. "Tell me about it."

"Do you want me to take you to the hospital?"

"God, no!" she groaned.

"Meghan said you've done this before."

"Tell me you didn't call Meghan."

"I didn't call Meghan?"

The couch shifted when he moved to get up. She quickly reached for his hand, snagging his wrist. She had to squint up at him, her eyes unhappy with their order to stay open.

"It's not your fault. I mean, well, it is. But it's not. I just...," she weakly dropped her hand, "Please. Stay. I just need a couple of minutes."

Jackson hesitated at her request, then sat. He honestly didn't know what to do. The first time she dropped on him like that he had a wound to treat and a soaking wet body to take care of. But not this time. He panicked when she fainted, immediately calling Meghan's cell, demanding to know what the hell he was supposed to do. He could handle a jungle ambush without thinking, but apparently Casey fainting was beyond all his comprehensive skills.

Meghan had calmly instructed him to just let her lie down with a cold compress and she would be fine.

That this wasn't the first time concerned him.

Had he missed something on the rooftop all those weeks ago? Had she been injured somehow? Was there something physically wrong? Mentally? If she was ill, why hadn't the colonel said something? Maybe he didn't know? So he called the only person Casey would never lie to. Meghan. And now he was frantic with not knowing what to do so he followed orders—Meghan's orders. His heart pounded out a scattered staccato rhythm to the slow tick-tock of the giant wooden clock hanging on the wall while he waited in agony for her eyes to open. When she finally sighed and moved he almost jumped off the couch.

She watched him now. He met her gaze, falling into the blue depths, holding still while she studied him, looking for an answer to a question he didn't yet know.

"Oh, Jackson," she finally sighed. Then she blinked and smiled—a tired, squinting, my-head-hurts smile, but it was a smile and he took it for everything it could possibly mean.

He leaned forward and cupped his hand to her cheek, lightly

tracing the edge of her jaw with his thumb. She placed her hand on top of his.

"What else did Meghan tell you?" Casey whispered.

He shook his head. "Meghan just said you needed to take it easy. Why?"

For a moment he thought he saw a flash of relief behind her eyes, but then it was gone. Her eyes were guarded. Worried. And something else. Buried deep inside he sensed...fear.

"Casey, what's wrong?"

She bit her lower lip but didn't answer.

"I swear," he said solemnly, "whatever it is I'm not going anywhere. Please. Tell me what's wrong."

His heart almost shattered at the tiniest of tears that slowly slipped down out of the corner of her eye. She squeezed her eyes shut and then focused directly into his.

He was locked in place, frozen, waiting for her to speak.

To tell him that it was over.

That she'd moved on.

That he'd truly lost her that night on the roof.

She opened her mouth, and he braced himself against the stabbing pain and almost fell off the couch when she whispered the words "I'm pregnant."

His heart skipped a beat. Stopped. Skipped again. Then pounded furiously.

"You're what?"

She closed her eyes and chewed on her bottom lip. "I'm pregnant."

Dear God. His entire body shook. A baby? His baby? Jackson suddenly forgot everything he'd ever learned about how to deal with women and blurted out the first thing that came into his head.

"Mine?"

Her eyes snapped open, and she sucked in a breath of air. "What? What the hell kind of question is that?" She struggled to sit up, but he scooped her up in his arms and swung around on the couch, pinning her into his lap. Then he jerked and released his crushing hold on her, apologizing profusely.

"I'm sorry, I'm sorry. I just, it's just...that's not what I meant. I mean, it's mine. Mine. You're having a baby. My baby. That's a dumb question, I suppose. Well, no, I mean, it's not, you're right, I should have asked you if there had been anyone else but I just thought that, well, you said you loved me, and I just really wanted to make this work, and the house—"

Casey threw her hand over his mouth. "You sound like Meghan."

He kissed her palm.

She slowly lowered her hand.

"You love me," he repeated, echoing her words from the rooftop.

She smiled and nodded her head. "Yes."

"You're pregnant."

She laughed. "Yes."

"I...." He blinked. "Wait." He slid forward to the edge of the couch, pulling her against him, and stood up. "There's something you need to see."

"I can walk, you know," she muttered as he carried her out into the foyer and down the long hallway to the back kitchen. A flickering glow cast dancing shadows along the walls.

She gasped, and Jackson stopped.

A beautiful café table sat in the corner of the kitchen, draped with a starched white cloth that pooled around the legs of the two matching chairs. Everything sparkled with the flickering of candlelight—the white china place settings, the silver, the crystal wine goblets.

In the center of the table swirled a rose-red floating candle, sailing across the water in a large etched bowl.

A sideboard had been set up with covered warming dishes.

It smelled heavenly.

He set her down gently in one of the chairs and took a knee in front of her. "This was supposed to be different. Our first date."

Reaching up with his hands he slowly ran his fingers down her arms.

"It's beautiful," she whispered.

"Meghan's idea." He grinned and shrugged when her eyes widened. "You're not the only one who needs help."

"You two planned this?"

"I went to see her yesterday. After she gave new meaning to the words 'tear a strip' she pretty much told me I'd better get my head out of the ground or I'd lose you forever."

"I see."

"So this," he angled his head towards the table, "was her idea."

"She has good ideas." Casey smiled, her hands resting lightly on his.

"This, however," he turned and grabbed a small blue crystal sphere, placing it gently into her outstretched hand, "was completely my idea."

Casey traced the exquisite lines of the small orb with her fingernail, watching as the light sparkled off the jagged and fine edges, creating a miniature mirror ball pattern on her upturned palm.

The top half of the globe slipped to the side with a small click.

She tensed, fearing she had damaged it, then smiled to realize it was indeed two separate pieces locked together to form the completed shape. She pulled away the top piece and found the inside hollow.

But it was not empty.

Resting in the bottom half of the split sphere was the biggest, most shockingly beautiful diamond and sapphire ring.

Casey sucked in all the oxygen her lungs would take, suddenly very afraid to let it out.

"Breathe, Casey," Jackson whispered.

Her gaze shot up to his. He looked absolutely magnificent in the candlelight. Hopeful. Anxious. And slightly worried. He knelt before her, like a seasoned knight kneeling before his queen.

He took the delicate blue crystal carefully out of her hand and extracted the ring, setting the pieces of the little ball onto the table. With a gentle caress, he turned her hand over and slid the ring down the length of her finger.

"I love you," he said softy. "With all my heart. I swear on everything I could possibly hold dear in this world that I will never, ever leave you. I will be your fiercest protector and your greatest champion. And I will do everything in my power to be the best damn father our child will need. Casey Marshall," he paused, searching her tear filled eyes, "will you marry me?"

With a small sob Casey threw her arms around his neck and buried her face against his throat.

"Is that a yes?" he laughed.

"Yes," came the muffled reply.

Once again he gathered her gently into his arms and carried her slowly down the front hallway towards the stairs.

"What are you doing?" She laughed softly, dropping her head down onto his shoulder.

"Taking you to bed where I plan to make slow, incredibly passionate love to you."

"And that glorious dinner?"

"Will keep."

She tilted her head back with a smile. "You know, I'm supposed to be moving tomorrow."

"Yes," he smiled, climbing the stairs. "About that. Do you think anyone might notice the change in destination?"

"That depends on who's going to tell Uncle Thomas." She giggled at the brief flash of worry on his face as he carried her into the master bedroom. "After all, we wouldn't want him sending in the troops, now, would we?"

He placed her gently on the bed and lay down beside her. "Rock, paper, scissors?"

She laughed and kissed him. "We should go see him tomorrow. I think it might be time to break the news about becoming a grandfather."

He groaned. "He's going to kick my butt, you know."

She leaned forward, her lips barely touching his. "I'll protect you," she whispered, watching his mouth curve into a smile. Her tongue darted out and teased his bottom lip.

Tangling his hands into her hair he tilted her head back. "I love you," he whispered fiercely.

Casey smiled.

"Well, it's about time."

The End

www.nikadixon.com

Author Bio

Nika Dixon is a freelance writer who graduated with a degree in broadcasting and spent years working in the television industry before expanding her roll to include that of a part-time educator and college professor. She lives in Ontario with her husband and son.

Red Rose Publishing

Second Chances-available in eBook and print

4956447R0

Made in the USA
Lexington, KY
18 March 2010